The
PROFESSOR
And The
STARLIGHT
PHOENIX

The Professor and the Starlight Phoenix
Copyright © 2019 by Nathan David Ward
Cover design copyright © Nathan David Ward

The author asserts the moral right to be identified as the author of this work

The Professor and the Starlight Phoenix by Nathan David Ward

This novel is entirely a work of fiction. The names, characters and incidents portrayed in it are the work of the author's imagination. Any resemblance to actual persons, living or dead, events or localities is entirely coincidental.

All rights reserved

No part of this publication may be reproduced or transmitted by any means, electronic, mechanical, photocopying or otherwise, without the prior permission of the publisher, except in the case of brief quotations embodied in critical reviews and certain other non-commercial uses permitted by copyright law.

9781794010390

Dedicated to *Barbara Leadbitter*,
Who passed away during the writing of this novel. Barbara was my mums much loved Aunt, who sparked the initial inspiration for this story when she bought me the wonderful Prisoner of Azkaban book as a young lad. That book will forever be treasured, along with the many fond memories of her.

CHAPTER 1
Endearing Beginnings

A small boy came running, panting, gasping for air as his tiny wire-like frame emerged from behind the shadows of the narrow side alley. His cheeks were glowing bright red from the cold that clung to his tender flesh as he came to a sudden stand still, glaring up towards the evening sky which was filled with oranges and swirly pink clouds while the sun was setting, descending beyond the distant mountain tops - tops which were covered by a thick layer of fluffy whiteness, like the village that surrounded the young boy, who was dressed appropriately, wrapped within a multi layered duffle coat and hand knitted bobble hat which matched, even down to the teenie fluorescent orange threads swirling around the seams.

  The boy began to follow the long cobbled street ahead, glancing up towards the tall cylindrical chimney stacks as they passed on by with every stride, disappearing behind him amongst the white, with only a foot length of clarity until everything became consumed by the frosty mist that was sweeping through the frail village.

Billboards seemed to have warned about the coming wintry storm but it was the first time in ten years that it had actually been accurate, which took most of the locals by surprise as they peered out of their windows, sat in the comfort and warmth of their homes, unexpecting and wide eyed to the icy flakes which were falling against the young boy's face as he ran past their window sills, crunching in to the spotless blanket of snow as he headed towards a frozen metal stairwell, attached to the street corner, beside the Reeds bakery, leading down to another row of shops where villagers suddenly appeared en masse.

They must have been stocking up on essentials before the shutters closed permanently for the Christmas period, the boy thought as he carefully climbed down the stone steps, avoiding the slippery patches of ice which were dotted along the slabs, while glancing at the people that happened to look like ants from a distance, blurred by the mist, darting in and out of shop fronts clutching onto their baskets and bin bags, all filled to the brim with luscious mouthwatering foods and novelty toys.

"*Oi! Charlie!*" called a voice from a distance, which immediately stopped the boy dead in his track. He quickly turned as a small group of children appeared in the middle of the misty cobbled street, stood underneath the orange warming glow of a street lamp as snow crystals settled upon their hats and hoods, fluttering down on the gentle evening breeze.

The skies darkened and pinks diluted against the vastness of the night. They waited for a moment, then Charlie, the small boy with the knitted bobble hat, emerged back on to the top step with his right hand grasped around the cold silver handrail of the stairwell, cowering ever so slightly.

"Oliver, I told you not to follow me...this could be dangerous!" said Charlie with his eyebrows raised, staring back at his friends awkwardly.

"We know, that's why we told you not to go out alone!"

"But you never told me why, I had to find out the hard way."

"You shouldn't have found out at all," claimed Oliver, staring with disappointment reflecting in his eyes.

"But why, why am I never included? It's not fair!" cried Charlie, still clung to the handrail as his so called friends remained at a distance.

"Charlie, you have no idea what you're dealing with here, rules are put in place for a reason, we've already been over this."

Charlie looked down at the ground, reminded of how he had always felt, never being included, falling between the cracks of friendship and having to persevere, to discover the secret enchantments surrounding the frail village of Vinemoore. But it never stopped him even with the constant warnings from the others, he just couldn't understand what made him so different, so unworthy of an equal opportunity to have fun like the other children. They didn't mean to sound nasty, they were just following instructions; instructions passed down by their guardians, but Charlie had never been *told* anything - his parents ran the local bakery, they were always up at the crack of dawn to get the dough in the ovens. Everyone loved a fresh loaf of bread with their morning brekkie in Vinemoore, but they had never told Charlie to keep a secret from his friends, they always told him that "*Honesty will always make you the greater man, Charlie Reed, as long as you're fighting for the right cause, honesty will always prevail and you can trust that*," they had stood by those words since his earliest memory of childhood, he was nine years old now and still abided by it, as much as he could, not knowing any better but Oliver insisted that he stopped.

Charlie could tell that the ordeal was reaching the end of its tether, Oliver was no longer smiling, concern now glistened in his eyes as he patiently waited for Charlie to make his way back towards them, back in the direction of his home.

"You know what has to happen now, don't you?" Oliver asked rhetorically, slowly reaching into his deep jacket pocket.

Charlie looked across from the steps as a teardrop fell from his face and against the snowy surface with a *splutter*.

"Please, it'll only happen again..."

"Oh, I'm counting on it," replied Oliver, pulling a long wooden object from his coat. He held on to it tightly as if his life depended on it, slowly raising it and pointing it towards Charlie, who stood opposite him with tear trails wet along his cheeks, knowing what had to come next. He glared at the pointed tip of the shaft, admiring its vine-like detailing spiralling from the handle area, which had a subtle trace of ivory that glistened as it remained clenched by Oliver, while Charlie tried to recollect his memories, remembering how it had felt the last time - trying to, at the very least, as figures of his imagination began to cloud, then vanish as if by magic. An alluring turquoise glow begun to illuminate the frosty night sky...

"It's here! I told you I was telling the truth!" yelled Charlie, with his face all ablaze, as trails of blue pulsated around the clouds overhead, dancing, and twirling to the rhythm of the winter wind that whistled by. The mass of children revolved and Oliver turned his head to look beyond his shoulder with his arm still outstretched, wielding the pointed stick like a weapon. His eyes suddenly widened like Charlie's had. They were astonished and frozen like waxwork as it passed, casting its ray of light through the endless blackness, like a beacon of hope, or perhaps a statement of terror as the very same expression transitioned on to the children's faces that were watching, as the large winged creature descended under the path of moonlight and faded beyond the falling snowflakes that littered the distant landscape, vanishing with all but a sprinkle of turquoise sparkle that lingered like twinkling stars.
"We have to tell Papa!" cried Oliver, turning and grabbing on to his younger brother beside him, "Run along now, inform Papa, tell him what you saw!" he concluded, watching as he scampered away in the direction that they had originally come, hopping over the mushy ice and disappearing inside, before slamming the hard wooden door behind him.

By the time Oliver had turned back around to deal with Charlie, he was nowhere to be seen. He had seized the moment but at the price of being seen as the others pointed towards the icy stairwell. Oliver frowned, before signalling with a wave of his hand, giving chase like a pack of rodents, scrambling over to the handrail and glancing down as Charlie hastily ran out of sight, delving in to the horde of oncoming villagers with their overflowing baskets of goodies and oblivious to the mystical creature that had just flown dangerously overhead, flapping away from the village with its entourage of youngsters just a few blocks behind in hot pursuit, scuttling along the market stalls and weaving in and out of shoppers, narrowly avoiding collision as they stepped out into the cold festive street.

Charlie came to a halt and clung on to the corner of a market stand, glancing back at his pursuers as they scrambled out of the crowd, snowballing to the floor in search of Charlie as he made his daring escape.

His legs had begun to tire and ache, but his heart empowered him onwards as he picked up the pace to his own discomfort, racing down a dim lit side alley with his sights set on the night sky as the turquoise glow strayed into the distance, towing Charlie forward with every heavy flap of its enchanting wings.

The pathway was free of ice, snow had begun to melt against the corners of the brick work as Charlie made a point of reverting his gaze, checking back on the cobblestones that lay ahead of him as he followed the direction of the winged creature that was now disappearing beyond the distant chimney stacks. Where the energy faded, so did the guiding light, returning the narrow streets into twilight once more, suppressing Charlie's ability to see as he stepped out from the alley and into the centre of the Vinemoore courtyard.

Here the odd shaped benches looked like gravestones from afar and the lack of lighting wasn't exactly helping as he held out his hands to feel his way towards the middle of the opening where he knew a rather tall and beautiful oak tree stood. It had been there all his life - and a few lifetimes before that. It was a magnificent peaceful tree, Charlie could tell it apart from the simple touch. It's grain was unlike any he had studied before, so as he bumped his snout against the solid bark and wrapped his arms around its trunk, he knew he was headed in the right direction, even its sap smelt like no other, it was natural and fresh, much like the crystallized spell that was whistling through the long spindly branches of the tree.

The boy continued on his way, guided by what was left of the shards of moonlight rays as they softened the sight of oncoming foliage and shrubbery that leant out from their resting places like the risen dead - who commonly rose within Charlie's nightmares, but he was certain they didn't exist as he pushed aside his fears and broke his way past the frozen greenery that was blocking his path. There was no sign of Oliver and his followers. This part of the village seemed unusually deserted as Charlie nervously wondered what the time could have been, disregarding the watch that was strapped around his wrist, because truth be told he knew his parents would offer some extra allowances, it was Christmas Eve after all and they'd be busy around the house preparing for the festivities that Christmas Day would bring. Another thirty minutes wouldn't hurt, Charlie decided as he broke in to a comfortable jog, observing the snow veiled vehicles and weary labourers closing up shop as he passed on by, sporting a heartwarming smile while the raw adrenaline and excitement raced about him, prompting him to catch the back of the turquoise trail that sparkled in the sky, up ahead.

Charlie leapt, his legs bounced like springs along the frozen pavement, slipping and sliding, dashing and weaving around the statue pedestrians as they flocked from one window to another, glaring at all the gifts and jewellery that sat seductively in their luxurious velvet cradles, brainwashing the typical human minds with their elegant charm. They sighed intently, dazzled by the shop display as Charlie pushed his way past, mistaking Mr Occamy for a shadow as he stepped out from behind the pharmacy porch and into the path of Charlie, who was beyond the point of return as he collided with the man, knocking the brown paper bag from his hand and crashing at his feet.

"Ouch!" Charlie remarked, rubbing his hand against the back of his head which was thankfully cushioned by the heavy knit hat.

"Where are you headed in such a hurry, does your mum know you're this side of the village?" asked Mr Occamy as he knelt down beside Charlie to make sure he was okay, disregarding the medication that was sprawled all over the pavement in little plastic bottles.

"I'm sorry Mr, I didn't mean to cause you any trouble, I was just chasing the bird, didn't you see it?" he asked, reaching for the bottles that rattled as he dropped them back inside the brown paper bag.

"I didn't, what did this bird look like?"

"It was enormous! It's wings were the size of a house, Mr. Occamy!" Charlie's eyes lit up as he painted the image of the enchanted bird back against his mind, "It made the skies sparkle with stars of turquoise," he added, as he climbed back on to his feet. "I shouldn't really let it get away, I was right on its tail, might never get the chance to see it again!"

Mr Occamy smirked.

"You enjoy yourself, Charlie. Just don't do anything or go anywhere silly," he advised as he picked the paper bag off the ground and ruffled Charlie's hat.

As the boy scurried away, the tall slender man stood observant, at one with his responsible instinct of being a parent, just making sure the coast ahead looked safe and clear enough for Charlie before he turned back towards his home, clutching tightly to the paper bag and pulling his scarf up around his mouth.

"He had better look after himself," he thought silently as he traipsed his way up the village, through the heavy downpour of icy flakes.

Robin Occamy was a pharmacist. He had built quite the reputation in and around the village of Vinemoore, making it his sole duty to aid and assist the unwell to the best of his unprofessional ability. Occamy had his own concoctions, experiments that were frowned upon by most, but there was always the select few who simply couldn't get enough, like an unhealthy addiction. It kept the pains at bay where all else failed, it was a necessity they could no longer live without, besides, relying on a drug was far more easier than attempting self discipline. But while stocks thinned and Christmas Day drew near, the users were left to other means of obtaining them, ways that forever put Robin's life in danger as he resorted to the shadows, disguising his face with the lip of his scarf.

Robin Occamy was quite a distinct man; tall, slender with slim fitting tweed coats that fell to the knees. He was the hay bale on a mountain of needles. His shiny brown brogues twinkled under the rays of moonlight and his slicked dark hair shined like a shimmering river on a summer's day, but he couldn't risk a day without the medication, no matter how blatant his image appealed, he had to get it home - Kirsten was relying on him.

The alley seemed clear at first, but as Robin continued, he sensed as if someone was following him, he could almost feel their determination breathing down the back of his neck as he picked up his pace, knocking aside the leaves and branches, arriving at the courtyard where a thin layer of snow had begun to settle peacefully.

The village was silent for a moment as Robin came to a halt, stood beside the oak tree, looking back in the direction he had come...but no one was there, it must have been his imagination?

"I'm going mad!" he confirmed, turning into the path of a dirty short man whose face remained sheltered by darkness. Robin gave a gasp in shock.

"I-I'm sorry, I didn't see you there," he stuttered, stepping back towards the tree, carefully drawing the bag of medication towards his chest.

"You know what I'm after, hand it over!" the man yelled, still hidden by the shadows being cast by the moon.

"You know I can't do that!"

"Pig! I said hand it over!" he repeated, becoming more and more aggressive in nature.

"If...If you don't step back, I'm warning you, I will..."

"You'll what? What are ya gonna do, Pharmacist…"

Robin took a breath as the vile man snatched away the brown paper bag from his possession, spitting down at the ground he stood upon as he stepped back to peer inside.

"Who's all this for then? There's tonnes in here…" the man asked, glaring up at Robin as he stood patiently, ready to knock the thief into next Christmas, and the one after that!

"It doesn't matter now, anyway. It's all coming home with me," he added, just as another silhouette figure appeared, descending down a flight of slabs and headed in their direction.

"Oi you! Yes you!" The mysterious figure called, distracting the attention of the thief who was suddenly victim to a swinging fist, as Robin knocked him to the ground - he fell like a sack of potatoes, knocked out cold.

Robin quickly knelt down beside him to make sure he was still alive as the third figure arrived at the scene, panting, short of breath - It was

Oliver's dad, Kenneth, armed with his wooden cane and military great coat, complete with brass buttons.

"Robin, it couldn't have been anyone else. Only you can pack a punch like that. Is he okay?"

"He's alive, I guess that's always a good sign," Occamy chuckled, sliding his arm from his sleeve and placing his coat over the thief's unconscious body.

"You've got a heart of gold, you have."

"Just a duty of care, Kenneth. He's not waking up anytime soon that's for sure, besides, that bundle of fluff was on its way out. It's going to be another cold night."

Kenneth watched as Robin gathered together the medicine and placed it inside the the battered paper bag again. It was much easier in just his white shirt and golden waistcoat, far more manoeuvrable. He collected his belongings and sprung back onto his feet, meeting Kenneth's weary gaze.

"Anyhow, what brings you this way?" asked Occamy with an eyebrow raised from curiosity, he was quite a distance from home with a blatant lack of breath as he continued to pant, placing his hands around his hips.

"A sighting, I don't suppose you saw it?"

Robin was instantly reminded of Charlie who had ran straight into him, claiming to have been following a giant bird, could it have been the very same one?

"A bird?" Robin asked with sarcasm in his tone; to which Kenneth's eyes widened even further. He looked worried, and fearful as his grip tightened around the handle of his cane that was firmly pressed into the snow.

"You saw it?" Kenneth asked with concern overwhelming him, taking a step closer to Robin whose face fell pale.

"No, no...I bumped into little Charlie, he said something about a bird with wings the size of a house, probably just in a world of his own, you know what children are like."

Kenneth's hand immediately eased from around the cane, "where was he headed?"

"Just back, past the shop...you know my place, right?"

Kenneth smiled behind his bushy moustache.

"Of course, thank you, Robin...you have no idea how important this is, but I'm sure, one day I'll be able to explain it all!" Kenneth suddenly took off, darting towards the alley and raising his hand to Robin, signalling his farewell before vanishing beyond the snow veiled foliage.

"Very bizarre!" Robin chuckled to himself.

He pulled his bag of medicine tightly to his chest once more as flakes swept in, riding the bitter breeze of Christmas as the day itself drew all the closer, reeling the father of one back towards the warmth of his home that waited upon a hilltop, looking over the village of Vinemoore and the mountains of Shoulders Heath, away from the weird goings on that even on this night, Christmas Eve of all nights, it never felt more apparent.

CHAPTER 2
The Occamy Household

The year was 1966 and the common folk of Vinemoore had never expected Christmas to bring the arctic. It was a sight unseen until now, the town immersed in snow - it had always melted away without the chance to settle. It was no surprise when the villages people erupted in to panic. Even as the metal gates clamped together and the shutters shuddered against the ground, they still waited eagerly outside the shop fronts, hoping to haggle a last minute score while the shopkeepers snuck out back, darting away in to the dark of the night, avoiding the usual drama that came with closing time. But this was different, everyone was out of character, as fear of waking to a view of solid white packed against their windows and doors, overwhelmed them. The thought of being sealed inside was just a worry too far.

Robin smirked as he neared his dainty cottage that sat peacefully upon the hilltop, like a crown jewel, sparkling frosty underneath the glimmering light of the moon that had risen into the night sky.

The flakes were still falling aggressively, landing against Robin's face as he climbed the frozen ground - he had grown numb to the cold, dressed in nothing but a thin cotton shirt and golden tweed waistcoat.

"The other guy needed it more than me," he murmured, engrossed in the thoughts of his retired coat - he liked that tatty grey coat very much, he realised as he approached the end of his journey, relieved to be back after a day that felt like it was never going to end.

Robin pushed aside the brown wooden gate which separated his land from the wilderness outside, leaving it to spring back in to its closed position while he continued on his way, traipsing up the cobbled footpath that led to his beautiful, oak front door.

Robin and his partner Kirsten always liked to prepare for the new year and this was no different even under the difficult conditions that they had found themselves in. But nothing had prepared them for the cold grey dawn, not after they'd grown fond of the waking mornings when they would draw back their curtains to be met with the warm rays of sunshine and colourful flower beds staring back at them. Pretty petals and luscious leaves danced in the warm summer breeze as the couple had embraced and stood in harmony, watching.

Robin could still imagine it, the summer just gone, he was convinced he could smell it too, as he stopped to peer down towards the frosted soil where bulbs and shrubbery sat stiff, frozen like ice as memories began to flood his mind, memories of when life had rewarded him with everything he had ever wanted. Delightful immortal memories that even at the slightest thought could cast a joyous smile upon his scruffy stubbled face.

Robin was undoubtedly one of the softest men to walk the town, and he had never understood what he could have done to deserve his recent misfortunes, it troubled him greatly, but he had the treatment, now, he suddenly remembered, as the sharp winds fluttered against the brown paper bag drawn tightly to his chest.

There was no way he was going to allow the darkness to rip the love and joy from his heart, not yet, not on his watch. He often repeated that to himself silently. This Christmas was going to be one of, if not *the* best Christmas that their family had ever seen, Robin chuckled, turning to make sure the gate was firmly jammed shut before knocking the snow from his shoes and heading inside; closing the heavy front door behind him, carefully, as quietly as he possibly could.

The metal latch clunked in to place and Robin was suddenly hit by the fiery warmth circulating his home. He could smell the fire burning and food cooking, he could see the orange glow flickering from inside the sitting room as he bent down, placing the ruffled brown bag beside his foot and proceeding to untie his shoelaces - or at least trying to, as his hands were like ice blocks. He could barely feel the waxed lace between his fingertips, so he simply grasped at what he could and tugged, hoping for the best - thankfully they were loosely tied and came undone rather quickly. So Robin slipped off his shoes and placed them inside the cupboard under the stairs, where the rest of his winter and summer attire belonged.

"Sugar, are you down here?" Robin asked, while distracted by his collection of tweed and boucle coats. He loved a quality coat and there was plenty to choose from on his rack as he cast his gaze along them. It was like a full spectrum of colour, there was simply too many for one man to enjoy but they would surely last him a lifetime, he considered, deciding what one he might take for a spin in the morning - once the presents had been opened, of course.

"Kirst?" he called again, then turned, closing the cupboard door behind him and stepping in the direction of the living room. The heat flowing from the room had already dried the dampness from his shirt and waistcoat, he noticed as he brushed his hands down his collar and across his shoulders, expecting Kirsten to be waiting for him in her leather armchair as per usual...which she was, to Robins delight as his gaze fell upon her, resting peacefully by the fire curled up in a ball of comfort.

Robin smiled and stared from afar with enchantment glistening in his eyes, and a sense of privilege as he recognised her undeniable beauty, a beauty that had always made his legs turn to jelly at the sight of her, since the moment they met, he had never seen anyone as pretty as her.

Kirsten's hair ran dark, silk smooth across her face while she waited, and slept - her face, body, gaunt and pale, colourless like the landscape framed within the living room window. She wasn't well, she had not been well for many months leading up to Christmas, but they didn't let it get the better of them, they still decorated. The tree was always important, it made the room feel complete and homely as it stood singularly, twinkling and sparkling, reminding them both of the old days when they were children. They were glad they could still enjoy Christmas the same way, besides, things were beginning to look up, Robin thought as he leant down and grabbed the brown paper bag and wandered over to his partner, who was still in a deep slumber, absorbing the warmth being given by the fire, as the flames flickered, burning underneath the chimney breast like the burning love shared within their hearts.

Taking care not to wake her, Robin quietly knelt beside the soft leather armchair and placed his warming hand upon Kirsten's forehead, then gently stroked away the hair that had covered her face, revealing her long, dark lashes and her dried pale lips that rested against the surface of the leather arm.

"Look at you," he said softly, "Best thing to ever happen to me, you are...don't know where I'd be without you, or Emily," he added as a rather excitable young girl came running down the stairs and in to the front room, chirping away - *Papa, Papa*.

She looked no older than five, dressed in a black and white polka dot skirt and hand knitted cream cardigan. She couldn't have looked any cuter if she wanted to as she ran, Blonde curls fluttering about her shoulders.

"Papa, you're home!" she said as she gently threw her arms about her father's neck, embracing him tightly, pressing her face amongst the prickle bush growing around his chin. Emily erupted in to laughter, her father joined in, beaming as he wrapped his arms around his daughter and chuckled.

"I'm home, sweet pea," he said warmly, "I'm home…"

Then Emily let go and stepped away, sprawling along the fluffy brown rug that sat in the middle of the room, looking up at her father's prominent brown eyes as love reflected within them.

"How was your day, Mr," said a croaky voice from the armchair as Kirsten blinked away the dust from her eyes and smiled warmly, watching as Robin had cradled his child and then turned around with a look of surprise.

"Hey, love! I'm so sorry, we didn't mean to wake you,"

"I'm glad you did, we've been waiting all day...well, since you left this morning, really," Kirsten blushed, looking down at Emily who was staring back, alternating between her mother and father. It needn't be said that she loved her parents sincerely, no matter how hard it had become to live in a house that was silent throughout the day, apart from the occasional ringing of china as Mrs Jillings put away the plates and bowls into the suspended cupboards over the kitchen worktops.

Mrs Jillings was a residential carer - she volunteered to help, she wouldn't even accept payment. Robin had tried time after time, he even slipped some notes in to her handbag once but they soon turned up on the kitchen table the next day with a hand written note on parchment underneath. It simply read, *You owe me nothing, and you never will.*

Robin wasn't prepared for that, neither was Kirsten. Those eight words had transformed their tear ducts into running taps, they couldn't contain the emotional delight they felt, knowing they could rely on someone without the need of waving cash under their nose.

She arrived at the crack of dawn as Robin was dressing for work and she left shortly after his return, once she knew they were settled - it allowed him to concentrate while working at the pharmacy, his mind at ease ever so slightly, knowing his family were in safe hands.

Since Kirsten had fallen ill just after the events of the summer she had become weak and frail, unable to perform her daily 'to do list' around the house - she felt so deprived even at the best of times. Everything was so tiring but she was thankful to still be able to move about her home on her own free will - but the stairs were out of bounds, for now, at least until they could find a medication that would help. Bone disease was very uncommon, so the possibility of one existing seemed slim.

Robin reached across the rug for the tatty brown paper bag.

"So how has your day been, miss and miss?" he asked, smiling at them both and rustling his hand about the paper bag, removing the plastic bottles and placing them on the wooden shelf beside him, beyond Emily's reach.

"It's been lovely, hasn't it Em?" Kirsten asked, met with a cheer from her daughter.

"YES! We were wrapping presents and singing and Mrs Jillings even baked us cookies, do you want to try one, papa? I decorated one especially for you!"

"I would love one, sweetie."

"I'll go fetch it!" Emily chirped energetically, jumping on to her feet and rushing out of the living room, her gorgeous blonde curls fluttering behind her as she raced down towards the kitchen.

Kirsten shuffled over and Robin slumped in to the gap, exhaling a sigh of relief as he buried his arm behind her and placed his hand gently down onto her stomach. Kirsten snuggled up to her partner, resting her face against his chest and playing with his bitter cold fingers, warming them a little while he sat silently, in harmony staring out of the window where snow was still falling majestically.

"How was work?" Kirsten muttered with her face squashed against Robins tweed waistcoat.

"Tiring, didn't think it would end," Robin chuckled, reverting his gaze down towards his chest where Kirsten's head laid comfortably.

"Was there any trouble?"

"Trouble?" he frowned.

"You know what I mean, it scares me, and I couldn't help but notice the bag is torn. The bag with my medication in..."

"Oh, no. It was already like that…" Robin said reluctantly, feeling the guilt rush through him as fast as the blood circulating his veins, it made him uncomfortable, but she didn't need to know, she mustn't know - not in her condition.

"It was like that after I ran in to Charlie, I mean, he ran in to me..."

"Charlie Reed?" Kirsten's eyes widened, surprised to hear his name. She wondered why

Charlie would be playing that side of Vinemoore, so far from his home - It was much unlike him.

"That's the one. I told him to get home, it was dark as usual when I left, I do often wonder how his parents sleep at night letting their child roam about the village like that, just think what could have happened!"

"It's hardly reputable right now, I think Emily is lucky to be allowed in the yard with all the recent goings on," Kirsten suddenly sat up beside him, "I'm scared, Robin. What if you don't come back one evening, what if something happens again…like last time?"

There wasn't much more he felt he could say, so he answered honestly, as best he could, "I won't, I think I made a name for myself. Anyone would be a fool to mess with me, wouldn't they?" Robin asked rhetorically, ending with a calming wink in Kirsten's direction, who had blushed again, cowering behind her hands, burying her head against her thighs.

"I hope Charlie gets back home okay, it's Christmas...who'd want to be outside in that?"

"I'll pop by his house tomorrow sometime, just to check in. You've seen what it looks like out there, haven't you? People are going nuts, you'd think it was the end of the world or something," Robin sighed.

"End of the world? A bit of snow?"

"HEY! I forgot, I passed Oliver's dad, Kenneth. He seemed in a hurry, chasing some kind of bird."

"Another one?" Kirsten yelped in surprise.

"*Oh* no, a *feathered* bird. Charlie also mentioned something about it, perhaps a rare breed. They seemed set on finding it," Robin then cast a look of confusion and stroked the stubble on his chin, "I really don't know what's happening here, it's bonkers, it's making me wonder if Vinemoore is the best place for us to settle," he remarked, glancing over towards the door frame as Emily returned, out of breath with a cookie grasped in her right hand.

"What took you so long, trouble!" he said, then chuckled as she slapped the biscuit into his palm with a cheesy grin.

"I was just saying goodbye to Mrs Jillings, she said she won't be coming tomorrow but I think she wants to," Emily whispered cheekily, then catching her breath she added, "I don't think she has anybody at home, she doesn't even have any pets."

She had lowered her voice to a hushed tone and begun to peer over her shoulder as Mrs Jillings arrived into view, opening the cupboard door and removing her sequin covered shoes. She seemed fit as a fiddle for a sixty year old lady, but no one knew much of her background apart from her loving nature and her lonely lifestyle, which was why she enjoyed it at the Occamy household.

Robin and Kirsten were not married but it was something they had always considered, just never gotten round to doing. They were both at one with each others mind set and knew that Emily was right as they glanced to each other, eyes glistening with sadness, knowing what Mrs Jillings was going home to - a dark, damp hole with barely any food or warmth. It was a horrible thought and one Robin felt he had to act upon as he called across from the armchair without a seconds thought.

"Mrs Jillings, could I speak with you for a

moment?" he asked, taking a bite out of Emily's biscuit and watching as she pulled her blue knit cardigan over her shoulders.

"Of course you can my love, is there anything you need before I head off?" she asked politely, not wanting to out stay her welcome as she noted the couple cuddled up, sunken happily in to the soft dark leather of the armchair.

"I'd like you to stay with us for Christmas, Ethel. And I won't be taking no for an answer...unless you've otherwise made plans?" Robin asked, looking smug as Mrs Jillings stood compliant under the door frame.

"Well I...I guess I could always reschedule, I was only going to treat myself to a lovely meal."

"You can treat yourself here, I'm sure we'd all love you to stay. It wouldn't feel right without you; besides, you have some spare clothes and a bed in the spare room, it would save you trekking home in the cold - It's ghastly out there, believe me."

Mrs Jillings smiled, unable to contain her joy and relief to be offered company at what would have been a lonely time of year for her.

"Thank you, Mr Occamy. You're just too kind. I'll be off upstairs to make my bed then if you don't mind? Just shout if you need anything, goodnight Miss, goodnight Emily."

"You can call me, Robin. I've told you…"

"And you can call me, Mrs Jillings. Now goodnight," she called as she disappeared up the creaky staircase, hiding her glee.

"Em, go with her...just in case she needs a hand, then I'll put you to bed, otherwise a certain someone might forget to pay a visit!"

Emily gasped.

"Don't be silly, Papa! I know the Christmas Phoenix doesn't exist. Plus, I've seen one of my presents already…"

"You cheeky monkey! Go on, off you pop now!"

Emily grinned, and jumped to her feet, disappearing up the stairs behind Mrs Jillings.

Robin turned to Kirsten who was smiling awkwardly, then suddenly they burst out in laughter, together.

"I'll put the presents down in a minute, no point trying to keep a secret that's no longer a secret anymore," said Robin, gracefully kissing Kirsten's forehead.

"She's a bright girl, I reckon she gets it from you, I'm too scatty for my own good!" Kirsten chuckled.

"Finally! Something we agree on," claimed Robin in a joking manner, quickly cowering as an expected and playful fist landed against his arm.

"*OW!* Steady on!" he chuckled, pulling her tightly yet carefully towards him, not wanting to inflict any further pain to what she was already experiencing.

"Here," said Robin, popping the lid off a orange plastic bottle and pressing down the cap, releasing a small red and blue capsule in to the palm of his hand.

"We're going to have a nice day tomorrow, nothing's going to spoil it," he smiled, handing over the capsule to Kirsten, who knocked it to the back of her throat and swallowed it with a gulp. She was used to taking them now, it was no hassle and they worked a treat, even though they didn't know what they were physically doing, it gave her a sense of calm at the centre of a terrifying storm.

Robin had been used to feeling useless, but now he had a means of helping, a duty of care that he could perform without endangering those around him. It was the least he could do and even if it meant running into the occasional low life, it was worth it, and they deserved what they got for interfering with the power of love. The mugger that slept underneath Robins tatty grey coat that night was lucky to be alive, he silently concluded. Others hadn't got off so lightly - if it wasn't for Kenneth, god knows what he would have done to the vile little man, he questioned, reimagining the mortal fear quaking in the depths of his glistening eyes, his disgusting dark eyes... Then Robin snapped back to the subject of Christmas and the wonderful gifts that needed planting underneath the Christmas tree.

He leapt off the chair, excited by the thought!

"I'll go get the presents!" He chirped, as Kirsten watched him scarper from the living room and up to their bedroom where all the gifts were stored, hidden away in different secret spots that they had mistakenly assumed were undetectable to young prying eyes.

But that wasn't a worry anymore, as Robin rummaged all of the gifts together into a pile on the bed - not forgetting the extra special one that had remained hidden in his top drawer since November. He pressed the small gift wrapped box in to his trouser pocket and swallowed the other presents into his arms before transporting them slowly down towards the living room where Kirsten waited patiently, sat beside the tree, staring blissfully out of the window.

"*Ta-da!*"

A giant mass of shiny presents suddenly appeared in the room, then tumbled to the ground.

"Careful, Robin! Some might be delicate!"

"You wrapped them, you should know," Robin claimed, kneeling and passing over the boxes to Kirsten, looking amused.

"Fine, I'm just saying there could have been…" then she smiled again, covering her mouth with her hand and turning away to hide her returned amusement.

"What - what's that in your pocket?" she quickly asked, pointing with her eyes a blaze with excitement. Robin awkwardly placed the last present under the tree then turned to Kirsten.

"That was going to be a surprise, but I guess you may as well have it now...it's nothing much, but it's the thought that counts, *right*?"

He pulled the gift from his pocket and tossed it over to his partner, who jumped up to grasp it from the air. Her eyes were wide now; and she looked as if she had just drank an endless mug of coffee - she was going to be awake for the rest of the night.

She tore away the beautifully crafted paper like an excitable puppy until all that was left was a small wooden box. It sat in the palm of her hand for a moment while she looked to Robin who had began to shy away, ever so slightly. Then she proceeded to lift what looked like a lid, unhinging the top from the bottom, revealing its content. Kirsten's eyes glistened as a single diamond sparkled at her from inside the box, it was a small silver ring pressed inside a velvet blue cushion, it was very pretty - at least that's what Robin thought as he wondered what Kirsten was thinking, she hadn't said a word yet, she was just staring as if she was in a world of her own. There was even a subtle motion from her jaw as it dropped ever so slightly. Robin raised his clenched fist to his mouth and cleared his throat to break the tension as Kirsten suddenly jumped and her eyes darted from the ring to Robin, who sat with redness glowing from his cheeks.

"Oh, my," she exclaimed as her eyes began to fill with tears, watching as her man hopped on to one knee and spoke the words that both had waited all too long to say and hear.

"Kirsten Mae Withers, would you make my dreams come true and accept my invitation of marriage? *Please*," he begged, then realising that his pleading was completely unnecessary as his lady approached him, using all her energy to climb over in to his arms and accept.

"I do," she whispered elegantly in to his ear, feeling relieved that he had finally asked before it was too late. Robin whimpered, then broke out in a stream of tears as he held tightly on to his wife to be.

The pair of them continued to embrace, sharing a moment of tenderness and passion as their lips touched under the colourful fairy lights that twinkled on the Christmas tree.

Robin removed the ring from the wooden box in his passing moment to take a breath, then slid it onto Kirsten's finger while she kissed him again, but this time on his forehead. She then smiled playfully and before they knew it, Christmas day had come, chimes could be heard as the second hand struck midnight.

It was then, Robin and Kirsten snapped to

attention, glancing over towards the hallway and back to each other, listening as the ringing sound echoed around the house.

"You hear that?" Robin asked.

"Yeah…" Kirsten nodded, confused as they looked to the hallway.

"Since when did we own a grandfather clock?" he added rhetorically, knowing that Kirsten was freaked out just as much as him - and it wasn't the first time they had heard it's chime.

It was strange, like the village, a clock of that kind was nowhere to be found inside the Occamy household - *so where had it come from for all these years?* They wondered on that question, laid together against the floor as Christmas Day dawned, blowing in on the icy white flakes that fell in to the early hours of the morning.

CHAPTER 3
The Morient Man

A peaceful *tick-tock* sounded around the Occamy household as the sun began to rise over the village, casting away the grey veil with its bright fiery glow. Not an inch went uncovered as Vinemoore looked like a Christmas card under the thick white blanket of snow that had fallen throughout the night.

The living room was now light again, and Robin could feel the warmth of the sun shining through the window and on to the side of his face as he laid comfortably behind Kirsten, embracing her as they slowly woke together, on the soft leather of the sofa, which was positioned against the back wall, facing the direction of mountains that sparkled in the distance - acting like a partition between Vinemoore and the mysterious land of Shoulders Heath that was beyond them.

His eyes took some time to adjust as they crumbled open, hazy for a moment, then the bold silhouette of the landscape sharpened.

"*It was morning already?*" Robin muttered as his gaze fell upon his clothing, which had gone unchanged - he'd never done that before, at least not since his teenage years which came as a shock at first, until the view outside enticed his attention.

The snow had finally stopped falling, the yard was white, the village at the bottom of the hill was buried under the frosty spell and all that could be heard was a cold, high pitched whistle as the wind swept against the walls of the cottage, kicking up the fluffy flakes in to the air from the mound that sat at the foot of the door.

It could have been worse, Robin observed as he carefully climbed over Kirsten and wandered towards the window, rubbing the dust from his eyes and untangling the nest that now resided on his head.

"It could have been a *lot* worse," he concluded, scrubbing at his head and breaking a yawn. The rest of the house was still fast asleep. It was only 7 am, which gave Robin just enough time to shower and change before Emily awoke, bright eyed and buzzing with energy.

"It's Christmas! It's Christmas!" Emily chirped as she bounced on her mattress. Unaware that her father was already on the move.

"Merry Christmas, sweetheart!" Robin called, dashing from the bathroom through to his bedroom with nothing but an Egyptian cotton towel wrapped around his waist, and hair dripping wet.

"Merry Christmas, Mrs Jillings!" he added, thudding his fist against her door as he passed, running down the hallway.

"Oh Robin, cut that out!" she groaned.

Then she rolled from her bed and reached for the silk floral dressing gown that hung on the back of the door. This was only a small box room, just enough for a bed and wardrobe but it was more than adequate for Ethel, or rather Mrs Jillings - which was what she preferred.

Once she had tied the gown around her body and slipped into her navy sequin slippers, she felt ready to face the festivity that was brewing down the hallway. Emily was still bouncing around her room, singing and calling out excitedly, and as Mrs Jillings released the wooden door from its latch, she took in a slow breath, taking in the air of Christmas morning, before wandering down towards the charismatic child.

Robin quite enjoyed listening to the sound of his daughter messing around as he fastened a violet cotton tie around his neck, under the collar of his fresh white shirt. He watched his reflection staring back at him through the elongated mirror, which stood at the end of his king sized bed.

He made quick work of his silky soft mop, slicking it back with a thick moist foam that he rubbed between his hands before attacking the wavy fibres, until they settled evenly behind his large, pointed ears.

Satisfied with his fresh and revitalized hair, he pinched at two strands of fringe, pulling them beside his cheeks where they dangled freely, framing his face, before grabbing his soft grey waistcoat off the duvet, and buttoned it around his stomach - it was a slim fitting waistcoat that hugged his body perfectly, defining the shape of his athletic physique and also the charming personality he had to go with. He then ran his hand down the hazel bristles growing from his face and smiled, glaring in to the eyes of his reflection as it continued to stare back - a tired misfit, a predecessor with a face like thunder...

Robin slapped his hand firmly across his cheek, launching himself towards the bedroom door and back through the gate of reality where his daughter's singing had finally stopped and turned into a deep conversation about fairies and plastic dolls as she latched on to Mrs Jilling's hand, making her way down the creaky staircase and in to the living room, which was filled with lots of hand wrapped presents, complete with ribbons and tags.

"Mummy!" Emily chirped, climbing carefully over her mother's legs and planting a long sloppy kiss upon her cheek as she tried to sit herself up.

"Good morning, you! You're up bright and early!"

"It's Christmas Day, Miss Withers, what did you expect?" Mrs Jillings chuckled, standing under the door frame with her arms crossed and eyebrows drawn.

"I'm gasping for a cuppa, anyone else fancy one?" she asked, as Robin descended down the stairs and pressed his way past, subsequently pecking her cheek with a festive kiss.

"If you're offering, Mrs J," he said cheekily, casting her a wink before diving upon the oval chocolate rug at the foot of the sofa, tensed and waiting for his daughter who he knew was moments away from one of her famous moves.

She'd already latched her sights on him like a hawk, then predictably lunged from the sofa and on to his stomach, where tiny hands wiggled and papa hands tickled, Emily's face erupted in to a blaze of joy and laughter which cast away the frosty spirits of tiredness and exchanged them for something warm and cheerful, as Kirsten and Mrs Jillings cast a smile, admiring the affectionate scene unfolding in front of them.

The whole festive season had seemed daunting at first, with Kirsten's nightmare diagnosis, and the fear of Emily not having a mother come Christmas Day. Robin had bent over backwards to make sure that nothing stood in the way of their united happiness - even Mrs Jillings felt like a member of the family, she may as well have lived in the Occamy household, they would have all liked that, she'd been the best thing to happen to them during their darkest hour and now she was sipping tea and ripping wrapping paper from her sack of gifts that Robin and Kirsten had insisted on - once again it was the least they could do.

It lifted the mood, everyone smiling and enjoying themselves, it was a sight that they only believed to exist in their dreams, but it was actually happening, and the most of it had to be made, Robin decided, reaching for his mug of tea and taking a *slurp*.

"Oh, it's wonderful...Thank you, all three of you - thank you," Mrs Jillings sighed, captivated by the glistening dark rubies shining up at her, "This is naughty, *very* naughty," she added as a tear silently ran and dripped from her flushed red cheeks.

The two small rubies were embedded in elegant silver earrings and cushioned inside a navy box with a single sequin glued to the lid. They were *beautiful*, Mrs Jillings thought, while feeling pleasantly, but more than a little, overwhelmed by the whole ordeal.

"You deserve it, you're like god's gift to us!" said Robin.

"You're like the phoenix in the story you told me, Mrs J. You're sparkly and beautiful and impossible, like a miracle...Right, papa?" added Emily.

"She has a point, you are like a miracle to us and I never believed in those. You're like magic, you make me want to believe in the impossible," Robin admitted, placing a comforting hand on Mrs Jillings shoulder, before stepping out of the living room and reaching for the cupboard handle and drawing open the door where behind it hung his vast collection of winter coats, beaming back at him like a tribe of children, competing for his undivided attention as they hung vibrantly. Robin began to run his hand through the selection in front of him, making judgment until he then stopped at the softest one available. The coat felt like a wool blend, basket weave pattern and had a deep purple hue while inside the cupboard, until Robin unhooked it from its hanger and yanked it out into the light of day. It then changed completely to an almost metallic, colour changing frock with turquoise sequins. *"Nah! It's just not me,"* he claimed, throwing it back inside and paying closer attention to the other competitors.

"How about...you!" he said out loud, reaching for another and pulling it out. This one was much the same pattern and soft to touch, Robin never liked anything too experimental, it irritated his hands - but this one was perfect, he decided as he set his gaze on the honey yellow weave and threw it about his shoulders, adjusting the cuffs for a better fit. It sure did suit him and it hung nicely at his knees - it even went with his grey waistcoat, shame about the tie though, that was overkill, Robin recognised, quickly untying it and throwing it amongst the shoe rack then slamming the door shut.

"So, what do you think? Not worn this one before have I? Might be a new look to go with the new year!"

Kirsten smiled, "I like that, a lot!" she said, then looking to Emily who wasn't bothered in the slightest, she was way too busy with her brand new dolls.

"You look like a lollipop man, Robin," Mrs Jillings remarked, holding back her laughter as his expression quickly changed to one of annoyance.

"It's mustard, I'll have you know. And it cost me a fortune!"

"Then why on earth haven't you worn it already! You mad man!" said Mrs Jillings with a look of confusion.

"Well that's easy, I was waiting for the right time. Kirsten, I'm just going to pop into town and check on Charlie like we discussed last night, is that okay?" Kirsten nodded, sipping at the juice concealed inside her china cup.

"Hopefully won't be long, but don't think you can't carry on without me!"

"Oh, we won't," Mrs Jillings chuckled, frowning comically in Robin's direction.

He wrapped a thick grey scarf around his neck, checked his pockets then cast his family a nod and a smile, before making his way towards the front door, ready to endure the winter spell that awaited beyond it. He hoped it would be a quick visit, expecting Charlie home, safe and sound - or was it too much to ask, he wondered... Not meaning to sound too greedy.

* * *

The village had already seen its fair share of strange ordeals, and they weren't becoming any less dangerous. The muggings, the disappearances, the dramatic increase in contagions - these were the least of the people's concerns, apart from those who were blind to the greater picture, the vastness that they had existed within.

Had Charlie really seen a bird with wings described as large as a house? Or was it just a figment of his imagination? It was blowing up a blizzard, surely it couldn't have been…

"*A Phoenix,*" echoed a commanding feminine voice, "A Phoenix flew to Shoulders Heath and hasn't been seen since. We can only assume that it's gone into hiding once again - but this time we know where it is!" she concluded, sat firmly in her bronze throne like chair, glancing towards the other members of the meeting who were also sat against large sculptural thrones that had been cast in metals that reflected the seated person's ranking amongst the chamber.

The Golden throne shaped in the form of a dragon was taken by a tall, heavy man, with a grand, bushy black beard. He wore a long purple velvet coat with silver stars sewn in to the sleeves like some kind of wearable weaponry. They definitely could have been used as throwing stars, if a time ever came - as well as his long curly cane that rested against the side of the throne.

He was known as Professor Grimtale, Head of the Institute of Morient kind. A school for the gifted, he liked to think, but others thought of it as more of a hospital, a means of looking after the unstable youngsters that were only just discovering their silent potential.

The children, the adults, the people who existed with Morient DNA were far greater in ability than any human. Magic circulated their blood streams, stardust twinkled in their eyes and love blossomed stronger than anything a Human had ever had to offer. A Morient - or ***magically orientated person***, had every right to walk the land of the Humans, but most forced themselves to remain separated, creating a sense of superiority, which Kenneth had always frowned upon.

Kenneth was present inside the chamber, sat in his bronze Bear-like throne and eager to add to what Miss Bilshore had said as glimpses of the appearance flashed before his eyes.

"I told you, Professor. I was not mistaken, I saw it! I followed the Phoenix to the border of Shoulders Heath, as far as I could climb. The Starlight Phoenix has returned, Professor Grimtale, you now have two eye witnesses," Kenneth claimed, wiping the sweat from his brow and adjusting his spectacles, looking flushed in the face as he glanced over at Sachester Bilshore - the gatekeeper of Shoulders Heath and the sacred land beyond the black mountains.

"Believe me, Mr Brown, I do not disbelieve either of you, it has merely raised concerns. And if what you say is undoubtedly true then we must prepare for the worst – and you both know what happens then..." Grimtale smiled dangerously, "Were there any other witnesses that we should know about, Mr Brown? Miss Bilshore?" he blinked, glaring across at the pair of them.

"There was a boy, and a man," Kenneth muttered, "But I dealt with them, there's nothing to worry about."

Grimtale gave a sigh of relief then ran his hand vigorously through his silky curls. Grimtale had a lot of love for his afro, more than what could be said about Sachester Bilshore's, whose head also sported a nest of dark curly fibres. She had just thrown it in to a bun, much like the black dress and corset she had slipped in to. There was never time to make an effort with appearance, but needless to say she was a beautiful lady and her lack of make-up complimented her natural curvaceous features, especially her rosy red lips and cheekbones. Her arm was *probably* the only part of her body that she had allowed a little extra effort. It had a brown leather bracelet curling around it, much like the body of a snake, where beneath it, the black ink etched into her flesh took the shape of a tree with branches bare and sprawled about her forearm. It kind of looked out of place where the rest of her body was bare.

The heavy chamber doors were opened, swinging forth and closing hard behind the two strangers who came strutting in to the circular room. One was female and wore a long, vibrant pink coat that fell to the ankles and swayed behind her as she strolled towards the open space at the centre of the chamber - where the council members sat in a circular sequence, surrounding a tall ruby statue of a bird, much the same as the one described as a Phoenix by Miss Bilshore and Kenneth Brown.

"Sorry we're late, Professors and…," she paused, looking across at Kenneth like the dirt on the sole of her pink diamond slippers, "- and whatever they call you," she added, with amusement in her tone as she slumped herself down in to the comfort of her silver seat, which appeared to resemble a strange looking snake with the body of a horse, most certainly not of the human world.

"Professor Magenta and Mr Silverstein, how nice of you to finally join us. Better late than never," Grimtale grumbled, looking over at Kenneth, who now had Magenta sat smarmy beside him.

"Apologies, Professor," said Silverstein - Magenta's companion who had followed her in to the chamber. Silverstein was tall and slender with a long colour-shifting coat wrapped snug around him, casting rivers of silver as the sun's rays glanced across him, beaming down through the glass dome lid that sat overhead, concealing the room and casting it transcendent.

His shiny metallic shoes clattered and echoed about the chamber as he stepped towards a chair, next to Magenta. This one was much smaller, and lacking personality in comparison to the others within the circle, but it was solid bronze like the majority of the seats that sat empty, apart from the presence of the silver and singular golden throne that Grimtale sat upon.

"Is this everyone?" Silverstein questioned, looking across to Grimtale, "Or would there be a lack of reliability in the ranks, Professor.

Wouldn't be a first now, would it?

The chamber fell silent as Silverstein and Grimtale exchanged a stern glare.

"Lillian Vargov, Professor Lint and Professor Yuri are otherwise preoccupied, Mr Silverstein. As for the fourth throne that sits empty, the one I assume your remark was initially intended for...I believe you know the reasons better than *I*."

Silverstein frowned, glancing over towards the solid silver chair, cast in the shape of a Phoenix bird, peering over the backrest.

"You're mistaken, Professor. Far before my time," he claimed as he ruffled his silver tipped hair into a standing mass and then slumped back, eye level with Magenta who sat amused beside him.

"Why is Kenneth here?" Silverstein whispered, leaning towards Magenta's ear as she peered across.

"I think we both know the answer to that one, that's if you're right…"

"Course I am, why else would he choose to live on *their* side?" Magenta blinked, lost in a world of thought while Professor Grimtale, Headmaster, clambered from his golden throne and marched to the centre of the room, pressing the shaft of his spiral shaped cane against the marbled dark of the floor beneath him, supporting his grand physique and dominating presence as he addressed the person's present within the chamber.

"For those unaware, the lady on my left is Sachester Bilshore, Gatekeeper of Shoulders Heath, the sacred land beyond the black mountains. Miss Bilshore, I'd like to introduce Aline Magenta, our expert in mythical creatures, and Leonard Silverstein, captain of the governing enforcer unit, protecting our borders from terrorist threats, be it Morient, Human or otherwise unclassified species."

Bilshore frowned as she looked to the captain.

"Then why has the Starlight Phoenix managed to escape again?" she yelled towards Silverstein, who suddenly jolted to attention.

"The Phoenix - It's here? Why wasn't this brought to my attention sooner?" asked Silverstein.

"Why do you think you've been summoned, Mr Silverstein!" Grimtale asked rhetorically, peering down at him.

"I apologise, but we have been searching high and low, Miss Bilshore. So the Starlight Phoenix is in Shoulders Heath?" Silverstein asked, wide eyed and now far more interested in the topic of discussion.

"It's what we are led to believe, yes," Grimtale nodded, sensing Bilshore's eyes burning into him as she shot him a look of disgust.

"And I want it gone! You brush aside the work I have done to make the town safe! We were even in talks to host field trips for the students next term, but with a Phoenix on the loose, it would be immoral to allow anything of the sort to proceed. We've all seen what they can do…" She explained, looking to Magenta who seemed eager to jump in.

"I don't know what planet you live on, love, but to think the children would want to visit that dump, you must be mad, and last time I checked you had much greater problems than a Phoenix. Were you just going to hope that the Veilers would stay in their holes and turn a blind eye?

You realise Shoulders Heath will never be safe? Quite frankly, I pity the *Phoenix!*"

Magenta smirked, amused by Miss Bilshore's outburst.

"In fact, how do you propose dealing with your infestation?" she asked.

"Enough, Magenta!" bellowed Grimtale with a stern look in his eye, "That is a matter for another time, we are here today to devise the capture of the Phoenix and its safe return to its enclosure…"

"Inside the institute? You want to put it back where it originally escaped from?" Kenneth said in surprise.

"It hardly escaped now, *did it*? We were betrayed! This is our chance to complete the rebuild that we have yearned for. The Vinemoore institute of Morient kind can be great again, I promise you all."

The room filled with silent concern as they all cast each other a look of worry.

"Won't the Phoenix's presence here just provoke an attack from...*them?*" Kenneth questioned, asking the burning question the others had not wanted to raise.

"When was the last attack? When were *their* kind last sighted?" interjected Grimtale, abolishing their theories with a reasonable question that most had no choice but to consider. The enemy responsible for the Institutes undoing hadn't been seen for many years, but it was safe to assume they still existed...somewhere, some place, watching and waiting in the shadows...

"How about we discuss what happens next, once we are in possession of the Starlight Phoenix, yes?" Silverstein chirped, leaning forward and resting his chin upon his knuckles, "I have a suggestion, if you will?"

"Go ahead," Grimtale nodded.

"Bring him in," Silverstein added, pointing towards the empty solid silver throne, "So the theories state, he was last to bond with the Phoenix. He would be the ideal candidate when we attempt to lure out the Phoenix," he smirked.

"no...That would be too dangerous, not to mention we would have to bring him here…"

Silverstein nodded, "Good job it's holiday season then, Professor!" he winked, twiddling his thumbs, waiting for confirmation.

"Any Objections?" the headmaster asked, turning to Kenneth, Miss Bilshore and Magenta.

"Do you even know where *he* is, Mr Silverstein? The man's a ghost," claimed Bilshore, sounding unconvinced by her tone.

"Well, that's where I was hoping one of you might know… Kenneth, for example?"

Kenneth suddenly bolted upright, casting Silverstein a nervous look as he recalled the man they were talking about.

"I'm - I'm afraid I've got nothing, it's been years, as Miss Bilshore said, a ghost," Kenneth looked away, knowing that Silverstein was still glaring in his direction for some strange reason, like he was suspected of something.

"That is disappointing,to say the least," Silverstein sighed, yet looking amused by the smirk on his face. Then Magenta spoke up.

"I know where he is!" she said, feeling quite empowered as the other four turned simultaneously, "I know where he lives," She added, as her gaze fell upon Leonard, who was sat loosely beside her, waiting anxiously for an answer.

"Vinemoore. He lives in Vinemoore," she confirmed, as Leonard Silverstein slumped back against the bronzed backrest of his chair and kicked up his feet on to the arm, exhaling loudly.

"Vinemoore, hiding in plain sight, who would have known?" Silverstein muttered under his breath, peering up at the crystal ceiling.

"Kenneth. Bring us Professor Robin Occamy," ordered Silverstein, conveying a look of fury through the fires of his eyes as they fell upon him, whose face had paled. In that awful moment, he had just realised the consequence of Magenta's admittance - his friend Robin was now in grave danger...

CHAPTER 4
Rise Of The Reapers

The ground was still frozen solid as Robin made his way down the hillside. Heading towards the pathway that ran directly to the village town centre. Charlie didn't live far from Robin's cottage, he passed it every day on his way to work - it was just on the corner, at the other end of the walkway, the part that was cast in shadow, dark and gloomy with the sound of water trickling down the side of the concrete walls.

Robin stopped as his gaze fell upon what was once a gravel path, but now a slab of solid ice, cracked and crystallised.

He scratched at his head then turned curiously, wondering if there was another means of getting to Charlie's house that wouldn't involve a fifteen minute detour around the back of the block. But the shop fronts ran endlessly as far as the eye could see, the walkway was his only option.

Robin sighed, exhaling a frosty white breath and turning back, meeting the eyes of his reflection that sat on the surface of the solidified water.

"One small step, slowly does it," he muttered to

himself, carefully placing the sole of his right boot on the surface of the ice, with his arms outstretched and placed firmly against the two brick walls either side.

Some of the guttering overhead had broken during the storm. It now had icicles hanging from them, drawing his attention up to their spear-like tips. Robin wasn't going to look up any longer than he needed to, he knew they were there, they weren't helping as he carried on moving, slowly shuffling towards the opposite side of the walkway, where Charlie's house sat peacefully, waiting.

Robin could see the front garden now, the fence was coated in a thick spell of snow, sat directly under the warmth of the sun's rays as it rose in to the sky.

"It's not that I want you to go, it's just that I don't want you to stay," Robin whispered, addressing the weather, trying to amuse himself as his feet started to slip and slide from side to side. He must have looked like a clumsy idiot, he was certain of it, but there was no one around to witness it, not a soul in sight. Vinemoore was silent, like most typical Christmas mornings.

But this was a first, never had Robin found himself traipsing through the wilderness of Antarctica on Christmas morning before. Neither had he felt so silly as he managed to bring his feet to a standstill, quickly holding his balance and launching his hands to the sides of the walls, supporting his weight and glancing skyward, directly down the frozen shafts of the icicles that were looming overhead, melting, dripping and cracking.

It was only a matter of time before they would become unstuck - and Robin was hardly in an ideal position, stood directly beneath them as the fracturing ice appeared to imitate a set of sharp, chattering teeth as they began to lose stability.

Robin held his stance for a moment, then bent his knees and launched himself out of the alley and straight into the bed of deep frothy whiteness that covered the ground of the surrounding cul de sac, leaving a body shaped indentation embedded in the surface of the snow, with no time to spare as the heaviest pole of ice plummeted in to the alley, shattering across the icy path.

It was as if by magic Robin had vanished - that was of course until his head slowly re-emerged, sprouting from the pit and peering around the neighbourhood to assure himself that nobody was watching. He then began knocking the frost from his coat as he got back to his feet, which had already lost their warmth and begun to throb as numbness set in.

"What a palava!" Robin grunted, patting away the last of the snow from his hair and trembling as a slither of ice fell down the back of his shirt and melted against his spine.

"Close call, as well. Better luck next time, though!" he chuckled, pointing at the shattered icicle that lay in pieces against the bottom of the alley walls. He then gave a long, weary sigh as he marched over the mounds of snow that hindered the path to Charlie's front gate.

Once past the snow, he had arrived, and the damp rotten gate creaked as Robin pushed it open and carefully approached the green front door that sat at the end of the salted pavement.

The heavy wooden door was framed by ivy and a bush that would have been full of blackberries back in the summertime, but now it sat weak and decrepit in the corner, sent to slumber by the chill of the season as Robin stepped up to the stone slab at the foot of the door, pressing his face against the glass before knocking.

He'd always done that, never did him any favours, the best thing to come of it was this one time when a little old lady opened up almost immediately - then Robin had to explain why he had ended up laid along her doormat - of course, he came up with something witty and walked away with a pork pie and cup of tea, poured into his thermal flask that he used to carry everywhere; however, this time there was no one there to spot him, but there was a light on in a back room, he could see it glowing warmly, then a shadow begun to move as Robin's eyes widened and his hand raised beside his ear and started to bang against the wood of the door, frantically.

"Hello!" he called out, "It's Mr Occamy! I was wondering if you had a moment, Mrs. Reed? Mr. Reed?"

He took a breath and watched as a figure moved towards the door. He thought it must have been one of the parents at first, but as the latch *clonked* and the door pulled away on its hinge, Charlie appeared in the doorway, looking up at Robin with curious eyes.

"Mr Occamy, it's good to see you! We didn't make any calls if that's why you're here," he said, sincerely.

"Calls? Oh no, I'm just here to make sure you made it home okay. Are your parents back there?" Robin asked, peering down the hallway.

"Yes, do you want me to fetch them?"

"No, no, you're safe and sound, that's all that matters, little man," Robin smirked.

Charlie frowned.

"What do you mean, exactly?"

"After last night, I was just a little worried. The streets are even more dangerous at night!"

Charlie blinked, feeling confused.

"But I've not been out, it was probably one of the other kids, we all kinda look the same when we're wearing our coats and bobble hats."

Robin looked to the ground, casting his mind back, certain it was Charlie who had ran in to him and knocked the brown paper bag from his hand. Who else could it have been? Maybe he had made a mistake? *No, it was definitely Charlie*, he had the orange fluorescent thread running through the seams of his coat, and he could see it hanging from the chair in the back room, as clear as day.

"You bumped in to me, you said something about a bird with wings the size of a house! Don't you remember?" Robin asked.

As he spoke he knelt down to look Charlie square in the eye - if the boy was lying, he would soon be able to tell, he was good like that, he could spot a lie a mile before it was told, he liked to think. It was as if a flame of negative energy would appear, burning within the pupil of the eye - but as Charlie shook his head, it remained extinguished, meaning he was telling the truth, Robin silently confirmed, scratching at his chin and staring down at the salted concrete slab where his boot resided, damp and firm.

"Not to worry, my man. Too much booze, probably. Never drink on the job, that is more than likely a reasonable explanation," he lied, knowing full well that he hadn't touched a drop of alcohol in over twenty four hours.

Charlie felt confused as Robin stood up and stepped back from the door, he was thinking of a bird with enormous wings, he could have sworn he'd dreamt up something similar...*but it was a dream, was it not?*

"Merry Christmas, Charlie," said Robin as he began to wander towards the gate, the boy quickly looked to Robin and waved, then slowly closed the door as he tried to make sense of it all, lost on a train of thought about dreams and giant birds...

"What's going on here then?" Robin muttered under his breath, frowning and staring in to the snowy abyss, "- *unless I was drunk on oxygen, I'm certain that Charlie Reed was outside the shop last night. Why doesn't he remember? Maybe he knocked his head harder than I thought?*" Robin wondered on his own question as he stood at the centre of the cul-de-sac, surrounded by houses and snowmen aplenty.

Maybe it would come back to him given a little time, or did it *really* matter? It had to be one of the most normal things to ever happen in Vinemoore. Usually someone would lose their memory, then the next day they were running along rooftops believing if they ran fast enough they could grow a pair of feathery wings and take off in to the sky, but instead, they just found themselves tangled in vines and branches as gravity took its handle. It was a good job the village had plenty of trees to go around, they were quite literally life savers.

On the plus side, now Robin had seen Charlie alive and well he knew he could go home without worry lingering over him. He couldn't wait to get back inside the warmth of his home and chow down on the lovely meal that Mrs Jillings must have been cooking by now - the turkey always took a good three hours if they wanted it roasted to perfection.

Robin could almost smell the scent of Christmas dinner as he tried to paint it in his mind, stepping back in the direction of that dreaded alley, which looked as dangerous as it did before, however as he peered towards the distant end, there now stood a person dressed in a long, black tatty robe, with a hood that hid their face by shadow.

Robin stopped abrupt in his path, biting his bottom lip as he began to wonder whether he should turn back and take a different, longer route around. But before he reached a decision, the figure started to step forward and so did he, ignoring the ice beneath them that surprisingly wasn't as slippery as before, it had begun to melt and turn to mush.

Robin didn't want to look the strange person in the eye, so he pretended to mind his own business, glancing down, making it seem like he was checking over his waistcoat that was now cold and wet from the snow. He pulled at a stray strand of cotton and patted his hand against a button for no reason at all.

But as they passed, Robin could feel the mysterious figure glaring at him from the corner of its eye. He continued to stroll towards the light at end of the alley, not looking back and hoping that there wasn't going to be any trouble - he didn't quite fancy another punch up, he thought to himself, finding the thought rather amusing.

He just wanted to be back home, with his family and that lovely seasonal food. Maybe if he pictured it for long enough the thought of the potential danger would vanish? He couldn't worry every time he passed a random person either, they were *probably* on their way to a family member's house - *Yes, that's exactly what they were doing*, he told himself as he stopped near the clearing to peer over his shoulder, trying to be discreet as his gaze fell upon the eyes of the dark figure staring back at him, with a winding stick held at arm's length, pointed straight towards the plastic guttering torn from the rooftop and arching over, exactly where Robin stood.

The stick wielding vigilante suddenly shrieked, muffled by what seemed like a opera mask that covered half of their face, except for the emerald green eyes that were wide and filled with hatred as the word "*Brexio!*" echoed down the alley and a bright green luminous energy began to manifest at the tip of the thin wooden stick that was grasped by the robed figure. It's voice seemed to be that of a male, quite young too, Robin noticed – then a bolt of lightning ejected from the stick and struck the arch of solid ice, breaking free the four remaining icicles that loomed overhead.

Robin looked up to witness as the four icy shafts plunged in to the ground, shattering simultaneously just inches from his toes. He then looked back at the robed man who was now pointing the scary stick directly towards him and advancing, chanting and calling out, "*Professor Robin Occamy! Confirm, Professor!*"

Robin frowned and stuttered as his nerves got the better of him, backing away.

"Doctor of medicine, preferably. May I be of assistance or do you just enjoy shouting like a lunatic?"

As Robin prepared to make his valiant getaway, he felt a rough hand clamp on to his shoulder and pull him from the aggressors line of sight.

It was Kenneth, the slender middle aged man with golden framed spectacles sat firmly on the bridge of his crooked nose, and a moustache the size of a slug, slumped across his top lip. He pressed Robin against the closest shop front and yelled in to his face.

"*Come with us!*"

Then he pulled him along sharply, as they darted away from the dark robed figure emerging from the alleyway, a figure that slowly looked about, searching and hunting for sight of its prey - they had already disappeared inside a run down building, just across the street...

Kenneth slammed the door shut and whispered what seemed like garble to Robin as he tapped the doorknob with the tip of his cane. The door instantly locked and Kenneth turned to the paled faced Robin Occamy who stood wide eyed and frowning as he could see beyond the broken glass segments, the robed man wasn't far behind, he was right on their tail...

Magenta, who was also present, grabbed on to Robin's arm and pulled him away, disappearing towards the back of the shop where heavy wooden tables and chairs were stacked as high as the ceiling.

"We can't go this way!" Magenta yelled.

She yanked Robin backwards, following the other three Enforcers who had already begun to ascend towards the second level. Here, it was far more spacious but thick with dust, the entire room was as grey as the storm that was riding in on the horizon beyond the black mountains. Robin had spotted it in the distance, through the multiple smashed windows as he glanced around the abandoned room, then saw the sky rolling over heavy and darkening rapidly with the approaching storm.

Kenneth was last to emerge on the top floor, listening out for the sound of intrusion while waving his cane about the air until it burst in an explosion of bright blue particles, fizzing and sparking like a firework, as it erupted and then absorbed into the rotted wallpaper.

"We don't have long, but we're safe for the time being. You two, guard the top of the stairs," Kenneth commanded, pointing at the two enforcers who acknowledged with a stern nod. They were Leonard Silverstein's personal guard, sent to assist Kenneth and Magenta who had finally got Robin in a reasonable position where they could begin to explain what was going on.

Robin didn't know where to turn, but an explanation would have been ideal right about now, he thought, staring silently at Kenneth who was making his way over, with his cane clutched tight in his right hand and his fair brown hair standing on end, swept back by the winter breeze that was whistling in through the broken windows.

"Robin, I might not have been entirely honest with you these past few years but the time has come, and it might be a bit much to comprehend at first, but that's okay."

Kenneth placed his hand on Robin's shaken shoulder as a sign of reassurance, casting away the terror from his eyes.

"*What the hell is going on?*" he roared, demanding answers.

"Robin, We need you to come with us, some place far from Vinemoore…" said Magenta, who had stepped in beside Kenneth, but minding her distance - she still wasn't too fond of him it seemed, as she cast him a disapproving glance.

"No, Magenta. He needs to go home, pack his belongings and run, as far from Vinemoore as physically possible, *away* from us! You listen here, Robin. It's unsafe, you've known that for quite some time, if there's anything you choose to do today, make sure you do *not* listen to *her!*" Kenneth interrupted, towering over Magenta, who was ready to take him on, assuming he was looking for a brawl - she wasn't easily intimidated, it was clear as she sternly met Kenneth's violent gaze.

"You still fail to surprise me, Kenneth Brown. Silverstein was right about you," she claimed, forcing herself against the rising tension between the two of them, until Kenneth surrendered, stepping back from the blonde bush of hair and turning his concerns back to Robin who didn't appear to be any less confused.

"We don't have time for this, out of the window!" Kenneth ordered.

"Out - *out* of the window?" said Robin, glancing behind him.

"YES! Jump through the pigging window, man!"

"Why can't she do it first?"

"Because, she's a woman!" Kenneth yelled, hoisting Robin by his mustard coloured collar and throwing him with force, out of the ajar window.

"That's not to say I *don't* want to throw you out of a window," he remarked, as he hopped on to the window ledge and lowered himself down the side of the guttering, into the yard where Robin was still shuffling his way out of a deep, prickly, thistle bush.

The branches crunched and snapped as Robin pushed himself through the sharp foliage and fell against the snow. His hands and neck were covered in thistle leaves, they were very sore and had already began to itch as he knocked the greenery from his flesh.

"*You could have given me some kind of warning!*" he yelled, glancing across at Kenneth, who was watching the window, waiting for Magenta to appear.

"No time for warnings, Mr Occamy."

"Marvellous," he replied, scratching away at the irritated skin on his neck.

Suddenly Magenta was now making her way down the guttering, glaring up at the window with her eyes a blaze with fear - she must have seen something that had sped up her desire to be back on ground, her hands were red raw as she jumped from the wall and in to the snow capped gravel beneath her, where Robin and Kenneth waited impatiently.

"*They're gone, the Reaper killed them. We have to leave now!*" she yelled, drawing her elegant, purple coloured stick from her deep coat pocket and pointed it towards the palm of her injured hand.

"Heal," she chanted, and the tip began to ignite, casting a mystical aura around her injured limb, until the broken flesh had bonded itself back together, looking as good as new. She rushed to do the same for Robins neck and the back of his hands, they were stinging and tingling from the thistles until the golden energy fused with his inflamed skin, returning it back to its original state. Then Robin stood stunned, frozen to the spot as he felt the irritating sensations disappear.

"How did you do that?"

Magenta barged past, pulling at Robins mustard coat.

"What are those things, why has everyone got magic sticks?" he asked.

"It's called a wand," Magenta replied, imagining the look of stupidity that had washed across Robin's face as she dragged him towards the furthest end of the yard.

"I knew that," he smirked.

The three of them raced towards the back fence, which was dusted with frost. There was also a large wooden gate that seemed to be unlocked, they noticed as they glanced back and forth, expecting the sight of the robed man, stood at the window that they had escaped from - but he wasn't there, he could have been anywhere by now.

Kenneth and Magenta had already recognised the power they were up against, it reminded them of a time long ago when the first of the Reaper kind had tethered the two realms, threatening both the human and Morient kind with their hostile antics and uncontrollable thirst for blood.

If only Kenneth and Magenta had been more oblivious, then perhaps they would have appeared fearful, however they had always lived in fear of the day when darkness would return, so they were somewhat prepared as they pulled open the gate, exposing a pack of Reapers, stood tall and menacing behind their shining face masks. Their dark robes had a frosty coating and their crooked wands were raised, tightly grasped and ready to attack...

Magenta slammed shut the gate as the others backed away, turning towards the abandoned shop. Their Shoes and boots crunched in the snow as they ran, until the alley Reaper dropped from the window, breaking his fall with a forward roll and then stood there, blocking their escape.

Kenneth pulled the group to a sudden halt, then stood staring into the green of the Reaper's eyes as they waited patiently for someone to make a move.

"Hand over Professor Robin Occamy, and perhaps...your lives will be spared," the Reaper threatened with its raspy, predatory tone.

Robin looked to Magenta and Kenneth who were stood sharp and rigid, ready to fight, then he spoke up with anger.

"You speak as if I don't have a tongue in my mouth. So for the lack of respect, I am forced to deny your request - sorry lad!"

The Reaper gave a disapproving grunt and sharpened his aim, pointing his twisted black wand towards Kenneth, whose gaze had fallen cold on the tip. A spoken word now stood between life and death as the other three Reapers approached from behind, also bearing their wands at arms length.

"*Now!*" Magenta yelled, casting a spell towards

the fence in time with Kenneth who had waved his cane, blasting the Reaper ahead of them with a blinding light.

"*Senteer!*" Magenta cried, then a ball of crystallized energy erupted out of thin air, like a passage, pulsating and sparkling as bright as ice.

"Robin, I need you to think of home, imagine your room, follow my lead," ordered Magenta, diving through the mass of energy with Robin and Kenneth in tow, avoiding the poisonous bolts of energy that shot from the reapers wands and exploded against the fence.

The three of them had now vanished and so had the passage, closing in on itself immediately before the Reapers could follow them through. There was no way of telling where they had gone, they had no idea where Robin had spent the last few years of his life, let alone where he was living. So the four faceless warriors had no other choice but to lower their wands and stand defeated - until next time, which would be different, they confirmed with a subtle nod of their heads.

The darkness was slowly returning, and with it came the Reapers and the opposition running scared, becoming terribly reminiscent of times long ago, when evil had enslaved both the Human and Morient world...

CHAPTER 5
The Spell Of Transportation

The walls began to tremor, the crockery on the table tops rattled and knocked together, chattering as it became apparent to Emily, Kirsten and Mrs Jillings that something alarming was happening upstairs as the ceiling broke apart in the corners, releasing a trail of plaster that trickled down, landing in a cloud of dust on the living room carpet.

"Was that an earthquake?" Kirsten questioned, staring towards the plastered ceiling.

Mrs Jillings looked confused, but then her face suddenly lit up as if she had just remembered, it wasn't an earthquake at all - at least she *hoped* it wasn't, as she climbed to her feet and slipped on her navy sequin slippers.

"I'm just going to check upstairs, you carry on drinking your tea, Miss Withers."

Then Mrs Jillings began to go up the creaky staircase, leaving Emily and Kirsten anxiously waiting as they peered out towards the top of the stairs, taking an occasional sip of tea from their china cups as they watched the sequins sparkle their way up the steps.

Meanwhile, the tremors may have come to a halt but there were still sounds like fumbling and knocking coming from Robin and Kirsten's bedroom. The sound became more prominent as Mrs Jillings neared the landing, but there was no one else in the house, *what could have been making that awful racket*, she thought as she slowly crept in the direction of the bedroom.

Robins door was chunky and coated in a thick layer of mustard yellow paint, much like the coat he had chosen for the trip to Charlie Reeds house, which he was yet to return from, but he wasn't home, *she would have heard the front door go if he had come back, surely?* Mrs Jillings queried as she wrapped her frail hand around the big brass door knob that sat cold and still as the banging continued to pound from within the room.

She paused, then gave a heavy sigh before bursting inside, pushing the door back abruptly on its hinge and entering the bedroom where all the noise had been coming from. But the room suddenly fell silent, there was no one inside so it seemed, as Mrs Jillings eyes fell back in to a resting scowl. She searched every nook and cranny of the bedroom, to be sure that she wasn't going mad!

She had *definitely* heard something and the house was fully detached so it couldn't have been the neighbours, unless it had come from the attic, she wondered, casting her sights up at the dusty lamp shade that was swaying ever so slightly, left to right.

Mrs Jillings had become frustrated but had no other choice but to give in, shrugging her shoulders and pulling the bedroom door to a close as she made her way back downstairs.

"Well, there's no one upstairs and everything seems to be in one piece. You may have been right, perhaps a minor earthquake," Mrs Jillings slumped back in to her armchair and reached across for her cup and saucer. Kirsten glanced over, meeting her gaze.

"It's nothing to worry about, is it?" she asked, sounding nervous.

"I wouldn't have thought so, it's Christmas! Don't let it distract you, my dear."

"No, I shan't. I'm just wondering when Robin will be back, he's been gone nearly an hour now. Charlie's house is only ten minutes down the road."

Kirsten turned her gaze towards the window where she began to cast her mind away from the tremor, as the sky was slowly becoming heavy and gloomy as the storm on the horizon approached, drifting from the direction of Shoulders Heath, beyond the black mountains.

However before her mind could detach from the fear of another earthquake, there it was again, the shaking, the walls vibrating and bumps and knocks pounding from upstairs.

The attic hatch suddenly became unhooked and swung open, releasing a bundle of bodies that dropped from the attic and crashed down to the passage floor.

It was Robin, Kenneth and Professor Magenta, they were now stacked upon one another, pushing and shoving as they climbed back to their feet and began to knock away the sawdust and cobwebs that clung to their coats.

"I'm sorry! I've never even been up there

before, I didn't know we had an attic!" Robin muttered, staring at the other two who were looking at each other and both furious.

"What did you think you were doing? You do realise how dangerous that could have been?" Kenneth roared, just inches from Magenta's face.

"We're safe aren't we? Besides, the Reapers couldn't have followed us, that's *not* how the spell works!"

Robin didn't understand a word they were going on about, he felt it would be best to remain silent and let them have it out, it seemed like there had been a lot bottled up by the way it was pouring from their mouths.

"Robin, dear, You're probably wondering what that was? Now, Kenneth listen up because you might learn a thing or two. Senteer is a spell of transportation, very handy if in a spot of bother like we were, but it's always good for covering large distances in the matter of seconds, just *don't* push your luck; otherwise you might end up in Shoulders Heath!"

Kenneth still didn't look amused as questions still burned in his mind.

"The only reason we ended up here is because we were protecting Robin," she added, waiting for Kenneth to have his say.

"And what if the Reapers made it through? What if they had managed to filter their minds and arrived in this very building?"

Magenta moved closer to Kenneth, once again invading his personal space to counter his argument.

"Look, I did something and we're safe...If it was down to *you*, Kenneth Brown, you'd be dead and they would have taken Robin. No offence,

Robin, but you wouldn't have been able to do anything about it."

"No offence taken," he muttered, looking down at the mess on the carpet, the splintered shards and mounds of dusts.

"You'll pick it up quickly, now, are you ready?" she asked, as Robin cast her a look of confusion.

"Ready?"

"No, he's *not* ready, Magenta," Kenneth interrupted, standing between them, "This is ridiculous! We have to report back to Professor Grimtale, he has to know that the Reapers are back, perhaps then he will reconsider Silverstein's ludicrous plan."

"Do I not have a say?" Robin piped up, reverting his position between the two flamboyant characters, "As mad as it sounds, shouldn't I be the one to decide whether I help or not?" he added, and for a moment there was silence as they collected their thoughts.

"I think that's fair," replied Kenneth, shooting a smug look at Magenta who stood beside him, reluctantly, not wanting to waste her energy by meeting his gaze any longer.

"Go ahead, just remember what's at stake…"
Robin frowned.

"What exactly *is* at stake?" He hissed through his teeth as Mrs Jillings began to climb the stairs again, alerting Robin, as the bottom step made a nasty squeal.

"Get out of here, both of you! And I'd prefer not to see you again, you understand?" He said in a hushed tone, waving his hands, prompting them both away as Magenta suddenly looked worried and Kenneth still looked smug, knowing that

Robin was no longer going to be returning with them - which translated as hope as the thought of Robin and his family safe, and hidden far from Vinemoore loomed bright in his thoughts.

"Ethel will make him understand, this isn't over, Kenneth."

Magenta blinked, then Kenneth cast the spell of transportation with his cane, slamming it against the floorboard and chanting "*Senteer*" as both stepped back, into the portal of crystallised energy that had suddenly erupted from thin air, illuminating the passage with a golden ray of light. The two figures quickly disappeared beyond the light, holding a strong thought of where they were headed, clearly in their minds as the energy closed behind them, concealing itself until there was nothing left behind but a weary man dressed in a mustard yellow frock coat, and a old confused lady, stood upon the landing, comfy and warm but also curious as her gaze fell cold upon Robin who was yet to notice her, frozen still on the top step.

"It's not what it looks like," Robin claimed as he turned awkwardly, trying hard to look casual, wondering whether she had seen what he had just witnessed.

"Don't suppose we have a dustpan and brush?" he grinned, his cheeks glowing bright red as he crept towards Mrs Jillings.

She still didn't look amused as she frowned at Robin, watching as he approached, stepping into the dying light of the sun that was shining through the landing window above the front door.

"I think it's time we sat down over a cup of tea, Mr Occamy," she said, sternly.

"You drink a lot of tea, don't you…"

"Of course, tea is good."

Then she led the way down the stairs, pulling the front room door closed as she passed and went on to the kitchen - Robin followed behind.

Once in the kitchen Mrs Jillings wasted no time running the kettle under the tap, and throwing it on the hob before taking a seat up the table.

"Do take a seat," said Mrs Jillings, signalling towards the chair beside her as Robin peeped his head around the door frame.

"Dinner smells good Mrs J," he said, winking at her as he removed his coat and placed it on the back of his wooden chair. Then as he sat down on the chair and brushed away the creases on his clean white shirt, he noticed that Mrs Jillings was still looking at him in a strange way.

"Is everything...*okay*, Mrs Jillings?"

She continued to stare, as if she was looking directly at the core of his soul.

"What did they have to say?"

"I'm sorry?"

"The Morients you brought home, what did they want?"

Robin's eyes widened.

"I didn't think you - I didn't think you noticed," he mumbled, awkwardly.

"I didn't think I'd see a Morient on Christmas day!" she chirped, still frowning and waiting patiently for the water to begin to boil.

"What did the Professor and Kenneth Brown have to say for themselves, Mr Occamy?" she added, leaning in so close that she could feel Robin's breath panting against her brow.

"Why am I seemingly the only one who has no

idea what the hell is going on? I ran into a strange man, a man with a stick - a *wand*, a magic wand!"

"Kenneth?"

"No! He has some kind of magic cane, this man was different. They called him a...*Reaper?*"

Mrs Jillings expression finally changed, Robin could almost see her second skin breaking away and crumbling as her face expressed a look of surprise and mixed anger to account for the breaking news, the return of the power that many had feared...

"If they are back, that can only mean one thing…"

"And that is?" asked Robin, reaching for Mrs Jillings hand to find it had turned cold and blue.

"It means things are going to change," she added in a shocked whisper, turning away as a tear fell down the side of her cheek, and the kettle began to whistle a stream of steam from its spout.

"Mrs J, what do you know of these Reapers?" Robin asked curiously, as she wandered over to the stove and lifted the kettle over to the side board where two floral coated, china cups waited with a tea bag set inside.

"Everything there is to tell," she said, "Apart from, it's *not* my place to say, and I'm sorry, Robin. It would appear that I haven't been completely honest with you these past few months…"

"Oh not *you* as well!" he remarked, reminded of Kenneth who had turned out to be some kind of magician.

"I have been watching over you and your family, but it was no coincidence. There is a man who wanted to make sure that you, Kirsten and Emily would be safe. So I pledged my allegiance to your family, not realising I would grow a fondness for you all."

Mrs Jillings stirred up the cups of tea and brought them back to the table where Robin was sat, listening carefully and trying his best to understand what was being explained.

It wasn't easy but even though it seemed silly and bizarre, he was still curious, after all, he had already seen a great deal with his own eyes, fallen through a portal of liquid energy, and watched as Kenneth and Magenta vanished through the fabric of reality.

Nothing was questionable anymore as he listened to all Mrs Jillings had to say.

"There is a lot that you're about to learn about the world we live in, and if I'm honest I think there's a lot to be learned about yourself, too. But I am not the one to tell the tales, Mr Occamy."

Robin took a sip of his boiling hot cup of tea and took a moment, casting his mind back to all the weird and wonderful things he had experienced since living in the town of Vinemoore. The more he thought about it, he realised that there wasn't a great deal of memories to recollect, anything beyond moving into the cottage was all a blur, a vivid image concealed by a cloud of hazy smoke that wasn't yet ready to disperse.

"You're wondering aren't you, perhaps realising that this makes more sense than what you had originally expected, but please if you take anything away from me, let me tell you that Kirsten and Emily are safe, and what may be required of you will not bring them to harm."

Robin now looked worried, taking another sip of his tea to hydrate the brittle skin forming on the surface of his lips.

"Do they know?" he asked.

"Of course not. They're lucky, they're amazing people and they shall never know."

"Are you one of them?"

Mrs Jillings sighed and looked down for a moment, then met Robin's gaze.

"I am Morient. But I am one of few, much like Kenneth who live in harmony with Human beings."

"Am I Human?" Robin asked, noticing that Mrs Jillings was slowly becoming more and more vague by the way she was turning away and peering out of the kitchen window that looked out towards the clear skies that would soon be overwhelmed by darkness.

"Mr. Jillings...You know, I *know* you do...am I Morient?"

She still looked away and sipped at her tea, avoiding the question.

"I've said too much already, I will not jeopardise what's been put in place. I don't have the right, and I don't want to see you or your family coming to unnecessary harm, do you understand?" she muttered, still facing the opposite direction.

"No, I believe I don't," he replied, stepping up and walking in front of the window, breaking her stray gaze that had now settled on his face.

"What were you really sent here for?" he demanded.

"To protect, to nurture your family, Mr Occamy."

"You've done that pretty well, now what else? What has been *put in place,* why did they say that they needed me?" he bellowed, towering over

Mrs Jillings, who was slowly slumping down into her chair and cowering behind her china cup and saucer that was raised in front of her face.

Then creaking on its hinge, the front room door slowly began to open, then a pair of curious eyes peeped and widened as Emily spotted her Father stood in the kitchen.

"Papa! You're home!" she chirped, jumping in to the kitchen and throwing her arms around Robin's left leg.

"Hello, sweetie. Are you hungry?"

She nodded, with a massive grin, sniffing at the smell of turkey wafting up from the oven.

"Can you go and tell mummy that there's not long until dinner…"

"Okay!" she then skipped her way through to the front room to deliver the tasty news, giving Robin and Mrs Jillings a last moment to revert their gaze and board the train of thought that had momentarily escaped them.

"Magenta said, before she left, you would be able to bring me around, make me understand," he said in a hushed tone as he heard Emily rambling away to Kirsten in the front room.

"My mind is open, there is no better time than now! You *have* to tell me, what is it you're keeping from me?" he hissed, becoming slightly aggressive as he leaned close to Mrs Jilling's face as all its warmth washed away and fear glistened from her eyes that was all too apparent to Robin as he glared at her, coldly - aggressively.

"Don't you *dare* speak to me like that, Mr Occamy. Don't you *ever* do that again!"

Mrs Jillings pushed Robin away, where he quickly realised his wrongs as he buried his head in his hands and pressed away his hair.

"Please accept my apology," he begged, which immediately wiped the fear from Mrs Jillings eyes, and it was as if the fires were reignited as she rose from her chair, clutching her cup and saucer that were now sipped dry of tea.

"When the time is right, you will learn," she said, placing her china in the sink then turning back to face Robin, still massively upset.

"When the Occamy household falls into a slumber, meet me at the grandfather clock, then and only then will I begin the necessary proceedings that you seek."

Robin anxiously stood in the kitchen, running his mind over the questions that still remained.

"But we don't have a grandfather clock, *do* we?"

"What do you think?"

Robin scratched at his chin, looking about the kitchen. He had definitely heard the sound of a clock for as long as he could remember while living in the cottage, but still he was yet to find it. *Perhaps it was a miniature sized clock? Or an invisible grandfather clock?* He thought, as what seemed like crazy ideas *yesterday*, were now no different to the norm as he fell on to his hands and knees and began to scour the kitchen tiles for a trace of the infamous clock that chimed at the turn of day.

* * *

During the time that Robin had been in search of a grandfather clock that may not even exist,

Kenneth and Magenta had arrived at their desired destination, stepping out from within the portal of energy spiralling around on the surface of a dark rocky quarry, surrounded by tall, dark mountains that sat vertical through the angry grey clouds overhead.

It was like home to Magenta as they stepped a foot back inside the Morient realm, allowing the Senteer spell to close firmly behind them, exploding like a bright orange firework, casting light upon the vast institute temple that perched upon the cliff edge, across from where the two Morients had come to stand.

"Ready for a climb?" said Kenneth, staring down in to the depth of the valley where the grand Institute for Morient kind sat peacefully at a distance.

Magenta had begun to chuckle as she glanced towards Kenneth - he was being serious, he must have forgotten, which only make it funnier, she thought, as she drew her wand and tapped it gently against her head, accelerating a pleasant gift that she had discovered back in the days of schooling. She was surprised that Kenneth hadn't remembered as he turned to catch a glimpse of Magenta, shrinking to the size of a bird and spreading her fluffy pink wings.

"Sorry, Kenneth. Must dash!" she chirped as she jumped from the cliff edge and swooped down towards the institute's courtyard, flapping away and disappearing in to the distance, leaving behind a trail of glistening pink sparkle that stung as it bristled past the glass of Kenneth's spectacles.

"Brilliant, just bloody brilliant!" he cursed, taking the first step of a long, painful journey, down the side of the rocky valley, knowing Magenta was probably already inside the institute and about to slate his name again. Convincing the chamber that Kenneth Brown was the sole reason behind the failure in capturing Professor Robin Occamy. *As if the day couldn't get any worse*, he thought, slowly descending, remaining vigilant as he feared by the time he arrived at the gates, the only reason to enter would to be faced by Silverstein, ready to cart his corpse to the deepest, darkest corner of the Institutes dungeons....

CHAPTER 6
The Unpleasant News

The heavy chamber doors *squealed* and *crunched* as they returned to their closed position behind Professor Grimtale and Sachester Bilshore. They were headed for the front gates which stood beyond the grand, golden decorated hallway with pearlescent marble tiles that were glistening like a river beneath their feet. The gates were tall and dark and made from the strongest of steel, because even in an alternate world, the primitive metals had their uses and had never failed in keeping evil at bay, not while they remained shut and sealed by one of Grimtales most powerful enchantments.

There was no way to emphasise the sheer size, they towered four times the height of the professor as he arrived at the foot of them, where his journey had come to its conclusion as he waved away the aura of energy that was binding the two steel structures like a mystical padlock.

"You know I wish you well, Professor. But my enthusiasm to find the Phoenix has come with its concerns, especially for the Institutes well-being."

Grimtale cast Bilshore a warm smile and placed

his hand upon her right shoulder as a sign of reassurance, "I think you'd agree that there's no better people for the job than us. This is what we have been preparing for…"

"However, I don't think you're ready. Silverstein seems confident enough, but bringing *him* here, you understand I cannot stay and it's not just him that worries me…"

Grimtale carefully raised his hand until it was gently resting against the side of Bilshores cheek. It was warm and it made her feel comfortable and relaxed as she let out a heavy sigh and looked up, directly in to Grimtales eyes that were fallen graciously. He hadn't broken eye contact, but Bilshore couldn't help herself as shyness washed through her, acting as a reminder of how she felt towards the man of magnificent stature as he stood towering over her, with his thick purple velvet coat hugging his muscular build and his bushy black beard, curling silky soft around the curve of his smile as he gleamed under the pinky sparkle of Magentas tail feathers, which had swooped through the black steel verticals and landed overhead, perched on the fingertip of her favourite golden sculpture that reached out from within the ceiling mural, like branches of a willow tree.

Grimtale was now more than aware of Magentas presence as he looked over his shoulder, catching the twinkle of her beady black eyes as she chirped and fluttered her wings.

"I'll leave you to get on, Professor," said Bilshore, with disappointment in her tone as she looked away.

"I'm sorry about this. You have a safe trip back, please take care of yourself and let me know as soon as you get home."

Grimtale leaned in and kissed the blushing Sachester on her warm, rosy red cheek. Casting away her sulking lower lip and replacing it with a gentle smirk as she pulled open the left gate that stood beside her, turning back to cast her eyes on him, just one last time through the vertical struts as she stepped back, in to the vast wilderness of the Morient world that lay beyond the Institute gates.

"I'll see you again," she said, before whistling, alerting her mode of transport which came with haste, launching from the hazy mountain ledge and spreading its enormous wings to break its fall as it landed beside her. Its neck like a serpents with the body of a horse and wings of a creature like nothing of the human world. The beast hissed, flailed its double ended tongue and lowered its head as Bilshore cocked her leg over the brown saddle-like leather, and held on tightly as it flapped its wings and made way for Shoulders Heath, ascending out of the valley pit, towards the sea that lay beyond the dark mountains. Leaving the Institute of Morient kind all but a blur in the distance as Grimtale watched her disappear, over the horizon, far from the dangers that were assembling across the land.

The steel gates clattered as Grimtale pulled them to, aligning them and chanting under his breath, which sparked the tip of his chunky wooden cane as he waved it between the structures. Lime green orbs spluttered and illuminated the steel until finally the enchantment wound about the verticals like a snake, an unbreakable bond.

Grimtale frowned as he glared across the land, observing the approaching storm clouds that had begun to blacken the skies.

"I fear there has been further developments, Professor Magenta," said Grimtale, as he felt the flutter of wings brush against the hair of his neck.

The rosy bird chirped, then sparkled as it began to grow in size, shedding its delicate feathers which drooped around her now humanoid looking body, morphing in to the shape of her soft frock coat as magentas face finally reappeared from the remnants of the bird-like features.

As she took her first breath, she coughed, launching a pair of pink feathers from her throat and in to the air, then turning to Grimtale who had now reverted his gaze as Magenta raised her hand to wipe her lips. He was staring coldly at the long fleshy scarring along her brow and cheek, which caused her some discomfort as she broke eye contact to pull her wand from her coat pocket and cast a spell over the deformity, hiding it from sight where it was best for everyone, especially Magenta who would rather it not be there at all, but it was something she knew she had to simply live with, now.

"I have news, Professor," she said, returning her wand to her pocket and taking a step closer to Grimtale.

"The chamber awaits," he replied, leading the way back down the hall, over the stream of marble and towards the golden entrance to the chamber throne room.

* * *

Inside the throne room, Silverstein was still waiting patiently with his feet kicked up over the arm of his bronze chair, watching the others who were talking amongst themselves, beside the central ruby statue of the starlight phoenix, which was twice the size of the average professor as it stood there, still, glowing bright red as the chamber slowly fell in to darkness where moody clouds drifted overhead, concealing the sun's rays.

The conversations were abruptly brought to a close as Grimtale returned to the sound of heavy doors slamming against the walls, with magenta following behind as they approached their seats.

"This session is back in progress, professors. If you would all retake your seats, we have news from the human world," Grimtale explained, sitting back against his golden throne, overlooking Silverstein whose eyes had widened at the sight of Magenta who made her way over, slumping beside him in her solid silver throne.

"Where is Kenneth?" Silverstein whispered, as Magenta shuffled to find her spot of comfort.

"He's on his way, you were bloody right about him, though. You'll hear the full story in a moment, anyway," she explained, as the other three professors found their seats.

They were designated to bronze seating, leaving only Bilshore's chair empty by her absence as the chamber settled, falling silent and allowing Grimtale to speak.

"Professor Magenta, as you can see we are now joined by Professor Yuri, Professor Lint and Lillian Vargov, which I believe you're familiar with. However, Silverstein with certainty, will not be."

Silverstein looked across and gave all three a subtle nod.

"Each will play a part in the capture of the Phoenix. Professor Flint Yuri is our tutor of innovations, anything new and quirky, he's the man for the job. Perfect when faced by a spot of trouble that perhaps was unforeseen."

Yuri gave a wave of his hand to address the others, pushing his glasses up on the bridge of his nose with his other hand as Grimtale continued.

"Professor Teppi Lint is our potions and enchantment master, who I believe is currently working on a serum to counter the reaction after a Reaper bite?"

"Correct, Headmaster," he confirmed, in an unusual accent, much like the robes that wrapped around his body. They were wax treated and fluttering as a gentle breeze blew through the crack of the chamber doors, whistling as it swirled about the room.

"And lastly, Silverstein. This is Lillian Vargov, the first of her kind. A mix breed between the rare elvish kind and the humans; but here at the Institute we hope you have settled in nicely, you will always be made to feel welcome, and to live without prejudice. Anything less is unacceptable," Grimtale smiled - Silverstein frowned, biting his tongue to make sure he kept his thoughts to himself.

"Thank you, Professor Grimtale, Headmaster. I may not have much to offer, however defending the school and keeping you safe is something I can assist with, what I'm *willing* to assist with," she replied, her pointed ears standing on end beyond the blonde of her bob cut hair.

"Right, you are. We shall need to round up what tutors we can, but by no means will we force anyone to stay. As we know, this is about to get dangerous my friends, and I expect no one to pledge their lives to this cause. However, we also cannot win without them, but we will do our damnedest!" Grimtale concluded, meeting Magentas gaze from across the chamber.

"Now, Magenta has further word from Vinemoore. If you will, Professor."

Magenta rose on to her feet and slowly wandered to the centre of the room, allowing time to recollect her memories of the events that had unfolded during the rescue of Robin Occamy, the betrayal of Kenneth Brown and the return of the dreaded Reaper kind. It sat prominently in her mind, so she didn't need long, and when she did begin to explain it seemed to unravel like cotton from a thread, it was exact and accurate even down to the point when they had fallen through the attic hatch of the Occamy household and were covered in dust, wooden shards and broken webbing.

"Kenneth prompted Robin to run, to pack his things and take off with his family. I did what I could to convince him but Kenneth had already planted too many ideas, the man was torn and sadly we were forced to return, without the Professor. Kenneth Brown has not only endangered our chances of success, but by fuelling a broken man in to believing he can run and live a normal life, safe and away from danger...he has brought forth the possibility of Robin jeopardizing the well-being of his family."

Everyone in the room seemed to cast the same expression as their perceptions of Kenneth became clouded.

"If that is not the actions of a Count fanatic, what is?" She added, pleading for action to be taken.

"Where is Mr Brown at this time, Professor?" Asked Yuri, leaning forward from his solid bronze throne.

"He's on his way down," she replied, glaring in to the shadows, not needing any words to express the lack of care she had for Kenneth as the others caught on, watching as Magenta slowly crept back towards her seat.

"May I be excused, Professors?" Asked Silverstein, rising from his seat and glaring across at Grimtale who had seemed like the most powerful presence, as he sat dominantly in his golden throne, looking down at his followers like ants, powerful yet intelligent ants.

"You May," Grimtale responded, watching as Silverstein's coat glimmered flakes of silver as he strolled towards the doors with haste, pulling the left ajar then crashing it shut behind him, leaving Magenta and the other professors curious as they wondered what had possibly been so urgent to get up and leave mid session.

Grimtale looked to the others, his expression enough to convey what he was thinking as Yuri shrugged his shoulders.

"Shall we continue?" said Lillian, softly.

"Reapers...The Reapers have returned as some of us predicted. Perfectly timed too which draws forth more concerns, concerns that we may be compromised, or perhaps it was just a coincidence? The Phoenix has forced many to surface including my faithful friends in this room. So the question that now stands, what are the next steps, professors?" Grimtale blinked away the dry of his eyes and turned his gaze to Magenta.

"We wait. Professor Occamy is now in the safe hands of Ethel Jillings. You hired her, headmaster."

Grimtale smirked, with a new sense of reassurance as he cast his mind back over the times when positivity was elevated by her doings, the joy that Ethel had brought to the institute, and if anyone could bring Robin round to see the light of the situation, and the possibilities that were achievable from a simple helping hand, she was the person for the job.

He was sure of it as he rested back in his throne and cast his gaze to the skies above, anticipating the fury and the darkness that was building. The tensions were high and hearts had begun to race as lightning suddenly struck. Casting a blinding white light inside the chamber and along the golden mural hallway, where Silverstein now resided, leant against a wooden totem, observing the gates, waiting as Kenneth made his way towards them.

He was curious of what would be waiting, but it was no surprise when Silverstein caught his eye, as he cast away the enchantment and pushed forward the dark steel gates that stood between him and a pathway to hell - or it might as well have been, he realised as the two of them locked gaze and begun to head towards one another.

"*Coll-Ructo!*" Silverstein yelled, as he drew his cold cast wand from his shimmering coat pocket and pointed it towards Kenneth, so it seemed, until the green energy slithered by, passing by

Kenneth's ear and against the steel verticals, binding them closed with a *hiss* and a *crunch*.

"Wouldn't want Reapers getting in, now would we, Mr Brown."

"Of course not," he replied, puffing up his chest and holding his head high as he neared Silverstein, who was still coming at him, slipping his wand back inside his coat pocket and glaring menacingly in to the dark of his eyes.

"I don't know what you think you're up to, but this has to stop." Silverstein continued to pace towards Kenneth who had slowed and begun to drift, not knowing what to expect as the next moment his personal space had been invaded as he looked down Silverstein's nose, which was pointed, sharp like a Reaper's tooth.

"I can assure you that the Count won't thank you for misleading his trust," he added, looking Kenneth dead in the eye.

"I do *not* work for the Count, Leonard…" Kenneth blinked, washing away the dryness of his eyes as Silverstein's breath brushed against his face.

"It's not me you need to convince, you fanatic. Assisting in the escape of Robin Occamy, I feel if *he* was to discover a man of your calibre abusing your position, whatever that may be, he would be most...upset." Silverstein paused for thought, "In fact, I'd count on your family being burnt at the stake for the errors of your ways, Mr Brown. Not to mention the chamber are most displeased with your attempts to lure Robin and his family towards an even greater danger that may lie beyond Vinemoore. Where exactly did you think he would go? How do you suppose we bring an end to the Phoenix plot without him?"

Kenneth's face had begun to boil with aggression, "I want to save the man, and his bloody family! I want him to be able to sit around a table and eat a fully prepared meal with his loved ones, not to live in fear like we have. He doesn't deserve the life that the Institute has laid to hand for him, he deserves better!"

Silverstein swept his hand through his hair and took a step back, then sighed as his eyes fell back on Kenneth who was pale and burning at the cheeks. His spectacles were barely clinging to the tip of his nose and sweat had begun dripping from his forehead.

"It's not me you have to convince, Mr Brown. Just remember where your loyalty lies and I'm certain there will be nothing to worry about. Unless you're telling a fib? Time will tell, you might already be too late, that is of course if you have betrayed your master," Silverstein grinned a horrible yet charming grin as he watched Kenneth back away.

"He wouldn't, he can't know…" Kenneth muttered, eyes wide and stumbling as his legs felt like jelly, as the horrors flashed before him. The sight of his family mangled and left for dead.

He suddenly picked up his pace until he was finally running in the direction of the tall dark gates. He was away before Silverstein had the chance to say goodbye, which disappointed him greatly; however, he gave Kenneth a wave as he slammed shut the gates and dispersed from view, racing toward the glowing crystallized portal that he had cast with his cane, holding it out in front of him as he ran, then disappearing beyond it, with a strong thought of the street he lived on, in the dead centre of the town of Vinemoore, which was still peacefully under a much thinner blanket of frosty whiteness.

The fear for his family's safety had never been so high as he imagined them, their bodies, laid still against the snow, left to rot. He wasn't going to let that happen, not ever, he thought as he limped his way down the centre of his street, casting his sights towards the dim lit alleys and openings as he passed. With his cane raised and spectacles pressed as far up the bridge of his nose as they could go. He was ready for whatever could be waiting for him as he neared the front of his home, expecting the worst, with tears streaming down the side of his face.

CHAPTER 7
Tick-Tock Goes The Clock

The cold, frosty wind whistled by his ears as they flapped and flailed behind him, like the tail of his brown umber coat that was damp and dirt ridden from the journey back to Vinemoore. He couldn't think straight, his mind was engaged in a never ending war of thoughts and threats which had began to cloud his vision in long, thin looms of spaghetti, like trails running before his eyes as he reached for the brass knob that protruded from his grand front door. He twisted it, then pressed his body against it, pushing back the slab on its hinges and hitting the inside wall of his home with an almighty *slam*. The house then fell to silence while Kenneth stood out of breath, panting under the arch of his living room as a dying orange light shone brightly through the front of the house, casting Kenneth's shadow long and spindly along the carpet, towards the furniture that sat in shadow at the far end of the room.

  His pulse had continued to flow heavy through his body, hazing his vision - so much that he failed to notice that something wasn't quite right - beside the fact that there was no sign of his family which had already sent him in to a state of increased panic.

An eerie atmosphere had fallen in a split moment, heavy like a sack of potatoes had fallen from the skies and gone crashing through the roof. It was an instant feeling, a cold sensation of evil that had began to linger through the halls and in the piercing breeze that whistled against the window frames.

"*Mr Brown*," said a soft voice from afar, lurking in the darkest corner of the living room.

"*Where are they? What have you done with my wife and children?*" Kenneth yelled. He grasped tightly to the shaft of his cane and slammed it against the ground. A *Crunch*, was the sound it made before aggressive splinters of orange and red energy erupted from the tip that was now firmly pressed into the raised bristles of the doormat. They dispersed and cast a warm glow of light across the room before finally extinguishing like a flame starved of oxygen, but the tiny remnants of magical energy had served a purpose, it was now only too obvious to Kenneth who or what was sat opposite him, slumped in his tatty single seater armchair, wrapped by a garment as dark as night with a metallic half mask clung to its face. It gestured towards the back room where what seemed like half a dozen figures were standing motionless.

"Correct my stubbornness, Mr Brown. But would I be right to think the Defence Minister is now plotting *against* the Count's movements?" The shadowy figure asked, remaining calm and collected with its body firmly resting against the faded pillow cases that were wedged along the back of the arm chair.

Kenneth paused before speaking, recalling what he had done - persuading Robin to scarper from Vinemoore, to detach himself from the solution that he had sworn to abide by. He had broken his word and now he and his family would surely suffer for his act of kindness. Because it wasn't in a Reaper's nature to be forgiving, the Morient world knew that all too well, especially Kenneth Brown...

He took a step towards the back room where the shroud of figures stood. Some small, some tall but all equally still and silent.

"Oliver, my boy. Are you in there?" Kenneth called, peering through the doorway and met with the harsh glare of the orange skies, shining through the wide kitchen window, silhouetting the band of people stood in the centre of the room.

"Are you out of your mind?" roared the voice of the Reaper that was now stood directly between him and the door frame, hindering the path to the back room, his breath gently wafting against the sore, dry skin about the left of his eye as he spoke with a raspy tone.

"To betray the Count, you must be mad. You're lucky to be alive, I was ordered to execute you the moment you arrived home, yet here you are, breathing the same air as *I!*"

Kenneth met the gaze of the Reaper, stood stiff and on edge. Tensions were rising as the two men took a breath.

"The Count does not need professor Robin Occamy, I know where the Phoenix is. I can lead him to it. Robin's story has been told, leave him be, allow me to bring the beast to him!" Kenneth begged, glancing over the Reaper's shoulder, trying to make out the shape of his wife and kids.

"Time is wearing thin, Kenneth. The Count's patience is at the end of its tether, we cannot be running in pointless circles forever. Recover the starlight phoenix before the eleventh hour of the final day and if you succeed, we shall release your family. Failure, Kenneth, will result in...shall we say, unpleasant consequences," said the Reaper, coldly and calmly. His emerald eyes glistened as the sun's rays cast long trails of light across the metal of his mask and the bare flesh of his face. He was certain that Kenneth Brown had received and understood the message by the rush of blood that had drained from his face, leaving it pale and chilled further by the breeze blowing past the ajar front door. Escape from the Count's clutches now seemed near impossible as Kenneth imagined the sharp, claw-like hands of his superior, clamp around his body and fondling his heart like a play toy, dangling by a whisker thin thread. He had no choice but to follow the command of the Reaper that had held his family prisoner, or ultimately lose everything, every purpose he had ever lived for, he realised as he slowly began to turn away and wander towards the front door.

"I'm coming back," he muttered, but clear enough for the Reaper to hear, who stood dominantly, watching as Kenneth drew back the door and latched it to its closed position.

The Reapers bare eye fastened to a slither as he cast a thought, wondering if it had been the right move to let the man walk free, at least if he valued the lives of his family and friends... He knew that Kenneth would have no choice but to return - but with the phoenix? There was no chance, and death most certainly loomed, riding the sun until the final day where it would be dealt out in more than necessary sums.

The Reaper smirked, then cracked a dark chuckle that echoed about the walls of the silent household, lingering like the endless fear that ran through the fragile veins of Kenneth Brown.

* * *

As a clap of thunder struck in the Morient world, the vast gold doors slammed together behind Silverstein as he strutted his way back inside the council chamber, surrounded by the institute's professors, perched on the metal of their personalised thrones.

Lightning flashed, zigzagging down from the angry skies, illuminating the transparent glass dome that sat directly overhead. The sight was majestic, the Ruby phoenix twinkled a rich red and light reflected from the gold and silver positioned around the room, lighting it up like the insides of an ornate jewellery box.

"Silverstein? W - Where's Kenneth?" asked Magenta, sat comfortably in her fluffy pink coat and vibrant cotton scarf wrapped around her neck.

"I'm afraid Kenneth, our associate of the Minister of defence, won't be joining us today, professors."

Leonard Silverstein continued his path towards his bronze chair and slumped back, addressing the others concerns with a flicker of his eyes.

"I questioned him, I set him up…" he added, looking to Grimtale nervously, who had already met his gaze with that of surprise.

"I used a simple scare tactic. We all needed to know, did we not? Kenneth Brown is no more than a fanatic, working for the Count's pathetic army. He has delayed the capture of the phoenix and now we run the risk of it falling into the wrong hands!" Silverstein reminded them, putting emphasis on the fact that they had all been betrayed.

Grimtale took a long deep breath then glanced across at Magenta before reverting back to Silverstein.

"What did you say to him?"

"I simply used an example, an example of what happens to those who betray the dark forces. The families that were found slaughtered in the Havana desert two years back were far from accidental, professor. He has been hard at work, the Count. Building his most trusted allies, waiting for this moment, and now we have flushed one of them from our close knit ranks. He will be on his way back to Vinemoore, but the fate of his family is out of our control..." Silverstein explained on as best he could, vaguely recalling past events before skipping ahead to the conflict in the hallway with Kenneth, not wanting to be reminded of the graphic sights his eyes were forced to be laid on. The Havana massacres, the truth that so little knew because it was better off that way. Better for the people that wished to live in peace, shut off from the world revolving around them.

"If this be true, Silverstein, the man is a fool, and must not be trusted to return," said Grimtale abruptly, casting his gaze to his fellow professors sat patiently around him.

"If he attempts to step foot back inside the institute, you can trust my people to deal with him, professor." Silverstein assured Grimtale, sparkling under the second bolt of lightning that suddenly lit up the chamber and the metallic fibres of his long silver coat.

"Thank you," replied Grimtale, then he climbed to his feet and approached the ruby Phoenix, casting his hand over its surface as he passed.

"Now, we wait. If Professor Occamy arrives in the Morient world, we must be ready. He won't be prepared for what he will witness inside these walls."

The others adjusted their clothing and leant forward, sharp and alert.

"What if he doesn't turn up? The old bats good, but she ain't *that* good!" stated Magenta, showing no sign of affection for the elderly lady that now lived within Robins' home.

"If she fails, and the professor chooses to take his own path, we will leave without him. We must not delay any further. For once we know the whereabouts of the Starlight Phoenix and we must act upon it, before time runs out, before the Count takes control and turns both the Morient and human world upside down. With every passing second I fear for those living under Shoulders Heath, exposed to a creature they do not understand."

"You mean Miss Bilshore, Sachester Bilshore, don't you?" asked Magenta, knowing full well of the affection he shared with her. It was all too apparent, made even more obvious by the turning of his bright red cheeks that had begun to glow behind his dark curly beard.

"Sachester is perfectly well trained for situations like these, but the people of the villages, especially those in the under dimension, are *far* from ready," Grimtale explained, taking a quick breath and glancing to the other professors. He knew in that moment, Magenta's eyes were still set on him like sharp, poison tipped daggers, nipping away at what knowledge was seeping from his extraordinary mind and being projected subconsciously through the language of his heavy, yet expressive body as she kept him in her sights, turning over all he had said, considering the seriousness of their situation...

* * *

Where the sun had fallen deeper, setting beyond the south horizon, the storm had been and gone. All that was left was the damp and the calming sound of icicles melting, drips and drops as the wet plummeted from the ceramic cottage guttering and splashed against the doorstep. Robin was glad to see the back of that ghastly weather, he thought to himself as his eyes strayed to the orange rays outside his kitchen window, watching the blackened clouds, pierced by the fiery glow of the sun as they drifted away towards the baron frozen coast.

"It's rough out there." Robin thought out loud, met by a look of confusion from across the table where Kirsten sat, her mouth filled to the brim with roast potato and steamed vegetables.

"It's winter," said Mrs Jillings as she rose from her chair and began to collect the empty china plates from the table.

"Did you enjoy that?" she asked in a child friendly manner, peering down at Emily, who was staring back with a messy grin, nodding her head frantically.

"It was lovely, Mrs J!" she yelped, reaching for her glass of apple juice with one hand and wiping away the gravy from her mouth with the other.

Robin was still anxious, glancing around the kitchen, taking advantage of the silence and listening out for the sound of the mysterious ticking that had been said to come from an old grandfather clock, one that had resided within the cottage for many years - yet no one had ever seen it. Perhaps knowing *that* was enough to encourage him as Robin felt the sudden urge to discover it by the evening - *which wasn't so far away*, he thought with the warmth of the sun cast along the side of his face, as it broke through the angry storm clouds.

While Mrs Jillings got on with the dishes, Kirsten and Emily had returned to the living room where all the toys and colourful gifts had spent the day, waiting to be played with, allowing Robin to get back on to his hands and knees.

Mrs Jillings had already sighed and rolled her eyes as she felt his stray hands brushing by her ankles, patting around the base of the kitchen cupboards.

"It's *got* to be somewhere. Let's just start small and scour the kitchen first...for the fifth time today," his mind spoke silently back at him, ensuring that he was taking the appropriate action to find the clock - no matter how disapproving the expression was, etched to the wrinkled face of Mrs Jillings as she wiped away the gravy stains from the china dishes and submerged them into the bowl of boiling water.

Hinges squealed as exploring hands pulled at the cupboard handles, one by one crashing back to their closed positions while Robin moved on to the next, then scuttling to the nearby counter where another pair of doors awaited, but much larger, double the size of the other compartments with a peculiar set of paper notes pinned to the inner panels. Robin paused as the parchment drew his attention and a curious hand proceeded to peel away the golden blank notes until finally, something to digest was revealed as the ink ridden parchment appeared, cast in a layer of shadow; and it read:

The perfect roasted spud
By Kirsten Mae Withers

Firstly, peel away the potato skin.

Drop the potatoes in a pan of water and place on the stove till boiling for fifteen minutes.

Take a deep ceramic pan and preheat with a block of cooking oil and any desired seasoning.

Once fifteen minutes have passed, rinse the pan dry, leaving the potatoes steaming hot. Now give the pan a shake until the potatoes are nice and fluffy, then place them in the hot pan of season, but don't forget to coat the potatoes with a spoon so they roast to a lovely golden colour.

Cook for twenty minutes then they'll be ready for turning over, spooning the oil back over them then placing back inside the oven for a further twenty minutes.

It wasn't what Robin had hoped to find under the kitchen sink but it had brought a smile to his face nonetheless, seeing his partner's handwriting hidden out of sight. He'd not known about these notes and they had been there all this time, he thought as he cast his eyes over the parchment once more.
"This explains how she always got it right, the perfect meal, time after time," he muttered with a charming smile, holding the papers between his fingers and admiring the scribbles that accompanied the written directions.

* * *

As time went by, the golden glow from the sun had now turned to darkness and Mrs Jillings was no longer cleaning dishes at his side, he noticed as he glanced over his shoulder. It was almost time, he wasn't going to find the clock sat on his knees at the centre of the kitchen, Robin realised, knowing he'd have to get a move on with the nineteenth hour drawing close. The parchments were pinned back inside the cupboard and door slammed shut behind them, bringing the kitchen search to a close, as sure as he had been, the clock was not there...

Robin climbed to his feet: patted down the white of his shirt, rolled his sleeves mid way up his arms and fastened them around his elbows before marching towards the foot of the staircase, determined to find the source of the mysterious ticking noise, the grandfather clock where Mrs Jillings was expecting to meet him.

"It has to be here, it has to be!" Robin repeated, ascending upstairs towards the dimly lit landing.

Here the moon's rays had begun to highlight the edges of the furniture and the door frames, casting its soft white glow through the upper window directly opposite the landing banister where Robin was still holding tight, catching his breath for a brief moment and listening out for the sound of the *tick-tock* motion that he had always been able to hear, just never thought anything of it. The sound had always been peaceful, but it was now a pain in his backside, he grunted, advancing around to the hallway. It was far cooler here, the light looked almost blue as it shone through the bedroom doorway and across Robin's face as he passed on by, moving towards the circular pane of glass situated at the end of the hallway. It was a round window that looked out in the direction of the black mountain and the land of Shoulders Heath. It was quite the sight, even at night as the tall, wide mass towered high at a distance, lit by the spotlight in the sky, the moonlight glow, reminding the villages people of its importance, forever dividing the land from the supposed nightmares that dwelled beyond it.

Robin leant against the wooden ledge and peered out across Vinemoore, lost on a train of thought that was far from the subject of ticking clocks. The view seemed enchanting by the distance his eyes had widened, glistening, almost twinkling like stars.

"I always knew there was more to this world. Now it's got me stressed beyond belief! But it will be worth it, if a greater power really does exist, then perhaps I really am the key to curing Kirsten," Robin sighed, reminded by the heavy ticking and the sound of a pendulum swaying in his right ear. It was like the rhythm of a heartbeat, a river of life thrusting against him, calling for him, begging for him to see it. He could feel it, Robin turned towards the sound expecting the clock to be stood there, smooth and slender as the smell of fresh varnish wafted by his nose - but he saw nothing. The energy he felt was unquestionable, but the image that Robin had painted in his mind was nowhere in sight.

"But I could have sworn..."

He blinked, rubbing away the blur from his eyes and scouring the hallway once more, certain that the clock was beside him. Perhaps it was, *maybe it was invisible*, he chuckled, raising his hand and slapping it against the air, where suddenly a sharp stinging pain electrified his palm as it came to an immediate halt, firmly pressed against the side of what felt like glass, or perhaps, *varnished wood*. Whatever it was, it was out of this world and transparent to the human eye. *After all this time and searching, had he really found the elusive, invisible clock?*

CHAPTER 8
A Painful Farewell

He wasn't sure what to make of it – the obstruction, the invisible object beside him.

There was that smell again, riding the draft that had crept along the hallway from the buckled attic hatch. The scent of fresh varnish with a pinch of mahogany, dry yet bitterly crisp and undeniably welcoming. Robin was not fearful, he was now curious and convinced that he had found the infamous clock that had tormented him for as long as he could remember. He ran his hand down along what felt like a side panel to the tall structure that was still cloaked by some form of enchantment, one that softened at the edges and rippled as Robin poked and rubbed his hand against the polished woodwork.

"It has been very well hidden!" Robin remarked, watching as the jelly-like cloak rippled.

As he remained caught in a web of fascination, Robin had failed to notice a streak of shadow ready to extinguish the twinkle from his eye - *A dark figure had begun its approach, carefully shuffling along the carpeted hallway, drawing closer, one short step at a time*. Robin could feel the further presence but it was one he felt at ease with, he needn't look away as the black mass closed in at his side, wrapped by a heavy navy cardigan.

"It would seem by accident you have discovered your past, present and future. The contraption that has left a charming notion, wouldn't you say?"

Robin shifted his gaze to Mrs Jillings who was stood at his side, removing his clammy hand from the clock and placing it upon her shoulder.

"How has it been here all this time? How have we not stumped our toes? Quite frankly none of this is making any sense, but it's bloody brilliant, *really* brilliant!" claimed Robin, reverting back to the transparent mass, listening closely to the swing of the iron pendulum.

"You see, Mr Occamy, it takes a powerful individual to bring forth something of such significance. You must have *really* wanted to find it for it to reveal itself in such a way, be it somewhat nervous but at least it made itself known to you. Usually a man with a past as vast as yours would go a lifetime not knowing the secrets that have been locked away, because it's not everyday you find perfection and no risk is worth taking, no matter how curious you become, but today as you reflect, it has never been more prominent that this life you have is on the verge of destruction. We don't know how long Kirsten has, and as each day passes for all we know, the next may be her last. What I'm trying to say is, in some instances a risk is the best chance you may ever have."

Mrs Jillings had spoken sincerely.

Robin scratched at his neck, riddled by irritation as he felt a cold wetness trickle down his cheek. As happy as he was, he couldn't help but wonder where the next moment would lead, what was going to be asked of him as he felt the world he used to know shredding away, crumbling under his feet while moonlight continued to filter through the cottage, shining from the bedroom windows along the wooden floorboards and on to the carpeted hallway as the invisible clock began to chime, striking the nineteenth hour of christmas day - a day that could have been a week for all Robin knew, it had been long, tiring and it reflected in his eyes as he broke a yawn, placing his hand against his widened mouth, his eyes sore and flesh as pale as a corpse.

"So what happens now?" he asked, weary eyed.

"I was going to suggest that you rest, but I fear we're already falling behind, Mr Occamy…"

"Please, Robin. Call me Robin," he replied, assuring Mrs Jillings.

"I was given strict orders to make sure you made it back, when the time was right. The other two couldn't have been much help," she added, rummaging in her cardigan pockets, searching for something particular.

"They pretty much said the same thing, only they sounded like they were somewhat relying on you."

"Did they really..." Mrs Jillings chuckled, distracted by the knick-knacks dropping on to the floor, spilling from her pockets as her hands scrambled around.

"Kenneth was more reluctant, he seemed set on me making my own decision on the matter, in fact he prompted me to pack my things and take off."

Mrs Jillings raised an eyebrow then reverted back to her search.

"However Magenta, let's just say she couldn't look Kenneth square in the eye for long, I feel there may well be history between the two?" Robin explained as Mrs Jillings finally drew a short looking chopstick from her pocket, no longer than the average pencil with tribal markings etched along the shaft. It was elegant and feminine, perfectly fit for Mrs Jilling's frail hand as she raised it in front of her.

"What you must understand about the two of them, they're both heavily set in their ways; however both perched on either side of the spectrum, they're not in the slightest way alike, except their unquestionable determination. Kenneth is the Informer for the Minister of Defence, not only for the Morient world but yours too, at least the one you've grown to know best. He chose to live here, marry a human and have children, a family. He settled down and ever since then he has been frowned upon by a minority. They say he's incapable of his job, some even go as far to accuse him of meddling with dark forces, the people you described in the cloaks."

Robin's body language had suddenly changed to a more relaxed stance, as for once what Mrs Jillings was saying had begun to process correctly and it was no longer as complicated as it first seemed. Perhaps it was just her tone, the way she spoke like the telling of a bedtime story, it was beautifully crafted and he was eager to hear more...

"Magenta I assume disapproves of Kenneth's antics?"

"Oh she makes it very clear, although I believe it's down to her other half. He can be somewhat, *manipulative*."

Robin couldn't help but feel curious.

"Who is he?"

"Leonard Silverstein, he works under the Minister as well. I know what you're thinking, it sounds crazy but Silverstein is part of a special order that is bound by the Morient world, he is Captain of the Enforcers but during the turn of events Kenneth had no authority over him, the Enforcer job role comes with its perks and the smallest of all men can be far more within those ranks. This is why you must be careful, Robin. Dark forces are at work, they never sleep, they never have. We've lived in fear for far too long, something must be done and it will take more than what you and I possess," her voice trembled as she gave a gentle wave of her wand, flicking it in the direction of the invisible clock that remained shielded by camouflage.

A bright green spark of light suddenly burst from the tip of Mrs Jilling's wand and flurried against the rippling transparent mass, casting aside the enchantment, the cloak of invisibility from the tall grandfather clock, revealing the deep brown wood grain and heavily varnished surfaces. It was now visible, Robin could finally see what had tormented him for so long, with its mysterious tick-tock sound and swinging pendulum, seeing it at last, it was far from disappointing, he thought as his face lit up with delight.

"It's beautiful!" he claimed, peering up at the

decorative hands as they sat five past the nineteenth hour on the face.

The build was impressive, it had to be at least a hundred years old yet it looked as good as new, now reflecting a moonglow sheen as moonlight flickered against the varnished wood panels and domed glass face.

"I feel like there's something important about this clock, the way it's been calling to me all this time, please tell me I'm right!"

"You are right," Mrs Jillings confirmed, reaching for the small hatch on the front of the tower unit and carefully easing it open, unhinging it from its stationary position against the clocks body, exposing the inner compartments.

An incredulous look washed over Robin's face as he peered inside. It seemed that there was something hidden, wrapped by a velvet cloth to protect it from the effect of years gone by - his excitement was building. Robin glanced across at Mrs Jillings, then back again, reaching inside cautiously, keeping an eager eye for any cobwebs or spiders lurking in the shadows before firmly closing his hand around the silky smooth cloth, drawing it out from the dark compartment and in to the subtle glow of the moon as it bathed the cloth in silver light that seemed itself, cloaked in mystery.

Robin didn't know what to do with the item, he was considering just handing it over to Mrs Jillings but curiosity had already got the better of him as he slowly leaned in with his hand held close to his chest, and his eyes cast over the surface of the dark velvet wrap.

"I don't know what I'm supposed to be doing," Robin admitted, standing awkwardly.

"Is this mine to open?" He asked, looking Mrs Jillings directly in the eye and unfaltering as she did the same, casting that expression of bewilderment as if she had never expected to be stood opposed to Robin as he clenched on to the most important relic of his time, as if it had only ever existed as a ghost of her dreams. She began to nod her head forward and back in a motion of acknowledgment while her boney, pale hand revolved like clockwork, urging Robin to unveil the findings beneath the shroud. He looked back down at it, allowing his thumb to wander over the silky texture, feeling his way around the items. One of them was soft to begin with but that could have been anything, however the shapes were rigid, almost rectangular and could easily fit in the palm of his hand, except for one, a solid elongated dowel with an exposed tip twinkling as moonlight caught the varnish coat that encased its inner beauty, the wood grain and the fluorescent green glow that seemed to seep through the cracks of ages - It was old, Robin knew that for sure as that incredulous look on his face began to soften, as silky coverings slowly fell away, leaving what seemed like the most important items he would ever hold, firmly in the centre of his hands.

There was a wand, a dark leather wallet fraying at the edges and a small round badge no bigger than a coin. Its domed surface twinkled as it rocked about in Robins sweaty palm, rattling against the shiny tin with its pin.
"What am I supposed to do with this?" He asked, glancing down at his hand.
"Well, what does it say?" Mrs Jillings huffed,

stamping her foot down on the carpet.

Robin raised his hand and drew the badge closer to his face while his other clenched firmly on to the wallet and wand, firmly yet gently, not wanting to damage them.

"There's nothing, there's nothing to read. It's just a golden foil star, what kind of relevance could it possibly have?" he asked with a puzzled look, turning it for Mrs Jillings to see.

Her eyes lit up, the golden shine seemed instantly familiar like she had suddenly been reacquainted - of course she knew what it was.

"Some items never require an explanation, for something such as this, it's presence is its meaning, a code of conduct that has once been achieved by said individual."

"Conduct? What kind? Good or bad?"

"That's something you'll later discover, Mr Occamy," she said in a tone of disillusion, a tone that barely registered as curiosity got the better of him and driven by the need to know. Robin closely examined the items, rubbing at the smooth surface of the deep dark wallet with his thumb, before popping the press stud and pulling the two halves apart. He peered up at Mrs Jillings one last time out of curiosity, she was still standing with a vacant expression yet he could tell, he knew she had a good idea of what he was about to find. She always did, it even seemed like she knew Robin Occamy better than he, however it wasn't an uncomfortable feeling, not at all. It was somewhat reassuring, he felt as he looked down towards the unknown and flipped aside the inner sleeve of the wallet, then he carefully moved it under the silver beam of moonlight where his gaze fell on the illuminated credentials that sat housed in a pocket, secured by a leather frame that pressed around the inked parchment with its foil stamp of authenticity - It read:

Name: Professor Robin Occamy
Hometown: Leadworth
Permit of Morient tutoring
The Vinemoore Institute - Defence class
Valid until the 1965 reassessment period.

"The sketch looks like me, why is my mug etched on this parchment? I've never been to Leadworth, where in the world is Leadworth?" snapped Robin, taken back by the glare of his inked face, stained in to the fibres of the permit.

"Robin, there is a lot that needs to be understood. You've already come so far but the rest is too much for one evening and I know for sure it won't be easy to digest."

"I've done pretty well so far don't you think? Wands, magic and mad men possessed by the devil himself, how hard could it be?"

"Yes, you've encountered things you never believed to exist, a taster of what's to come and I must ask this of you, please, place your absolute trust in me to advise the next step you take."

Mrs Jillings met Robin's gaze, carefully placing her hand behind the leather wallet and lifting it to a close, concealing the curious credentials.

"You must not worry about those, however I strongly urge you to keep them safe," she added, pressing Robin's hands against the warmth of his chest.

"And, what now?" he said coldly, standing tall, dark and silhouetted by the window frame that had cast a glow along Mrs Jilling's brow.

"Now is where the real adventure begins, Mr Occamy. The question is, are you ready?"

She asked with a smile, with an uncertain future laid ahead with a seemingly willing Robin, unfaltering to the idea of tackling the impossible as he dropped the tin badge in to the deep itchy pocket of his trousers, followed by the wand and wallet that slipped perfectly inside his waistcoats breast pocket.

It'll soon be morning, by the time I've packed and said my goodbyes, Robin thought, staring out of the window where the town lay dormant, sleeping and oblivious to unfolding agendas. It was never easy for Robin, leaving for work every day, let alone for some place he had never set foot - or heard of for that matter. His stomach churned at the idea of going alone, stepping beyond the front door at the crack of dawn and leaving his family behind.

Being dropped like a stone in water was the very least of his concerns, even the likes of the monstrosities that dwelled in the pit of the land were nothing in comparison to the cold dark fear that had now risen up like a shadow that covered him - the thought of not coming back.

"It wouldn't be fair," he paused, "unless, you mentioned a possibility of finding some miraculous way of helping Kirsten. A stop to her suffering - tell me the chances," he begged with an unsettled quiver of the bottom lip.

Mrs Jillings stepped forward, her eye twinkled a spell of courage as Robin met her gaze.

"By all means there is a chance. Pushing aside the horrors that surround that place, the ever growing darkness, if you can look beyond it, it's rather marvellous, really." She said, pulling her cardigan tight around her neck and burying her arms against her chest.

"Wake me before you leave, this old girl requires her beauty sleep and I'd urge you do the same, get some sleep, that is."

"Yeah of course, don't stay up on my watch; however I doubt I'll be getting any sleep tonight, I'm too busy running over everything I'm going to need, what to expect and what I'm going to say to Kirsten… if only life was simple," said Robin earnestly - listening to the rhythm of the cottage, the creaks and fumbling patters as Mrs Jillings disappeared in to her bedroom. She closed the door quietly, kicked off her sequin slippers and slumbered in to her soft silky bed sheets. Before a moment's passing, she was already sound asleep which left Robin as the last soul awake in the house, stood in the hallway as the clock slowly faded beneath its enchanted veil of invisibility; however the pendulum could still be heard, swinging to and fro, the floorboards creaking as Robin's feet pressed gently against them, making his way carefully towards his bedroom at the end of the hall.

The space was silent and empty, the bed sheets untouched like the ocean calm and a folded striped pyjama set laid unworn upon the wooden drawers.

The heavy door delicately came to a close, then there was finally peace, no longer any need for words, just comfort calling, as Robin planted himself on the edge of his mattress, head in hands, taking short, snappy pants of air which then transitioned in to long, heavy breaths that brought calming relief. Robin could now relax and lay across the vast surface of the bed. He laid there, still and peaceful, the whites of his shirt luminous against the dark that dwelled within the room.

Never had the sight of bland, blankness been so satisfying, nor so deep and dark and softly inviting to induce rest. For however long he chose to remain staring up at the ceiling, there were no worries, no concerns... no thoughts at all, just the absence of everything. It was like being swallowed up whole and suspended within a void of nothing - it was perfect.

He didn't enjoy sharing it alone, far from it, but it was a required escape.

If only I could take Kirsten and Em with me and run as far as our legs would take us, he thought, imagining himself afloat in the vacuum of space, hand in hand with them, both.

Kenneth advised doing a runner, he reminded himself, thoughtfully.

Now he was fully aware that the comfort he sought was beginning to wear thin as his mind began to unwind and set itself back in motion, there was no stopping it, he had suddenly become restless - it was no good.

Only ten minutes had passed before he was back on his feet, he jumped off the bed and fell to his hands and knees, reaching under the bed frame in to a cloud of shadow that lurked beneath it.

As his hand clamped about an object and he drew it clear, a empty green satchel emerged, its heavy canvas fabric creased and faded. Its age was more than apparent, it and Robin must have gone back a long way by the look on his face as he examined the inside, pulling at the lining. He shook the satchel and knocked away the last standing dust with his hand.

"This will do."

Robin rose from behind the bed and quietly began to pack away his essentials. He couldn't help but include a family photograph, the thought of leaving without one was already too painful to think about. He slipped it out from under his pillowcase and pressed it inside the outer pocket of his satchel where it would always be safe, then secured it in place by the two dark press studs, firmly popping them together and dropping the bag on top of the bed.

Perhaps now he could manage a nap, he thought as he laid back down, hands behind what felt like a clearer head than before. But he still had to face his future wife and his daughter - that would be the next challenge - but until then, he could feel himself slipping away in to a world of dream and much deserved rest.

* * *

When Robin eventually came to, it was no longer dark. Bright orange shone along the ceiling and water droplets tapped against the window sill, dripping from the overhead guttering that ran along the front of the cottage. The ice and snow had melted, the ground was now damp, littered by puddles that glistened. The sun was rising from beyond the ocean and edging its way over the tops of the chimney stacks that lined along the quiet streets of Vinemoore; all staggered like the motion of waves, soaring along the land.

Robin yawned, rubbed away the dust from the corner of his eyes and perched himself beside the bedroom window, watching as the morning arrived with a flutter; a swarm of pretty birds, darting high and low and chirping, singing the most sweetest of melodies.

Their red, yellow and blue feathers swooped past the glass aperture like a blast of neon energy, then disappearing beyond the cottage and in to the naked branches of the trees that arched over the garden fence.

Robin cracked a smile - a weary one at that. He stretched across his pine drawers and grabbed a hold on his silver pocket watch. It was dusty, the faceplate had a beautiful decorative pattern etched in to it, and it still shone bright as new after a gentle rub.

He gave the top a press and the faceplate popped open revealing the inner workings, the cogs, the domed glass face and the petite hands that told the time. It was quarter past six in the morning, he had slept for a considerable few hours which came as quite the surprise for Robin. He felt great, still a little tired but it must have done him a world of good. He gave his face a rub and yawned in to his clenched fist, glancing vaguely across the room at his satchel that was bulging at the seams and slumped at the end of the bed exactly where he had left it.

Slowly and gradually, reality began to strike as deep as heartache could reach as the situation at hand became vividly apparent. If it could have been a dream that would have made everything just perfect. But it wasn't a dream at all, time was of the essence - and didn't he know it. Soon he'd have to say his painful farewells. *What excuse could he possibly make*, he wondered, feeling lost as he searched for an answer.

"*It will surely keep me awake*," he muttered, with a face sunk by deep thought as he wandered away from the window and began to head for the door.

He turned the brass handle as quietly and carefully as possible, pulled the door open and crept down towards the bathroom. The hallway was still dark, but the landing was cast in the soft radiance of the morning sun as it pierced the window panes and fell along the staircase bannister. He was the first awake it seemed, even Mrs Jilling's door was still pulled to, he noticed as he staggered past and entered the bathroom.

He grabbed his comb from the sink and began running it through his wavy brown hair, brushing away the mess that had accumulated overnight. A dash of water was all it needed and it sprung back in to a life of its own, perfectly coiffed and tucked behind the ears. He ran the comb one last time then splashed his face with a handful of chilled water from the tap, then patted it dry with the towel that hung beside the sink.

A tiny mirror posed on top of the toilet unit, glaring up at Robin who couldn't help but take a glance, not from vanity, but just to lay his eyes on a man that was about to leave everything and everyone he had ever loved, man whose life was about to be turned on its head. He stared deep into the dark of his eyes and took a breath, before turning away from his reflection and emptying his bladder in to the pan beneath him - it was a satisfying relief.

The toilet flushed, he washed and dried his hands and the bathroom door swung open. Robin returned to the hallway, fastening his shirt buttons and stretching his limbs as he marched back to his room where he grabbed the green satchel from his bed then began his descent, downstairs.

* * *

Kirsten and Emily were snuggled together, asleep on the sofa. The Christmas tree was still aglow, casting pink and blue stars upon the living room walls. The orange scented candle on the fireplace had eventually burned out in the night and the television set was playing to itself - Robin crept in quietly and turned it off, then pulled one of the curtains aside to help lighten the room.

They looked so peaceful, he observed as he moved around them.

"They're just perfect," he said softly, kneeling at their side and gently stroking the hair away from their faces.

Emily smiled, lost in a dream of her own. Robin just had to remind himself and remember the reason for leaving, the hope he held of a better life for them all. Kirsten's health restored - the chances of that made everything worthwhile, no matter what he had to endure to get there...

In that moment, confidence had returned and his overactive mind fell at ease as he sat there, mesmerised and paralysed by his unconditional love for his family.

It was now time, and the opportunity to dare to reach for the chance to alter the course of fate would never come again. He knew he had to take this chance.

He rose to his feet, left the living room and entered the dimly lit kitchen. He turned on the kettle, took out four mugs and a handful of tea bags, then placed them on the counter. His mustard yellow coat was still hung from the back of the chair that sat at the side of the dining table. He pulled it free and flung it around him, his arms slotting in to the sleeves and ending perfectly against the white of his shirt. He gave it a quick pat down, knocking away any dirt and dust before slipping on his brown leather boots - they were very worn but the distressed look about them reflected his mood perfectly, he took no shame in noticing as he pulled his laces tight and tied them into a long and loopy bow.

"There, that should do it."

The kettle clonked and steam hurtled from the spout as the water reached boiling point. Robin poured the water in to the ceramic teapot and dropped a couple of tea bags inside before giving it a quick stir, listening out behind him as he heard the sound of Mrs Jilling's slippers scrunching in to the carpet as she approached the kitchen.

"Good morning, Mrs J."

"It is, isn't it. And to what do I owe this pleasure?" she asked, gesturing towards the four mugs.

"Call it a going away treat. Fancy some toast to go with it?"

"Oh no, the tea will do just nicely, thank you,"

She smiled.

"I - I need to ask a big favour… don't think I'm trying to sweeten the situation, I just genuinely need help."

"I know you do."

"It's not been easy trying to think up an excuse to be setting off like this, but I was wondering, could you just say I've gone to check on the store? Then when I'm late back, just make out I said something about a special surprise, because let's face it, where I'm going I'm certainly bound to bring something back that will cause a rather exciting stir, eh?"

Robin began to pour the tea in to the four mugs and Mrs Jilling's somewhat vacant expression turned in to a devilish smirk.

"I think that will work, perfectly," she added, giving Robin a pat on the shoulder.

"Kirsten's going to be suspicious no matter what, but when she's eventually told the truths of this mad situation, she won't question it…"

"Robin, she can *never* know the truth. There are laws in force that keeps both worlds apart, leave it with me, I will find a way to put her at ease. Even if it means the use of a mild sleeping charm!"

Robin turned abruptly and chuckled.

"We'll be having less of that!"

He grabbed the satchel and lifted its strap over his head and twisted the bag against his back, then looked back at Mrs Jillings who was stood at the counter, casting him an encouraging look of respect.

"Why did you do four cups of tea, Robin?"

He shrugged his shoulders.

"My mistake," he chirped, making a turn for the

front door.

"Oh, Robin!" she called, remembering something important, "I never told you how to gain access to the Institute, in the… *Morient world*," she whispered, scuttling over on the tip of her toes, "It is essential that you take the secret entrance. It was a specific requirement from Grimtale. Only then would he be able to trust that you are who you say you are."

"But my face is on the parchment, the credentials," he raised the wallet and flipped it open, right under her nose.

"Well, if you were using some kind of disfigurement charm, it would make things a tad difficult, however, I do stand corrected. You look dashing, just like the man inside the wallet."

"The man, being?"

"You of course, just not the Robin that I've had the pleasure of knowing in recent years, let's leave it at that!"

Robin returned the wallet to his waistcoat pocket as intrigue grew.

"Now, the gateway will be found at the foot of the oldest tree to stand in Vinemoore, which I'm certain you know the whereabouts of. A flick of the wand should do it, but keep it discreet. Under no circumstances should you enter if being followed, no matter who or what it is. One witness is all it takes before the location becomes common knowledge and I know you're not stupid, you know what can then happen…"

For once, Robin understood the severity.

"Those things, the reapers. They have a crushing advantage, not to mention the additional lives that would be endangered, lives that stand protected. You've really nothing to worry about,

I've got this," he assured her with an alluring wink before taking his leave.

It felt as if time had eased as he made his way down the hallway, past the staircase and between the open door frame. It was like a picture frame, frozen in a moment that depicted the love and joy that their lives were now filled with. Kirsten and Emily were safe, they would always be safe with Mrs Jillings. Then as swift as the turn of a handle, the decision was made, his brewing adventure was now in full swing, at last.

CHAPTER 9
Puddles and Predicaments

He stood on the concrete slab outside his cottage. The air was brisk and the skies were polluted with swirly, pastel coloured clouds.

Winter had never been his favourite time of year but it did at least offer a choice of many gorgeous coats to wear, and a beautiful morning sunrise with the occasional event of snowfall - nothing could beat waking up to a fresh blanket of snow - but that had all gone now.

The pathways were almost dry, even the icicles had gotten a little hot under the collar, they were all but a tiny snub, still latched on, hanging underneath most of the steel gates and window ledges that lined the cobbled high street.

There sure were better days to be traipsing across town, but time was forever fleeting and the thought of a soggy sock wasn't going to deter Robin. He was already on his way down the hillside, slipping, sliding and splashing.

The streets were so peaceful, there was not a soul in sight, just the sound of the wind, gently brushing by and whistling down the alleyways. Robin had considered leaving before sunrise, which would have been ideal, he could have slipped by unseen, but there hadn't been so much as a curtain twitch, he noticed, headed for the steps beside the bakery.

Thankfully the steps were no longer a hazard, so they didn't slow his pace as he descended in to the market district, the heart of the town. It was vast and ran all the way to the Black Mountain that sat tall and grand in the mere distance, like a powerful god watching over its creations. Robin felt awfully small as he shot the mountain a curious glance. Even being sat miles across the land, it still towered over the tallest points in Vinemoore. It was quite the sight and had forever struck an enigma with the town's people, those yet to venture as far as the mountains ascent. There had never been one known in history to make the journey across Shoulders Heath and return to tell the tale.

It was fear, it was unquestionable fear, Robin decided as his mind wandered, while his feet continued in motion, carrying him on, down through the damp narrowing street where rusty signs pivoted from the closed shop fronts, swaying in the mellow breeze and screeching a metallic squeal, thirsty for oil as Robin passed beneath.

He pulled his collar high around his face as the pathway cooled, dark and water clogged. The walls glistened and the remaining stubs of icicles dropped at his submerged feet, reminding him of the unpleasant events that followed the last time he was anxiously passing down a silent, gloomy alleyway.

"It's just a coincidence," he reassured himself,

constraining the urge to turn around.

"We'll be out of here in a jiffy," he added reassuringly as he climbed the final two concrete steps that led up and out of the flooded alley and in to the sunlight that had begun to beam a warming light, down through the spindly branches and on to the courtyard slabs as it rose higher, into the morning sky.

The smell of change filled his nostrils as he emerged from the shadows and into the light. He first noticed a strange, singular puddle at the base of the old oak tree. The ground around it was bone dry and there was no sign of damp for a good few yards. It seemed awfully deep for a puddle and it was moving, rippling as a soft wind swept in from the east - but there was not just the one peculiar sight that Robin had unearthed, there was another.

The walkway he always took to work, the one with the overgrown bushes and zombie-like branches, it was as dark as the night and a smokey fume was rising from behind the wall.

Was something on fire, or was it a trap?

The option that seemed most obvious was no longer the logical choice. Robin watched carefully as the black mass begun to set in motion, drifting along the top of the crusty foliage. It was moving towards the courtyard - towards *him*, he realised before surveying the area for some place to hide. He leapt for the closest and safest spot, the bright red post box outside an old abandoned building, where he was out of sight to whoever, or whatever was on its way out.

Robin stepped back a little further, pressing

himself firmly inside a open porch that overhung from the abandoned shop. The wood was breaking away and the door was boarded up, so there wasn't much choice but to hold his position, peeping across at the walkway, waiting while the mass of energy neared, just a few metres from the clearing.

He could feel his body trembling, he was tense and a cold sweat had surfaced as his most recent fear returned - they were back, the sight of those familiar dark robes and silver faceplates had stemmed an uncontrollable frenzy. Robin pulled himself out of sight and froze, hoping that the group of reapers hadn't spotted him as they gallivanted around the open courtyard space.

Each of their cold disguises were unique. The leader of the pack was distinct by the way she carried herself in to the centre of the courtyard, with a slight hunch and wielding her wand loosely in her right hand. Her hair had escaped from under the hood that sat heavy over her head. It was long, wavy and almost white. Strands were caught in the wind, whirling around and clinging to the chrome of her mask like spiders legs - They were terrifying, and in force...

Robin took a breath, then stupidly glanced around towards the tree. Thankfully they hadn't noticed him, but there was certainly more than three this time, there had to be five or six, restless and waiting in close proximity.

He hadn't the foggiest why his wand was in his hand, he didn't know how to use it.

All it was good for was twiddling as an attempt to keep the growing nerves at bay - but it wasn't working. It was just defecting his concentration, so he carefully put the wand back in his waistcoat pocket and decided to bide his time, listening closely to the sound of the Reapers boots, thudding far and near.

"You've lost him! I told you we should have struck the moment we had him in our sights!" bellowed the largest of the group from behind the ranks, making his way forward in to the centre of the courtyard.

The white haired Reaper turned to address him, watching his approach, her chin rattling beneath the mask as she restrained her inner urges.

"What do you have to say for yourself, Saph? Oh, what's this… you're trembling, maybe we can give you something for that."

She remained defiant, glaring coldly at the fat rebel, who was now stood level, eye to eye, believing his presence was enough to intimidate her - well, how wrong he would be about that. Their stand-off was short lived as Saph brought it to a sudden close, launching her head forward, like a rocket, knocking the rebel off his feet.

Robin gasped, his eyes wide as he heard the clang of solid metal and a splash, followed by a *thud* as the Reapers body hit the ground.

"No, no, no…," Robin muttered, with his mind aglow with visions of the enemy discovering the entrance. For all he knew, it may have been the puddle, but he could think of far worse disguises.

"Stand, stand goddamnit! Because if it's a brawl you're after, then let's be having it, you brute of a man!"

The rebel Reaper quaked in his boots, still damp and suffering from a mild concussion. His vision was a blur but he could make out the dark outline of Sapphire, knelt beside him and reaching for his throat.

"I'm going to offer you something - a choice. But before I do, let's not forget why the master entrusted me to lead this legion."

He wiped dry the exposed side of his face, coughing and spluttering, finding his long lost composure.

"I bet you think you're better than us? Why should we follow a *woman* of all people?"

Saph bit down hard on her tongue, her restraints now beginning to show signs of cracking.

"I don't see that being a problem, or am I mistaken?" she replied, glancing up at the other Reapers, who stood obedient as the rebel panicked, calling out to those he had considered his friends.

"*You fools, You bloody fools!*"

He yelled, realising that things were about to turn ugly as Sapphire directed her vicious looking wand down, towards his chest, its razor sharp tip like a pin, ready to inflict pain.

"Treacherous kind, like yourself, do not belong in the ranks of my legion. Your services, as of now, are terminated!"

She explained in a monochrome tone, watching as the life drained from the rebels face until all that remained was a skeletal corpse, wrapped within the endless layers of black, damp fabric. The remaining fragments of the Reapers soul slowly relinquished into the light at the end of Sapphires wand.

"We have no cause for concern, do we?" she asked, quietly, glancing over towards each of the remaining Reapers, who gave a subtle shake of the head.

"Good, now disperse. Find the professor!" She ordered, rising to her feet to witness the four dark figures disappear behind a ball of dark, smouldering vapour.

Robin could feel his body slowly relaxing, knowing that the Reapers were passing; however he still had a gut-curdling feeling that he was being watched. He could sense her eyes burning in his direction but she didn't approach, instead, she turned away. The sound of metal chains rattled from her boots as she vacated the courtyard, evaporating under a thick cloud of dark matter.

Robin could just make out the misty, organic fragments, floating towards the sky as he peered over to observe the courtyard, now safe and free of evil. He cautiously crept out from behind the porch, watching over his shoulder and in every direction, just to make sure for certain that the Reapers were gone and not reeling him in to a devious ploy.

The heavy oppressive cloud felt as if it had lifted, there was no trace of them at all, even the mist had now vanished, but the body of the fallen Reaper remained, lifeless and inhuman looking, left in a pile for the towns people to discover, which didn't sit well with Robin. The sight of the corpse was frightful - it wasn't for the faint hearted, neither any child, it was certainly the stuff of nightmares.

He crouched down beside the body and pulled the hood down over the Reaper's face.

"You may well have been on the wrong side, but in death, even an enemy is owed some respect."

Robin placed his hand down on the robes and paused, looking over towards the puddle beside him. There was something calling, something alluring Robin to that silly little puddle. It was almost as if it was trying to communicate with him, pulling at his seemingly endless attention.

He grabbed his satchel, just to make sure it was still attached, then began to pull the wrapped body along the ground - it wasn't as heavy as he had expected, after all, there was hardly any muscle or fluid left inside it. It wasn't pleasant, but to Robin, it seemed the right thing to do.

The robes became immersed by water, the same with Robin's trousers as he knelt beside it. The wet surface rippled around him and sparkled as the sun continued to beam down through the oak tree branches overhead.

He shot a vague look about the courtyard, one final act of assurance before removing his wand from his waistcoat - this time with reason.

He gave it a gentle flick, directing it down towards the water that clung heavy to his trousers; and then he waited, holding tight to the Reapers corpse with fluttering nerves.

It felt as if time had suddenly slowed, like it was trapped in an endless moment with the fear of being discovered: *Were they on their way back? Perhaps they had heard the sound of the body being dragged along the ground?*

They might have had eyes in the back of their heads, or super enhanced senses for all Robin knew, but the uncomfortable wait had paid off as he felt a hand grasp his ankle, then another, until he could feel his entire body being pulled down towards the shallow water.

"*No! Let go of me!*"

Robin glanced down at the hands, but they weren't what he had first expected - they were masses of water, rising from the puddle and taking the forms of appendages with long, spindly, water-clear fingers. They squirmed like snakes, latching on to Robin's body and tugging at him, pulling him down, fighting all of his efforts as he tried to break free. They were strong and nothing that Robin mustered had any effect. He was a sinking ship and he could feel pressure against his body as he sunk, like a chain might have been wrapped around his chest, drawing him deep into the ground.

He gasped, he spluttered and panicked as water rushed up around his neck and into his mouth, flooding his lungs. His eyes widened as his face slowly disappeared under, submerged beneath solid concrete - he was gone, and so was the puddle for that matter. As if by magic, Robin, the corpse and the puddle were without a trace, leaving nothing to tie them to the place or time. They had been taken somewhere far beyond the realms of reality, precisely where Robin had been summoned.

* * *

The sun sat low in the sky, just over the snow capped mountains that surrounded the vast, magical landscape. The ground was damp and soft, making the climb less of a struggle as Robin's hand rose up out of the dirt. He pulled himself from the soil, dragging the Reapers corpse behind him until they were out in the clear.

"Well, that was something!"

Robin rubbed the muck from his face and patted away what he could from his mustard coloured coat and soggy brown trousers, while setting his sights over the canyon, down towards the bottom, where the Institute resided, embedded into the mountain.

His eyes lit up, he could make out the shape of the enormous gates and the tall steel fencing that lined the pit. *It was quite magnificent*, he thought as the sun's rays caught the surface of a million gemstones, lodged in and around the rockery. Red, blue, green and orange, they twinkled and gleamed which made for a delightful journey as Robin descended down the spiral slope, pulling the corpse behind him, yanking at the robes as exhaustion set in. He huffed and tugged, then suddenly what had seemed like a tiny gateway from afar, was now slowly moving into perspective. The lower Robin trekked, the larger the scale grew, until he was at the deepest point of the pit and the dark, steel fencing towered over him. It had to be at least nine feet high with sharp, jagged tips - some heavily stained by bile and brightly coloured bodily fluids - certainly none of a Human.

"I don't fancy meeting whatever they're meant to be keeping out," Robin remarked, amused yet equally terrified, looking up at the spiralling rocky path that he had travelled down, observing the glistening stones as they woke from their sleep, while the sun crept overhead, partially casting light at the base of the pit where the Reapers corpse was laid, wrapped by the now rather tatty robes.

"And now I guess, we wait..."

Robin couldn't help but check on the body, even though it was no longer living. As strange as it seemed, it was the only company Robin had and it kept his mind from wandering. Being able to focus on something that was somewhat important allowed him to cast away the worry of what could be waiting inside this infamous Institute for Morient kind - whether that be an impossible creature, or a person. Perhaps it was the tall, sleek figure that was now on the approach from behind the enormous gates. His jacket had begun to flap, projecting beams of silver rays as his lining caught the sun.

At first glance, he seemed like someone that Mrs Jillings had described. His boots clomped against the gravel, moving with a confident swagger as he neared the centre of the pit where Robin was stood - he definitely seemed familiar.

Robin continued to watch, judging the silver man down to his simple choice of fragrance that rode in on the powerful breeze of ego.

"Robin - sir. Robin Occamy," he announced, holding tight to his satchel and patting at his pockets to make sure they were still full of his findings.

"Professor, at long last. We've been waiting for you," said the silver man, as he arrived face to face with Robin.

"I'm Leonard - Leonard Silverstein. Now, you had better come with me."

CHAPTER 10
The Informal Congress

His boots remained glued to the gravel as the silver man directed him towards the entrance.

"Are you in charge?" Asked Robin.

Silverstein fell curiously silent with one brow raised, turning back to look at Robin.

"I believe I'm fully capable of making my own way inside, with the utmost respect, sir." Robin didn't want to sound rude, it was the last thing he had wanted, but by the look on Silverstein's face, he hadn't come across as polite, either.

"Credentials… *please*," he said sternly.

"But you know who I am. You said it yourself, you've been waiting for me," he paused, staring Silverstein dead in the eye - but he wasn't fooling around, it seemed he was deadly serious.

"- oh for goodness sake," Robin said in annoyance as he began rummaging in to his waistcoat pocket, drawing out the leather wallet and flipping it open for Silverstein to see.

"Happy?"

Silverstein smirked.

"Just doing my job, sir. With the dark forces back on the move, we have to be sure. we have to ensure our defences are up for the challenges that the Count may throw at us."

Robin shot a look around the pit, observing the fencing.

"Good. Nothing better than feeling safe and secure on foreign land. So, inside, there's no one I need to be wary of, is there? No nasty surprises?"

Silverstein glanced towards the entrance, then back to Robin.

"The Institute? They're the most docile bunch you'll ever meet, and you can take my word on that. They wouldn't harm a fly." He scratched at the stubble on his chin, "- and perhaps that's the reason we're in this bloody mess," he concluded in a hushed tone. Robin hadn't heard the last part, but he was smirking as his eyes strayed down towards the forgotten robes at his feet - then he suddenly remembered.

"I need to ask a favour. There was this poor soul left out to rot, his body is under those robes. Would you bury him for me? It would mean an awful lot, that's all I ask."

Silverstein cast his gaze down towards the dark, tatty robes.

"You knew him?"

"Afraid not, I was just a passing, but thought he deserved a little...respect? I assume he was attacked, but I have to warn you now, it's not at all pretty under there. I really don't know what happened to him."

Silverstein crouched down beside the mass, examining the texture of the damp robes.

"I'll sort this," he said abruptly, "- you'd best be getting inside, Professor Grimtale will be most pleased to see you."

He continued to stare down at the shape of the

body, unveiling the face of the Reaper corpse, lost in thought as he wondered: *What on earth could have happened?*

The Reapers mouth was wide open, frozen stiff in his moment of passing. Silverstein carefully placed his palm on the forehead of the Reaper, sharing a moment of silence as Robin made his way towards the gates, watching over his shoulder to make sure that Silverstein was treating the body appropriately, the way he had requested, before he passed on through the gate that was left ajar, and then disappeared beyond the second doorway - the main entrance to the Institute.

Silverstein let out a sigh of relief as his body fell back in to a slump.

"Respect… don't make me laugh! How many people's DNA lie trapped under those grotesque finger nails? All of that bloody residue... *that* even looks like a hair!" he muttered aggressively, closely inspecting the Reapers decrepit hand, almost as if he had expected the deceased man to take a breath and hurl a response back at him.

"He thinks you deserve respect," he chuckled quietly, checking over his shoulder,

"How many families have *you* denied the decency they deserve, sir? How many children have knelt and begged you for their lives? I'm no saint; however I sense we have a lot more in common than we think. That's how I worked out precisely what you *deserve*. What we all have coming, now the great Count is finally rising from his slumber." Silverstein pulled his wand from his brown, leather holster that sat strapped firmly around his hips.

"There's going to be a war, we're going to need the space to bury our dead. It's better this way, for us both."

He lowered his wand, pointing the tip between the Reapers milky, white eyes.

"*Pirontious*," he said delicately.

Then a sudden burst of orange shot from the tip of his wand and ignited the robes in front of him. The corpse was suddenly engulfed at the centre of a fierce blaze that lit the darkened corner of the pit with a red hot glow. Silverstein watched as the corpse slowly degraded to bone, ash and dust, observing with a finger raised to his lips.

"Shush, now," he whispered, his gaze fixed intensely on the remains, his face reflecting burning crimson as the body crackled and snapped. He seemed almost fixated on the sight, but his aggression was slowly sweeping away with the bright embers. Torching the deceased Reaper had become a convenient release for all the anger and grief that had amounted within him - he felt at ease as the flames died down, leaving nothing but a blackened patch of gravel and a mist of particles that crumbled from the scorched remnants of the robes.

It had felt like a stride towards the cleansing of both worlds, no matter how small it was, the riddance of evil in whatever form it took, it made the chance of peace seem far less out of reach. A chance for order and unity, everything Silverstein had stood for. He held on to that thought as he rose from the ground and ran his hands through his elaborate, silver tipped hair.

Turning towards the entrance, Silverstein broke in to a light purposeful stride, making his way back to the Institute where he expected, by now, the foyer would be livening up with the presence of its latest arrival, the family man from across the realm - Robin Occamy.

* * *

Besides the rattling of metal coins as wildlife rummaged from inside their golden pocket hives, it was silent inside, eerily silenced like sacred land as Robin lumbered in to the main foyer entrance. The shiny marble floor beneath his soles glistened and mirrored the ceiling like a river of gold with the statue animals sat at the side of the embankment, glaring up at their physical counterparts then down as Robin reverted his gaze. They were perched high along the decorative frame of the walls before the ceiling began to curve by a body of solid gold that concealed the foyer corridor.

The ruby, sapphire and emerald gemstones that were buried in the mountain were also present, high overhead, embedded in the gold and twinkling, alluring Robin further inside, reeling him forward like a stupefied child.

His eyes were a blaze with magical sights. Everywhere he looked was decorated with parchments: medals, beautifully crafted statues and tapestries. One wall was covered entirely by a long woven shroud with a depiction of Vinemoore, his town, intricately stitched across it and embellished with a mixture of vibrant wool.

"*That would look lovely on the living room floor,*" he thought, smiling in admiration, reminded of the endless view outside his bedroom window, overlooking the towns cottages and allotments.

"I'd very much like to meet the person who made this," his voice echoed gently around the foyer as he turned to the glass cabinet beside him.

"Maybe they can make me one, I'd pay a pretty tuppence, for sure," he added as he leaned in to examine the three crystal cups that were suspended inside the glass cabinet, presumably by some kind of levitation charm.

He noticed each of the cups were carrying a different silver plaque at the base with an etched explanation of what they represented. Admittedly, he wasn't entirely interested, it was just the fact that they were dancing around inside the cabinet that caught his attention; however he made an effort to read off the plaques, frowning and squinting with his face pressed firmly against the glass:

Formidable conduct: Heightened levels of innovation in alchemy classes, and a superior understanding of magical creatures from the wild land to the enclosed habitats within the Institute.

"*Humph*, quite the achievers," he loosely remarked as his flesh popped unstuck from the pane of glass.

"And one day, we hope to add to our small collection," spoke a thunderous voice.

Robin turned towards the sound of the deep burly voice, glaring at the tall, heavy man that was on his way over; his cane clunking against the marble tiles with every stride.

"At last, we finally meet. For too long you existed in my mind as a character of fiction, it's damn good to see you in the flesh, sir."

Robin held out his hand with a wide grin etched on his face. The tall bearded man snatched up his hand with a slap and clung tightly, giving it a thorough shake.

"Professor Harold Grimtale, Headmaster. And you… well, you haven't changed one bit, besides the stubble and the newly discovered sense of acceptable fashion, to which I must highly approve!"

Robin could feel his cheeks burning as he quickly patted away the remaining dust from his mustard yellow coat and fastened his bag strap around his chest before finally clearing his throat.

"It's a pleasure, Professor. But I must apologise for the lack of knowledge of how I fit in here. As far as I'm concerned, we've just met…"

"And perhaps that's for the best, a clean slate for the both of us."

Grimtale rested his hand gently on Robins shoulder and gave a reassuring nod, to which Robin suddenly began to wonder, what kind of history was sealed between the two of them, *how far back did they go?* It was odd, he felt like a stranger and looked like one too, but as they exchanged a look within each other's noble eyes, the grand doors behind Grimtale were suddenly flung wide on their thick steel hinges and an excitable crowd of three began to flood their way in, followed closely overhead by a vibrant, pink feathered bird that fluttered and swooped its way to the front of the group as they raced for Robin's attention.

The bird was first to arrive, landing delicately

beside Grimtales cumbersome boots and reverting back to her eccentric, human-looking form.

"I'll never question the existence of magic again, that was bloody marvellous! And your name is?" asked an excitable Robin, looking in wonder at her familiar pink coat as she knocked away the remaining feathers from her luscious blonde hair - which only took a second or two, then she reached for Robins cold, pale hand.

"Magenta, we met back in Vinemoore?"

"Oh! Of course, how silly of me. Yourself and Kenneth, the Reapers! I'm awfully sorry, it's all still quite a blur to me, but it's lovely to see you again."

She smiled warmly back at him.

"It's ok, it wasn't pleasant. I assume a lot has happened since then?"

"A day from hell." They both chuckled, then Robin took a long, deep breath before slapping his hands firmly against his cheeks, hoping it would snap him from his dream - but it was no dream, it was really happening, he soon realised that as the laughter continued.

"So is Kenneth here? With you guys? Or does his involvement not stretch as far as this place?" asked Robin, peering over Magenta's shoulder where a group of fans had waited patiently, relishing the presence of *the* Robin Occamy. All were silent now.

"Kenneth Brown?" he added for the puzzled faces, breaking the awkward silence.

"I'm afraid, since his return we made quite the discovery," Magenta paused reluctantly, turning to Grimtale for approval, to which he gave a subtle nod of the head, allowing her to continue.

"The reason he insisted on you abandoning us and *saving* your family, was so *he* would stand a far better chance of surviving this. But he soon crumbled when Silverstein brought to light the severe consequences he would be facing if the enemy caught wind of his indecisive allegiance. Silverstein said he'd never seen anyone scarper so fast, he was straight out those doors. We haven't seen him since."

"And he is no longer welcome inside our walls. A necessary precaution, for everyone's safety." Grimtale added as Robin's look of confusion changed at once.

"To say I'm shocked would be the understatement of the century. I never would have taken him as a traitor, but what do I know, he was only a baker to me," he scratched at his chin, "if I may ask, what - what was the consequence?"

Magenta and Grimtale turned to one another, then sharply back to the curious Robin.

"A forced existence without love or trust. One where each passing day you beg for it to be your last until it inevitably begins again, over and over…"

"*Enough of that, Magenta. You'll give the poor man nightmares. You can't be doing with those, not on your first night in this creepy place,*" echoed the distant voice of Silverstein as he began his journey towards them, his metallic shoes clapping sharp against the marble and his perfectly coiffed hair standing rigid like daggers as the light caught the silver tipped fibres.

"It's morning, sir," replied Robin, forcing a smile and raising his head in hope of deterring the oppressive ego that had begun to radiate from

Silverstein's inflated chest as he flounced by, arriving beside Magenta, who couldn't help but inhale his bitter-sweet scent as it wafted from the inners of his jacket.

"I stand corrected," he grinned, "- but it's been an awfully long night, we're running on empty. So perhaps we'd all benefit from a little shut eye?" he said rhetorically, throwing up his hands and glancing over his shoulder to what he must have considered his personal audience, still waiting patiently to greet Robin.

"I'm sorry, Robin. Will you be ok if we take a quick nap?" asked Magenta, with a sincere look of concern in her eyes.

"Hey! Of course I will, I was one of the lucky ones who managed to get a little kip," he chuckled, feeling ever so slightly bad for everyone as they stood wearily before him. He could see the exhaustion reflecting in Grimtale's eyes, they were slightly bloodshot and there wasn't a doubt in his mind that he was suppressing a yawn, but he disguised it well, rustling his stubby fingers through the wiry texture of his beard.

"Professor Yuri… " called Grimtale.

"Yes, Headmaster," he replied, squeezing between Silverstein and Magenta, delighted to finally be a part of the gathering that had formed around Robin.

"Am I correct to recall you saying earlier that you were going to pass on bed rest this morning?"

He quickly fastened his bow tie and pressed his delicate spectacles to the bridge of his nose, "well, yes I had considered it, Headmaster. I believe I can sleep when I'm dead, and especially at a time like the present I think it's only morally correct for me to watch over the grounds while all of you sleep -"

Yuri nervously switched his gaze between Grimtale and Robin, he had never been the most confident, always a shy boy and no matter how well he tried to hide it, it was always distinguishable through subtle mannerisms. Like the rubbing of his hands as his eyes flickered from Grimtale to Robin, and occasionally to the ground where there was no one to glare back at him. It was like a safety net - a product of the inadequate self confidence.

"- besides, I have errands that require completion. I believe you will enjoy my recent discovery, Professors." He added, standing awkwardly in his tatty, multi coloured waistcoat and dark, hole ridden trousers that levelled just above the ankles, exhibiting his bright white socks and well worn brogues.

"Then if it's not too much to ask, would you show Mr Occamy to his lodge and perhaps spare some time to answer any burning questions he may have? I'm sure he will feel more comfortable asking, when not overshadowed by strangers."

Yuri nodded frantically, "most certainly, it would be an honour. Am I to take him to *his* lodge?"

"*His* lodge, Professor."

"Very well," he concluded.

Magenta had already been swept under Silverstein's arm as he impatiently waited for the others to finish.

"We shall be off, but we'll congress again at

midday."

Grimtale stepped forward, "Yes, we will all gather inside the chamber. Those who are sleeping, rest well, we have troubled days to come."

As Grimtale brought the reunion to a close, Silverstein and Magenta were the first to disperse. Robin had caught a smile and a delicate wave of her hand as she was swept away. The rest were still waiting to introduce themselves as Robin, Yuri and Grimtale slowly began coasting towards the giant chamber doors that were left ajar, following the sound of Silverstein's shoes, clapping against the marble, then granite floor.

Lillian held out her hand, walking in synch with the group.

"Lillian Vargov, It's a pleasure to see you again, Mr Occamy."

Lillian was predominantly the youngest, no older than twenty five, which Robin recognised as he collected her unwrinkled hand and smiled, taking a friendly note of her elvish looking ears and elongated nose. He wasn't accustomed to seeing such features, but he chose not to pass judgment - she seemed kind.

He shook her hand, "Lovely to meet you, Lillian."

She had a sharp sparkle in her eye and seemed to somewhat admire him - if only he understood why, but he was certain things would fall in to place now that he had arrived where answers resided. Everything about the Institute excited him, so much so he had shamefully forgotten about the realm where he had supposedly spent his entire life. The sights, the people, the looming journey of self discovery, it had suppressed his heavy heartache and welcomed him with open arms, when all along his greatest fear was being apart from the ones he loved, but now he knew for certain, he was going to be fine.

As the five of them made their way in to the council chamber, the fifth and final professor stuck his head forward and glared intently at Robin.

"Teppi Lint, charms master…"

Teppi was short, middle aged with a obvious Asian heritage and a plaited patch of facial hair that hung from his chin.

"- I shall catch up with you later in the day, good sir." There was a clap as he threw his hands together. He took a bow and then he was gone, before Robin had a chance to speak, but once again, he seemed nice, he thought as he witnessed everyone disappearing beyond the hidden segregated exits, behind the shining thrones that surrounded the Phoenix monument which sat as a centrepiece, a crown jewel at the heart of the council chamber.

Silence had fallen, it was then just the three of them. Robin, Yuri and Grimtale, staring up as the premature sun rained down on the sky dome, illuminating the ruby Phoenix, its streaky crimson hues cast raw across the flesh of their faces.

"I would highly encourage you to explore the grounds, but you must remember if you do, the two realms are nothing alike, you will make discoveries and cross paths with things you won't yet understand; however, the realm you now crave was only ever temporary - this is where you belong, Robin. This is where you made your name."

Robin continued to look up towards the sky

dome, his thoughts latched tightly on to his fiancée and daughter, who were locked firmly in his heart.

"Stick with Professor Yuri, or if you're feeling brave, take a wander. It might do you some good."

Robin caught a trusting sparkle in Grimtales eye, then he reverted his gaze back up at the sky and the pinkish storm clouds that were revolving violently, triggering Robin with an overwhelming realisation - he was much further from home than he had ever hoped to be.

CHAPTER 11
Between The Towers

It didn't take Robin long to realise just how loquacious Professor Yuri was, he could talk for both worlds when he was in the right frame of mind. He hadn't stopped since they left the council chamber and by now it was clear to conclude there didn't seem to be a bad bone in his body. By the way he so keenly chatted as if often starved of company it was all too obvious that perhaps he didn't have many friends he could entrust, but somehow, for some reason, Robin had been on the receiving end of details of quite an array of Yuri's top secret experiments. He had listed them as they made their way up a long winding stairwell that led high into the Institute towers.

"It feels strange," Robin said, "I'd be at work on a normal day, yet it still doesn't feel right. I look out of the window and I see a sky that *they* cannot. It's a little disorientating, you know?"

"Well it's only a reflection - the sky I mean. The Morient world is like, well, imagine turning a jumper inside out. We're just on the inside and your partner, is on the outside," Yuri explained, stopping beside a viewing ledge.

"I'm not sure how that would make me more comfortable," Robin chuckled, edging closer to Yuri, capturing the sight, "- just look at those clouds, I've never seen anything like it before. They're beautiful, enchanting but... it's *not* home."

Yuri glanced across at Robin, his eyes glistening with the electric pink of the flossy masses as they drifted overhead.

"It's going to be tough, the next twenty four hours. Assuming that's all I'm required for?"

Yuri removed his spectacles and rubbed away the trapped dirt from his nose.

"I believe so, however the size of the task is somewhat ambitious, but with you now at hand, we'll be in and out before the Reapers have a chance to respond."

There was that curious look in his eyes again as Robin turned to Yuri.

"We'll be in and out of where?"

He had asked the question but already had a good idea what the answer would be, but even so, it was just a hunch until Yuri confirmed with his reply.

"Shoulders Heath, the land situated beyond the black mountain."

Its whereabouts didn't need explaining, as Robin knew of it all too well. He was always reminded of its sinister presence on a weekly, sometimes daily basis when missing posters would materialise on the lamp posts and shop windows - missing persons as the result of curious expeditions. *No one had ever returned. None had ever been found, dead or alive.* The thought didn't sit well with Robin, it churned his stomach and made him feel rather sick, but the calm in Yuri's voice was somewhat inspiring; after all, maybe there were forms of protection for Morient kind, secrets yet to be shared that would suggest not all was doom and gloom, as they continued on their way, up towards the alchemist lodges.

* * *

The alchemist lodges were rather unusual pieces of architecture. They were round solid stone structures dotted in a zigzag pattern along a gloomy, torch lit tunnel that connected the two institute towers. Each had a heavy wooden door and was home to the professors that worked there, like a holiday home away from home; for some, it was the only comfort they had ever known. Working there meant that a roof over their head was a given, and that kind of security was something that no sane man or woman would have passed up, no person with Morient blood inhabiting their veins. Togetherness was strength, it was power in a time that was threatened with the return of the darkest of evils ever known.

Magenta loved living inside the institute, and now had finally slipped in to something less vibrant, something rather thin and delicate that complimented the curves of her body perfectly. Silverstein had noticed, admiring her from afar as she sat at the foot of their large, luxurious bed while he stood at the dresser, casting an intense expression as he brushed through his soft silver hair.

"You look nice," he remarked.

Magenta smirked, flicking her wand at the heavy fabric curtains which suddenly drew to close, concealing the stone window and the rays of light from the sun. The room was now lit only by candle light. Thick orange candle sticks were dotted around the room in various locations: tabletops, bedside tables, the dresser and they were oozing graciously as the flame burned away at the wax. They had cast a warm, romantic glow about the bedroom as Silverstein began undressing: first removing his jacket and then his dusty shoes.

"These will need a clean. Still, it was good to meet the man," he said, bending over to untie his laces.

"Yes, it's good to have him back. It's been too long," she agreed.

Silverstein looked up at Magenta as he pulled off his first shoe.

"You'll have to tell me more about him, so I know what to talk about when I see him again."

"Well, there's not much to tell, not really, nothing you don't know already," she explained, slumping back in to the bed and placing her wand upon her chest.

"I noticed a little tension between the two of you," she added.

Magenta watched as Silverstein made a chuckle, still bent over, untying the second strand of laces.

"We're men, it was merely a clash of egos.

Please tell me you noticed that..."

"Noticed what?" she asked with a look of confusion.

"How self-righteous he was. Strolled in as if he owned the place!"

"Maybe it's his way of dealing with fear. He's a long way from the human world. It takes a lot to put on a brave face." Magenta watched Silverstein intently as he rose from the end of the bed and made his way over, their locked gaze matched depth and equal understanding.

"I really don't know what people see in that human realm."

"Leonard," Magenta said sternly with a frown of disapproval " - just because you've had the privilege of darting between both, doesn't mean you can assume you know what it's like to live there! It's the only place he's known, he's bound to be fond of it now, his family are there."

"Privilege? But didn't you say he's from here? The Morient realm?"

He asked that question as he slumped on to the bed, leaning in with his silky white shirt unbuttoned, and his fist resting firmly against his jaw, looking intently into Magenta's eyes.

"Some time ago."

As lost as she wanted to be in his gaze, Magenta now looked away, to the deep red curtains with golden floral embroidery as her thoughts shifted to another time and place.

"It's funny because nothing's changed, not much anyway. Just that our hearts fell heavy that day."

Silverstein wrapped his arm around Magenta's shoulder and pulled her close. He waved his hand over her face and her perfect skin began to quake as a charm slowly disintegrated and dispersed like a stream of fairy dust, pulling away from the frame of her face and sparkling bright as embers, glowing as warm as a candle flame.

"You need not look back on that day as one of dismay," he gently ran his hand down the side of her cheek, then across to the long raw scar that split her eyebrow and ran thin along her forehead, "- only the beginning of great things to come. Revenge, revolution... peace. It's purely a reminder of what you're fighting for, Magenta."

Her eyes briefly reflected a longed for victory as she imagined herself making the final blow to the devil. Succeeding where he had failed, gauging away the eyes from his mutated skull...

"The Count will regret ever coming to Vinemoore."

Magenta glanced up at Silverstein as he held her in a comforting embrace.

"I can promise that much and I don't speak empty words," she added with buried rage, boiling deep within her.

Silverstein pulled gently on her chin, raising her head in line with his and then he pounced, locking lips with his lover, to extract the darkness from her soul and ignite a flame of love and desire that simmered, then burned in long lasting passion as the two of them held each other tightly. Only the walls of the room shared their intimacy as they stole this precious time to own in celebration of their love, nothing mattering but each other for as long as they held on together.

Damp from the heat of shared paradise as they began to cast the world outside away and lay in a lasting embrace, Magenta silently realised, no matter what was saddled to the day ahead, there was nothing better than time alone with her lover. Whatever fate had in store, she knew as she ran her hand down her partner's chest, that she felt free of danger – at least for now - but all the same, she was afflicted by the fear of a future without him, sleeping alone, with the cold nipping at her spine. She'd swiftly decided that this temporary mortal life was cruel, but she was now the happiest she could ever be, wrapped in his slender arms that caged her like a prison, a prison that she had no hope or desire to break from.

Her lover had also been thinking, and as he kissed her again, he had drawn a conclusion of his own. For a man who enjoyed bathing in his own appreciation, Silverstein knew in her arms, he had softened, exposing his most vulnerable side as he silently accepted that even the world's greatest men and women required a spot of sleep - in good time, of course.

* * *

The sun was shining weakly, casting beautiful trails of dim pink light through the slender gap between Grimtale's purple velvet curtains. His lodge bore similarities to Magenta and Silverstein's. It was oval shaped but slightly larger, allowing for more furniture and decoration. But Grimtale wasn't one for bare and bland - within hours of being promoted to Headmaster, he'd stitched a handful of metallic silver stars to the curtains. They still hung heavy across his viewpoint, now a little faded, reflecting the twenty years of sunrises.

Even the cold brick walls were hidden behind rugs and tie dyed fabrics that he had hung up himself, each with a recurring tone of luxurious purple, contrasting the rusty browns and inky blue hues that inhabited most of the designs. There was also a selection of moderately sized, rectangular mirrors dotted around the room, with a selection of different coloured scarves draped over the tops, adding a little warmth to their cold metallic frames. At the foot of his large wooden bed was a tatty brown trunk, with a pair of heavy duty padlocks restraining it closed.

Beyond that was an opening, followed by two small stone steps that descended into a smaller pocket room that none of the other lodges had. This was where he housed his tall oak cabinets, the books that sat upon the cabinet shelves and a large chest of drawers, which also doubled as a station to work at - one that was currently in use.

Grimtale was sunk on his stool, arched over the surface of his desk space with a quill in one hand crafting words on parchment, and the other outstretched, gently petting his companion, Quibble. She was a small penguin-like creature with pearlescent purple coloured feathers, a long, sharp orange beak and two beady black eyes. She sat quietly perched on top of Grimtale's golden ornate burner, glaring down at the parchment beneath it, following her master's hand under the glowing amber. The small room was dark and the silence was only disturbed by the sound of Grimtale's quill, etching away, and an occasional chirp.

His eyes were growing heavier after carefully

wording the letter, but after signing at the bottom with his name and a kiss, he began a final read through, occasionally whispering a sentence or two, just to ensure it sounded as good as it did in his head:

Dear Sachester,

I find myself reaching the end of another sleepless night, wishing you were at my
side.
I write to you bearing good news. Robin has returned and we have high hopes of
him joining us tonight, to help evacuate the Phoenix from Shoulders Heath.
I know you've never been fond of Silverstein, but in less than twenty four hours,
Robin will have his post back, if he chooses to stay, that is. Then Silverstein will
have no choice but to move on, to which I hope you reconsider my offer and join me
at the Institute. You belong with us.

P.s the cavalry arrived safely. I owe you a great deal. Thank you my love, and keep
safe.

P. H Grimtale X

"That'll have to do."
Knowing there could have been a million other ways to phrase it, he returned his quill to the

inkwell and drew his secondary wand from the top drawer that was already left ajar. It was a short eight inch wand with a pebbly handle and vicious looking fangs sprouting from the bottom like roots. It was an off white colour and the shaft had a hint of silver that shimmered as he held it close to the parchment, under the radiant glow of the lamp.

The Quibble made a snappy chirp, hopping from the lamp, on to the desk then up to Grimtale's shoulder, cowering behind his fluffy jacket collar.

"Oh, there's nothing to be afraid of Nibble, just some pretty sparks and then I'll be off to bed, and that's a promise!"

Nibble peaked her beady eyes out from under Grimtale's collar, watching as the tip of his wand began to illuminate as he cast the transportation spell:

"Senteer..."

He then pictured precisely where the letter had to go, painting an image of Sachester's bedroom and the pillowcase he wanted it to materialise on. It was strong and vibrant in his mind as the parchment began to wind itself up nice and tight before evaporating behind a popping explosion of yellow sparkle.

"It's just quicker that way," he assured Nibble, who had usually delivered all his mail; however Shoulders Heath was no longer a place for the cute and fluffy. One half was delightful, where Sachester lived - but it wasn't worth the risk of sending Nibble, not after the Phoenix sightings, she'd barely serve as an appetiser. Grimtale felt most comfortable knowing she was safe in his lodge, perched on her favourite branch which stemmed from a potted plant beside his bed.

"Yes, I know what you're thinking. If a Reaper was on the other end they could have torn their way through to the Institute - but Sachester is safe, her entire town is protected."

She chirped again, swaying on her stick thin legs as Grimtale rose from his stool with Nibble still firmly latched on to his shoulder.

"Nothing bad can filter the defences, it's been *field* tested."

He turned a knob on the desk lamp and the flame slowly shrunk until the room was dark with a hue of pink glowing around the door frame.

"What do you mean '*am I certain*'?" he asked in reply to her chirp, "I trust in Professor Yuri's capabilities as inventor. He had the stone at hand to help with his research, with thanks to Sachester. So yes, I'm more than certain, my feathered friend."

He made one last effort to smile as he approached his bed, he pulled back the fresh linen, then after Nibble had hopped on to her branch he slumped down on to the soft mattress, exhaling a sigh of relief as his head sank deep against plump pillows.

"Goodnight, Nibble," he whispered, already slipping away into a deeply desired dream.

Nibble remained perched on her branch, watching with her beady black eyes as her master slept and the morning began to slip away.

* * *

A little further along the winding corridor that connected all of the lodges, a weary Flint Yuri appeared with Robin Occamy in tow. He now had a large rusty key in one hand and looked pleased to finally be on the top floor after a long and treacherous climb.

"Just out of curiosity, why do you still use keys? I mean, I thought you'd just zap the locks with your wands," Robin went to flick his wand as a means of demonstrating what he meant, but Yuri suddenly snatched it from his hand and tucked it away back inside Robin's waistcoat.

"They're not toys, okay? And yes, we do use them for locking doors and unlocking padlocks; however, it doesn't work on them all, especially yours."

"M-mine?" Robin asked, scuttling along behind Yuri.

"Your lodge, " he replied as they arrived at a dark wooden door with deep grain running from high to low. "This lock had an enchantment cast on it. Magic doesn't work on it, as it seemed for the best - just in case anyone got curious. But here, we have this…"

He handed the rusty key over to Robin as his eyes registered surprise, seeing something he had not expected – before him was a long metal stamp nailed across the top of the door with an engraving that read:

Professor R. Occamy.

CHAPTER 12
Professor Occamy

The silver plaque shimmered as Yuri's wand began to flicker, emitting a harsh white light. He lowered it towards the rusty doorknob, illuminating the sharp edges of the key hole underneath. There were no windows or open viewpoints along the corridor, it was usually lit by old torches that hung from the walls, a few meters apart from tower to tower; however, everyone had gotten lazy on this particular day and deprived of sleep, they hadn't bothered to light them, even though it only took an effortless swish of the wand they preferred their own ludicrous methods, which as expected ended with twisted ankles and profound language being hurled at thin air - much to the amusement of the tiny critters overhead, who watched from their enormous sticky webs that stretched from wall to wall.

There was a heavy *clang* of metal as Robin began to force the rigid key into the door, bypassing the protective charm that rippled rays of green energy as his hand sunk through it like jelly. He then turned the key and the door *clonked* as the latch retracted, releasing it from its locked state.

"Here you go, Professor."

Robin went to hand back the key to Yuri, who immediately pressed it into Robin's palm.

"You'd best hang on to that. This old place will have you coming back for more."

"But I won't be staying long - twenty four hours and I'm back through that puddle. So please take the key, I'll only lose it."

Yuri decided he wasn't going to argue, so he retrieved the key and dropped it back in to his waistcoat pocket.

"You know you won't have to travel that way anymore. It's just because you hadn't seen the institute before, there wasn't a memory to lock on to. I take it you know how it works?"

"I've been told how it *doesn't* work, the risks that accompany it. Seems pretty simple to me."

Robin returned his attention to the door as a spark of excitement ignited within him. Not wasting any time, he grabbed hold of the doorknob and gave it a push, glancing over his shoulder at Yuri.

"It's been a while, ok... "

"You might need to be a little more vigorous."

Robin smirked and drew a deep breath, inflating his chest before throwing his body against the door. He fell straight in to the room and flat on his backside as the door swung inwards and slammed abruptly against a nearby bookshelf. The sudden impact kicked up a thick cloud of dust which reached every corner of the room, it became incredibly difficult to see anything in the dust cloud as Robin jumped back to his feet, standing directly in the centre of sunlight that blazed through the window opposite him.

"*It's been a while?*" said Yuri as he quickly slipped the key in to Robin's satchel, then began to pat away the dust from his coat.

"I wouldn't worry about that."

Robin gave that reply as he walked on through the haze, towards a shape that resembled a bed, running along the wall under the beam of light that was reflecting through a pane of distorted glass in the window.

Slowly but surely, as Robin stood at ease, the dusty particles began to settle and the spirit of the room came to light after many years of being stored away. Yuri was silent, recollecting memories as they sprung from the woodwork.

Robin had noticed a dark wooden wardrobe beside the bed, then a small gas fireplace in the middle of the room with an extractor running high into the ceiling.

Where many other rooms had luxurious curtains draped in front of the windows, Robin's did not; however, it did have a means of keeping warm on those oh so cold winter nights.

Robin looked relieved to see it. He crouched in front of the grill and turned to Yuri, "Do you have a spell for this?" he asked, pulling his wand from his waistcoat pocket.

"Yeah, it's - *Pirontious*," he replied, smiling as he pressed his spectacles back to the bridge of his nose.

Robin looked down at the wand held firm in his hand. He took a sharp breath and pointed it between the metal slats, then screamed "*Pirontious*" in an overly dramatic tone as clearly as he could - just to be certain.

There was a rusty squeal as a small lever shot forward, releasing the gas in to the chamber. Then a short bolt of fire shot from the tip of Robin's wand, igniting the fireplace. There were already coal leftovers inside, so plenty of fuel to begin warming the stone cold room.

Robin looked satisfied, gleaming with the orangey glow from the fire, painted against his face.

"Well isn't that just marvellous!" he exclaimed as he removed his satchel and threw it on to the bed.

"I think we're going to get along, me and you," he added, regarding the wand between his fingers, "- I think I'll be ok now."

Yuri moved a little closer, "Well, if you need me, you'd best come find me, or failing that just wait till I return, because you'll only get lost. It's like your first day back to school, most exciting," he chirped, rubbing his hands together, "Everything there is to know lies within this very room. Best of luck."

He reached for the doorknob and slowly pulled it to; as he left the room Robin was still sat on his knees, enjoying the warmth and the low roar of the flames behind the grill of the fireplace.

There was finally a sense of homeliness as Robin observed the surroundings, studying the paintings and ornamental junk on the shelving. Everything could do with a good clean, now that dust had settled again. The brass telescope was dull, the globe of the world didn't spin anymore - it's pivot had seized up entirely. *If only there was a quick spell for effortless cleaning*; there had to be a simple solution, the rest of the institute was spotless, even the golden statues in the foyer were sparkling, and they were suspended twenty feet off the ground. He couldn't imagine anyone dusting those, but as his mind wandered, he found it quite amusing, the idea of a tiny man, running along the ceiling with a bright fluffy duster - it seemed the only other logical explanation, he chuckled, shifting his gaze from the brass ornaments to the heavily worn, yet beautifully decorated floorboards beneath him.

He hadn't even noticed the drawings - wonderfully detailed drawings, smeared into the wood grain - now far less evident as their inconsistent forms reflected the passing of seasons and the years of abuse, served by the rubber soles on Robin's boots.

"These are old - very old," he disclosed as he made his way back beside the bed where the artwork was far less faded. That side of the room was slowly warming, so he swiftly removed his mustard frock coat and laid it beside his satchel on top of the bed.

"I'm seeing a pattern with these!"

He got back down on his knees and began examining the drawings, running his hand along the grain to help identify the hidden segments.

"Whoever drew them had some form of fixation with freakish looking birds, assuming they *are* meant to be birds..."

As he inspected each drawing, one particular doodle caught his attention, half hidden by shadow, half caught in sunlight. The colours only confirmed his suspicions as he took a closer look and realised he'd seen it before, he'd seen *something*, anyway - the blue and turquoise feathers, he remembered it as clear as day...

"He was telling the truth. *You're* what everyone saw over Vinemoore on Christmas Eve!"

Robin stared intently at the drawing of the bird, he recalled the colours in the sky that night and Charlie Brown, insisting that a giant bird had just flown over the village.

The dots were beginning to join, but a question amongst many had arisen to the foreground of Robin's mind:

What does this have to do with me?

Given a moment to wander, as the sound of the wind whistled down the chimney, he inspected the floorboards closely. Then his eyes fell still, slowly widening as they became fixated on a gloomy wide crack under the bed. He hadn't noticed it up close, it must have blended in with the dark shadowy mass, but after taking a few steps back in surprise, they were there again, what he thought he had seen the first time, two electric-yellow irises staring back at him from beneath the floor. They seemed to be glowing, following Robin as he carefully negotiated his way around the fireplace, backing as far away as possible. He pulled his wand from his waistcoat pocket and pointed it in the direction of the looming, sinister eyes, hoping for no hostility.

"I - I can see you, under there," he called, "I don't mean you harm, however I'm not so sure that's a mutual intention."

The eyes suddenly snapped shut, the yellow glow vanished behind darkness, then the floorboards began to tremor as the unidentified being shot in Robins direction, knocking the woodwork from the ground in a recurring domino fashion as it rapidly approached.

Robin dived away from the wall then scrambled

to his hands and knees, while watching over his shoulder at the floorboards coming undone behind him. He had spotted his wand rolling in the corner of his eye, but as he went to reach for it, there was a scamper of footsteps that swiftly passed under him, then a fleshy mass exploded from under Robin's nose, up from beneath the flooring and into the lodge. Shards of wood clattered back to the floor, powdering the pinky figure with a light layer of sawdust.

Robin carefully looked up, not knowing what to expect as he felt the heavy presence standing over him, holding him in his vulnerable state, glaring down with its powerful sharp eyes. He could only make out the silhouetted shape of the being as the light from the skies flared through the window, capturing the last of the dusty particles, lingering in the air.

It had to be human, or something similar, Robin amended as he turned his sights to the dirty, smelly foot, placed firmly beside his head. It's yellow nails were *so* long, they had begun to curl in on themselves; and their edges were splintered, each as sharp as pins - they weren't very pretty.

"Y-you could do with a manicure, my friend," Robin muttered, as he began to find his footing. During his ascent, he noticed the dark figure beginning to shrink. It was eye level with his belt buckle, no taller than his daughter, Emily - which he found somewhat amusing. He'd even go as far to say it was cute, at least until it began to speak, stepping aside in to a softer light that complemented its piercing yellow eyes.

"I would never harm you, Professor!" it snarled, in a rough and viciously sore tone.

But Robin struggled to understand as his attention was somewhat lost, in deep analysis of the creatures long, pointed nose, and large swept back ears that were almost the size of its face.

He was completely mesmerised by the tiny creature that stood before him - so much so, he was still standing in silence, glaring at its body, awkwardly. Only then did he realise how inappropriate it must have looked when he arrived at the tight white underpants, clung around its groin.

"Oh!" he jolted forward in embarrassment, "Do forgive me, how awfully rude of me."

"No need to worry, I have that effect on people," said the small creature, to which Robin smiled, shuffled forward and began to pat the creature on its wrinkly head, ever so gently, like he would a cat or dog.

"No, please don't do that," ordered the creature, with a irritated look on its face. Robin stopped immediately, then took a step back.

"Sorry. I do have a question though, what exactly are you? I mean, where do you come from?"

The creature waddled beside the bed and reached for Robins wand that had rolled underneath it.

"Arlie is an imp," Arlie looked Robin in the eye as he held on to his wand, "Arlie has lived here for as long as he can remember. Robin doesn't recognise Arlie?" he asked with a frown, staring at Robin who looked uncomfortable as he tried to think up what to say next.

"I'm sorry, I'm afraid there's not much I remember at all."

Arlie looked down in disappointment, pressing

his tiny fingers in to the detailed crevasses of the wand. "They stole your memories," he began wiping his nose with the back of his arm, then jumped on to the bed, "- Arlie is Robin's friend," he began again, with his legs dangling and hand wandering towards Robins satchel, "- Robin let me share his room."

"Then was it you who did the drawings on the floor?" Robin asked, sitting down beside the fireplace, pointing down at the artwork.

"These are not Arlie's."

He jumped back down and pressed his body against Robins to inspect them.

"You drew these."

Robin frowned, and Arlie dropped the wand and began rummaging beyond the crack between the floorboards.

"I couldn't have done, I'm not at all artistic. A stick man is probably the best you'll ever get from me..."

"A stick man?" Arlie asked. "Yeah, a picture of a man, made up of lines. These birds were drawn by a professional artist."

Arlie drew out a black plastic headband from beneath the floor and placed it on his head. There were two yellow crumpled ping pong balls attached by springs that flopped and bounced as he moved his head. He smiled at Robin, who chose to remain silent, holding back laughter with great difficulty as he was reminded again of his daughter and the funny things she would come out with back home.

"You know what, I'm not surprised I let you share my room. You remind me of my daughter, Emily. Please don't take that the wrong way, it's just you hold similarities that... let's just say they brighten my day."

The springs on the headpiece squeaked and rattled as they rocked from side to side. Arlie's eyes were wide and fixed on Robin.

"Robin has child?" he asked, sounding surprised.

"Robin met a *lady?*"

"A beautiful lady, and her amazing daughter. I couldn't get enough of them. So yes, Robin has a wonderful child, now. Her real father never seemed to want anything to do with her," he frowned, glancing at the window.

"Arlie is happy for Robin."

"Thank you, Arlie." Robin looked back down at the drawings. "So, I have lots of questions and such little time. Are you up for the challenge?"

Arlie grinned, exposing his sharp jagged teeth. "Arlie loves challenge, Arlie will do his best to help."

"Perfect. Then let's start with this..." Robin pressed his finger in to the teal coloured bird.

"What *is* its significance? I feel like it means something, like it wasn't a coincidence that something similar flew right over my shop."

Arlie shuffled until he was comfortable, crossing his legs and peering down his long crooked nose at Robin.

"Long before Robin lived in the Human world, Professor Robin Occamy lived here, inside the Institute for Morient kind. He was both a lecturer and captain of the Morient defences within the grounds. Arlie knows of Leonard, but Arlie much prefers his predecessor." Arlie smiled. "Professor Occamy always had a fascination with rare mythological creatures and taught the young all there was to know of those that had been sighted throughout history. Arlie thinks it is for the best that you cannot recall these times, especially the day that Robin lost his sister to the dark forces."

Robin's Eyes widened as he leaned in towards the Imp.

"*I had a sister?*" he asked in surprise.

"Well, Arlie does not know what happened to her. Robin just told Arlie that she was gone and that he would do everything he could to save her. Robin left that day, it was still term time, the children were left confused and Grimtale hadn't the slightest clue what was happening; however he knew that his colleague, his friend would never desert him. But he did, and from then on, no one knows what happened, only that Robin found his sister and brought the Count and his evil followers to Vinemoore, to the Institute."

Robin could feel his face burning, his cheeks had turned a rosy red. He felt an unforgivable embarrassment for a memory he no longer retained access, along with a creeping sense of dread at the thought of the consequences that may have followed...

Arlie continued to explain, cautiously.

"Everyone thought that Robin had betrayed those who had accepted him like family. Nobody knew he had a well kept secret, even Arlie was not told till the day he returned, ordering us to unlock the dungeons. He hadn't only given a home to a formidable creature, he had bonded with it, under everyone's noses."

History was beginning to slowly fall into place as Robin's Eyes narrowed and his fist cradled his chin.

"And this Count, he wanted the Institute or the creature?"

"*The creature*, The Starlight Phoenix. For those who bond with the bird will forever retain heightened strengths until it moves on to another host. Arlie believes that the Count had been craving the phoenix's power for many years, years that took their toll on his appearance. Even today, no one knows what he looks like, only that the last time he was sighted, his face was described as a reflection of something unimaginable."

The hairs on both their backs were now standing on end as a supernatural chill filled the confines of the heated room.

"Do not underestimate his power, Robin. Nothing will stand in his way; those who did, we lost. Arlie is still grieving for the little ones who lost their lives that day. Arlie knew of the Counts murderous ways through stories, but when Robin released the Phoenix, when all hope was thought lost and his power cast away the dark forces, back in to the deep, bottomless holes that they had climbed from, nothing could prepare anyone for the sight that was waiting."

Arlie broke eye contact to wipe away the swelling from under his eyes. Robin was silenced, his face turned pale and was suddenly overwhelmed by guilt, embarrassment and anger. A raging ball of emotion curdling within his stomach.

"No one expected the Institute to reopen for teaching. But we were the last hope for Morient children in Vinemoore. So, the Defence enforcers allowed us to return to duties, on the condition that you were exiled to the human realm with no memory of your past, and that the Phoenix be caged and taken away for experimental purposes.

But you'd already been sentenced to a fate that must have felt like death, and with strong disapproval you gave the Phoenix a fighting chance, releasing it into the skies."

Robin took a deep breath.

"I was a monster," he claimed, failing to meet Arlie's gaze.

"Arlie knows that what happened was devastating for all, but no one blames you primarily for what happened. The Count was hurt and he never returned."

"Until now?" Robin interrupted.

"He still hasn't been sighted - only the Reapers. Which can only be a sign of what's to come, and we know why they're here. Arlie has heard of the Phoenix sighting in Shoulders Heath. Its people are panicked, and now the good and the bad are looking to engage, to keep its power out of the opposition's hands."

"But why can't she be free, why has this got to be settled over one man's greed for the unthinkable?" asked Robin, fiercely.

"Wouldn't we all love to be free? Only, we know that there are people from both worlds who may choose to harm, or use the Starlight Phoenix. Arlie is certain that Professor Grimtale will explain it better than me, but one thing is for sure, you'll need these..."

Arlie rose to his feet and waddled over to the shelf beside the door with Robins wand held between his fingers. He gave it a swish, and two dusty books pushed themselves from the shelf and fell in to Arlie's hand.

"One of these is a book of spells that you favoured. The other is a short journal that may help you recollect lost memories. Arlie knows that you won't remember, but it should help you rebuild the picture. A stepping stone for the new day."

Arlie handed the two books to Robin, who was still sat beside the warmth of the fire.

"Thank you, Arlie. I appreciate everything you've done for me."

Arlie smirked as he pulled a tatty gown from the crack in the floor and wrapped it around his body.

"Arlie must return to work now, Arlie has to clean the main foyer and the dining hall."

Robin sniggered.

"You mean all of those golden statues? Do you have a feather duster as well?"

"Robin would like that, wouldn't you..."

He said sarcastically as he made his way outside, dragging a wooden bucket behind him and closing the door quietly, leaving Robin sat in the centre of the room, with only himself for company and the sound of the roaring flames, keeping the chill from his bones as his long lost past caught ahold, tying his gaze to the Phoenix drawing on the floorboard. He could never look at it in the same way again, surely, as the sight of the artwork ignited an overwhelming sadness. There was no escaping the guilt, knowing he was living a life in the shell of nothing less than a murderer. But he had realised with his presence back at the Institute, he had a chance to redeem the title that many looked up to, even if it was considered another life back then, he knew the man he was today was someone that the Morient world deserved - even if he had no intentions of staying.

Then in that sudden moment, Robin rose from

the ground, breaking his mental ties and reaching for his satchel that was laid on the bed.

"Let's get this show on the road!" he said with a spark of enthusiasm as he pulled a pair of dark purple trousers from his bag and began changing in to them, replacing the dirt ridden pair that were still damp from the journey - even after being sat beside the heat that was bellowing from the fire, the trouser fabric was thick and would take a while to dry out completely, so Robin carefully laid them over the bed, right beside his coat, leaving just enough room to perch on the end of the bed and begin the insightful journey of witchcraft, alchemy, and this:

Common spells for beginners, written by Professor Robin Occamy.

CHAPTER 13
Lessons Learnt

An hour had passed since Arlie had left the lodge and the fire was now beginning to die down as Robin turned the final page of his ink blotted journal. It had been written in 1959, so it held a rather interesting and detailed account of the days he spent as professor. In fact they were so precise that he now knew exactly what he loved for breakfast on a gloomy Monday morning within the confines of the Institute, which was somewhat perfect timing as he began to hear the sound of footsteps, patting by his door.

Robin slapped the leather binding together, threw down the journal and leapt off the bed, reaching for the doorknob and yanking it wide open just in time to catch Grimtale as he slowly wandered by, acknowledging Robin with a delightful smile as he stood under the door frame of his lodge with curious eyes a blaze.

The curvy corridor was now lit by fiery torchlight that lined the walls illuminating the pathway, down towards the stairwell. Robin could just about make out the pink fluffy collar of Magenta's coat and Silverstein's silver shimmer before they disappeared from sight, down in to the stone tower.

"*Professor Grimtale! Hold up!*" Robin called as he ran back to the bed and began to scramble his books in to the satchel. He assumed it would be wise to tag along and not get lost trying to retrace his steps.

"*Just one moment!*" Robin's voice echoed from within the lodge as he threw his mustard coat about his shoulders and hung his satchel from his arm.

"I've been reading," he said as he reached the corridor, slightly out of breath.

"My journals - *everything*. Only before I didn't quite understand my importance - but now it's safe to say, I sure as hell do!"

He pulled the door to a close, leaving his damp brown trousers behind to dry. Then he turned to Grimtale with a look of relief - he was still standing ever so patiently, watching Robin's fluster as he made his way over.

"I'm set," said Robin, adjusting the strap on his satchel and patting his pockets to make sure they were still full.

"Then you'd best follow me," Grimtale replied as he turned and continued along the corridor towards the tower stairwell the other professors had taken.

"I assume you had the pleasure of meeting Arlie?"

Robin suddenly picked up his pace.

"The Imp! Yes, strange little fellow, doesn't hold anything back - information overload!"

"Precisely the reason that you were reacquainted, Professor."

Robin bit down hard on his tongue.

"No, no. Don't call me that, just call me Robin. I'm not ready for anything like that."

Grimtale paused for a moment, placing himself in another's shoes to understand why Robin was reluctant to take up the title that consumed his younger self, as he needed reminding of the reasons - the things believed to be best left behind, he thought, glancing across at Robin. It was then he realised he no longer saw the man he used to know, the man who was caught by temptation. He felt a dangerous overwhelming trust like a time long forgotten had been recalled, only now he knew it would be different, this time Robin belonged elsewhere and Grimtale knew for certain he would stand by his word, if it meant returning to the ones he loved. He wisely made sure that in his silence he understood what Robin had requested, casting him a subtle nod of the head.

"Come, a spot of breakfast is in order."

Robin smiled and gave his headmaster a pat on the back as the enticing smell of hot porridge oats wafted towards their nostrils, luring them down to the warmth of the dining hall, situated at the foot of the tower.

As Robin neared the bottom of the stairwell, he began to hear the sound of chatter and cutlery clattering from the hall. It was quite busy from what he could gather, which came as a surprise, having only expected half a dozen professors, but as he reached the bottom and turned the corner, his sights fell upon a whole host of characters lining the oval tables.

Sat at the far end of the hall were a bunch of rather peculiar looking folk dressed in dark grey trench coats, huddled together and minding their own business. Most of them were munching down on buttered toast and warm croissants as they nattered across the table to one another. Then closer to Robin were the familiar faces of Professor Yuri, Lint and Vargov, they were also sat tucking in to their breakfast, keeping the conversation strictly within the confines of the table space. Robin had already spotted Magenta and Silverstein across the hall, they weren't hard to miss as they stood chatting to strangers - or so they seemed to Robin, who was still rather surprised by the turn out as he slowly wandered towards the nearest unoccupied seat.

"Is this one taken?" he asked politely, looking across at Professor Yuri who was the most familiar of the group. Remembering the great lengths of conversation they'd already had. Yuri looked up and met Robins gaze with a smile and waved his hand towards the seat as he munched down on a mouthful of toast.

"It's yours, my friend. You've not met properly..." he looked over to the other professors sat across from him, then back to Robin as he began to pull away the wooden stool from under the table.

"Oh, it was awfully brief. Professor Lint and Professor Vargov, wasn't it?" he asked as he lumbered down on to the stool and pulled his satchel on to his lap.

"Yes, and what would you like us to call you?" Said Teppi, who was sat directly beside him.

"Robin is just fine, however I'm not opposed to Mr Occamy. What I am reluctant to hear is the title *Professor*," he explained, keeping a watchful eye over Teppi's shoulder where at a distance, Silverstein and Magenta looked to be wrapping up their conversation, "- that may have been a thing some time ago, but as of now, I am no longer security and I am most certainly no *Professor!*" he added, reverting back to the table where an understanding was waiting from all three professors.

"By the sound of things, you're well caught up," said Yuri, sat opposite Robin, with a plate of toast held in his hand.

"Well, thankfully I found a few diaries and a rather terrifying yet knowledgeable Imp lurking under my floorboards. So I'd say I'm off to a good start, but it's still a lot to process. In fact, I've brought a few books with me that I'd like to get through, is it okay to be a little unsociable?"

"Knock yourself out, my friend. Fancy any breakfast while you're at it?" asked Teppi as he scooped up a large spoon of porridge oats.

"I think I'll go for pancakes and maple syrup," he declared as he clicked his fingers.

To the tables sudden surprise, there appeared a stack of pancakes sat upon a white china plate, with a side of syrup and a knife and fork to go with.

"Now that's what I call service!" Robin remarked excitedly, glaring at the hot plate of food steaming under his nose.

Teppi's eyes were wide in shock, but a grin stretched along his face wide and tall as he stared back and forth to his fellow professors who were also beaming with delight.

"That was always your favourite dish," Lillian said warmly.

"We'd best keep an eye on this guy, next he'll be hustling for our jobs," joked Teppi. There was a roar of laughter around the table, even Robin gave a chuckle as he rolled a slice of pancake around his fork and crammed it in his mouth.

"We all know that will never happen, I'm not that kinda guy, Teppi."

"Funny, that's what you said before..." Teppi looked away and the table fell to a awkward silence. Robin didn't seem phased at first, he was too busy enjoying his delicious breakfast to argue.

"I'm sorry, forget I said anything. This is a time for positive attitudes, the past is no longer relevant…"

"No, Professor. The past is very relevant. Excuse me..." Robin dropped his fork abruptly against the plate and sprung off his stool, directly into the path of Silverstein and Magenta who were on their way past.

"Good morning, Leonard - Aline," said Robin as he leaned in to greet them both, quickly pecking at Magenta's cheek then reaching towards Silverstein whose hands were already occupied with plates of food.

"Oh, are you taking those back to your room? It's just I was going to ask if you fancied joining us?" he added, glancing over to the other professors sat around the table.

"We have some last minute arrangements to make before the briefing, but thank you, Robin. I'm certain if there was one table to be at, it would be *this* one."

"Is that a compliment?" Robin asked, realising he'd probably never get to know, as he watched Silverstein press his way past with his sights set firmly on the stairwell in the corner of the hall, his shoes clapping like thunder against the stone floor as he disappeared in to the distance.

"Smarmy git..." Teppi muttered, glaring across at Silverstein with his spoon held tightly and eyebrows raging.

"What's gotten in to him? I get that he thinks a lot of himself but that was just bloody rude," said Robin, looking to Magenta in confusion.

"He's - just - stressed. This is a big deal. Today is going to be a monumental task, something that's been in the making for literally years," she explained, whilst keeping eye contact with Robin to avoid the glare coming from Teppi's eagle eyes. She could sense it, silently scolding against her flesh.

"I'd best be getting back…"

Magenta was about to hurry away but then she realised she still had an unanswered question that was burning at the back of her mind as she came to a sudden halt, stood beside Robin.

"How exactly did you find out my name? Aline..."

Robin smirked, pausing to relish the moment of mystery before pulling a crumpled diary from his satchel that was still hung over his coat.

"I guess I've always been the inquisitive kind."

Magenta shot a look at the tatty cover. There was no doubt in Robin's mind that she had recognised it instantly. She fell silent and her left eye had began to glaze over, almost as if she was about to burst into tears.

"Are you okay, Magenta?" Robin asked, reaching for her arm.

"Yeah... of course," she drew a deep breath and wiped her eye with the back of her hand.

"Just carry on reading, we're going to need you today. Those books and diaries are essential, don't misplace them!" she ordered, before following the path that Silverstein had taken, hurrying up the stairwell towards her room.

Robin looked about the hall then returned to his stool where his open book rested.

"Did you see that?" he asked, hoping the others were paying attention to Magenta.

"They're an odd pair, what else can I say, there's a reason we don't mix anymore. They never have time for anyone else but each other," explained Lillian, struggling to suppress the sadness in her tone.

"Let them be. They're hardly gonna change now, we don't even need them! We work together, but we - us three - we live together, we're like family."

Teppi tapped the back of Lillian's hand and smiled, luring Yuri and Lillian's attention with his warming, comforting aura which always existed in times of need.

Robin had felt a bond very similar, it was the very same one he had back home, with his family. It helped him settle as he began to turn the pages of his book, but he couldn't help but think about the divide, it wasn't so apparent till now, everyone was segregated. There were at least four different groups already from what he could gather just glancing about the hall, and this was a place of peace, a home to most who worked there.

"Urgh," Robin grumbled, "I'm not even going to be here long enough to worry about a dysfunctional community!"

We had enough of that trouble back home in Vinemoore, he thought to himself, trying to focus on the written text in front of him.

The book was hand written and seemed to house a vast list of spells and enchantments, ranging from the simplest gimmick to the safety precautions necessary - it was perfect for the budding alchemist. This all seemed well and good to Robin, who was taking a careful note of each and every spell he felt he may require, but there was something curious slotted amongst the back pages that suddenly caught his attention - it looked confidential. Robin's heart began to race as he carefully pulled the parchment away, taking a glance as he held it beneath the table, making sure that nobody else could see. There were two words pressed against the parchment in a waxy-red medium:

Brexio and Vanphineer, Robin whispered as he ran his fingertip over the type.

"What's funny is, it seems like the past knew the future would find its way back," said Robin, projecting his voice across the table space, "All these diaries and handwritten text books. Don't you think that's odd?"

Now he could see it in their eyes as they strayed away towards the table surface - the others had drawn a blank.

"The only person you can truly ask that question, is yourself. It's the same mind beneath that skull, same habits, same dress sense. You're just better, and so is your understanding of right from wrong," Yuri explained, not knowing what else to say but speak his mind plainly. But it seemed to have enlightened Robin, who suddenly slammed shut all of the books on the table and began cramming them back inside his satchel.

"It just so happens I did ask myself, and I would have done the bloody same thing!" he cursed with joy, determined to discover more as he leapt off his stool and threw his bag over his head.

"Spot of training?" he asked as he turned back to the table, waiting in anticipation for an answer.

* * *

Silverstein reached for a second pairing of curtains and pulled them apart, revealing the curvature of a stone door frame, bridging the bedroom to an elaborate balcony that overlooked the vast Morient landscape and a long winding canyon where heavy clouds were drawing in - an endless storm of white, falling across the two realms.

The man of silver stepped out in to the brisk air with a steaming cup of tea held in one hand and a saucer in the other. His metallic hair waved in the breeze, his shimmering tailcoat flapped and rippled around his neck, exposing his bare chest as he raised the China cup to his soft warm lips. His gaze set with intent towards the grounds below as the warmth of the tea took away the chill against his flesh. He felt untouchable up there, watching beyond the haze of snowfall where the ruins of the old abandoned Institute had laid to waste.

Magenta knew that something was wrong but the worry had to go unspoken, out of fear of losing him - *because no one likes a worrier*, she reminded herself as she arrived back inside the bedroom, noticing the chilly draft as she turned to where Silverstein was stood, beyond the flailing curtains. She quickly folded back the bed sheets then made her way out on to the freezing cold balcony, glad to be wearing her thick pink coat as the icy breeze lashed against her face, before she wrapped her arms comfortably around Silverstein's waist and rested her head upon his back.

He seemed to be in awe of the beautiful landscape, looking towards the grounds with an eye of intrigue as he noticed a band of blurry characters wandering out into the open landscape.

"He knows everything, he's been reading the diaries," said Magenta, hiding her face against the metallic fleck of Silverstein's coat.

"Well that's what we want, isn't it? The man is expected to perform, is he not?" asked Silverstein, still fixated on the people down below.

"I guess so. I just didn't want him getting involved with that lot. I thought we might be able to help him, guide him a little better."

"You mean, *manipulate* him."

"No - well - yes, I just don't want to lose him again to the same urges he had before."

Silverstein slowly turned to Magenta, taking one final sip of tea before leaning in to meet her gaze.

"You mean, trying to save his sister..."

Her face fell heavy, her eyes slightly bloodshot from the lack of sleep.

"I do," she replied, then her body shook, already exhausted by the cold and the stomach-churning worry that lingered deep in her gut.

"He was so foolish before. But he doesn't strike me as a fool anymore."

Silverstein reverted his gaze back to the ruins with intrigue, glare down at the mysterious goings on.

* * *

The snow showed no sign of stopping as it battered between the ruins, pillowing on to the rubble that laid scattered across the grounds; however, the unfriendly conditions had not discouraged the four dark figures that had traipsed through the midst of the storm before emerging from beyond the haze with their wands in hand and their eye on the game.

A sudden bolt of colourful energy erupted from the end of each wand then hurled against a tall dismantled tower, blasting away the loose rubble from its exposed innards and launching the rocks across the snowy circular platform that laid ahead.

"Let's move in!" ordered Teppi, calling forward Robin, Lillian and Yuri who were stood at his side, peering on towards the unclear shapes that were darting in and out of the obstructed shadows.

Robin quickly wiped the ice from his face and begun to carefully advance towards the ruins, keeping a watch on Teppi's footing and the others around him, not wanting to mistake them for something else.

"Keep alert!" Teppi reminded them, nearing the debris at the foot of the tower, back to back and vigilant. It felt as is they were trapped at the centre of a tornado as their snow blown white surroundings hurtled around them. It didn't help that Robin hadn't a clue what they were hunting, his mind had already begun to draw demonic silhouettes and crystal avatars, pouncing from boulder to boulder, back and forth, using the snow as a means of camouflage. But most disturbing of it all, he wasn't an awful distance from the truth, he soon realised as a giant humanoid figure rose from beneath the ground and launched itself high overhead, on to the tallest plinth overlooking the mere mortals as they tracked its movement and unloaded a flurry of powerful spells that blew the top of the structure into shards of dust.

"It's circling us, Robin. Any ideas?" asked Yuri with his fogged up glasses hampering his vision.

The four of them had bunched together keeping a tight grasp of their wands as they waited, sizing up the opposition that was lurking closely, using the environment as an advantage.

"Its body looked to be made up of crystal fragments - like ice," explained Robin as he slowly became more and more paranoid of the shifting snow beneath him.

"Typical of a Celestial. Powerful and intelligent - but not unbeatable," said Lillian as a pair of large footprints suddenly began to appear, charging towards her.

Yuri dived across in to Lillian, pushing her away from danger as the celestial creature scrambled past, narrowly avoiding Robin who had leapt aside and met the creature with a rather timid glare opposed to the terrifying form as it turned back around with its eyes burning orange like a ball of fiery rage.

Robin suddenly froze, his entire body was stiff to the bone.

"*Somebody!*" he yelled, unable to raise his wand as the Celestial advanced, preparing to charge, its face growing larger and its eyes lighting a path through the storm as cumbersome feet pounded against the ground. Robin could feel the earth beneath his shoes moving with every lunge, he could feel the fury scolding his face like dragons breath. Then as the creature emerged from the haze, a flurry of energy struck violently against its face, knocking it awkwardly off balance and into the nearby ruins. There was a heavy thud, then Lillian and Yuri stepped forward and pulled Robin back with haste.

"Are you alright?" asked Lillian.

"I just froze up, it won't happen again," he said, nervously glaring at the mound of body and rubble.

Teppi made his way over, carefully avoiding the assumed deceased as he passed the tower ruins.

"Nice work. That was really brave of you, Robin," said Teppi.

Robin looked to the others awkwardly, "Just doing what anyone else would, but in all honestly I think it's these two who deserve the praise," he said as he turned back to Lillian and Yuri whose eyes were suddenly wide with fear.

"*Teppi!*" yelled Lillian, pointing down at the ground, too late to warn off the oblivious professor as he felt a hand clamp tight around his ankle and pull him off his feet. Robin swung around just in time to catch a glimpse of Teppi being dragged away with his long silky robes fluttering under his chin.

"I've got this," said Robin, holding out his arm to disengage the others.

He watched as the creature slowly vanished behind the raging blizzard, then a new found source of courage ignited within Robins heart, shattering the fears that had leached his body and held him still and cold. He quickly raised his wand and aimed for the creature's enormous crystal head as it bobbed - now barely visible. Then Robin remembered the hidden text and howled the first word that came to mind:

"Brexio!"

An electrical rocket of energy shot from Robin's wand and soared through the powerful winds and ice before impaling the Celestial creature between the eyes. The ball of energy pulsated and sparked for a moment, then blew the head clean away from its shiny body, eliminating all odds of survival.

The creatures headless body fell backwards in the snow, where it remained as Teppi was pulled to his feet by the others.

"For a moment there, I thought it was gonna kill you," said Robin.

"For a moment there, so did I!" replied Teppi, "- only that would be mad, considering it wasn't real. Perfect for those who require a little seasoning!"

"You mean that thing - the Celestial or whatever it's called, it was a imitation?" asked Robin.

"An elaborate manifestation with a taste for blood. Just a charm, but don't go getting any ideas, I'll have you know the definitive article is far more ruthless. They are not so easy to take down in person," explained Teppi, casting away the Celestial remains.

"But this Count guy. On a scale of one to ten, the Celestial being a nine point five, just how scary is he? A five or six?"

"If only that were true," said Lillian, leading the way back towards the Institute walls with a worried looking Robin now in tow.

"That spell you used, it takes quite a powerful wizard to conjure it to that strength," remarked Yuri, trailing behind.

"I saw it in the back of a book. But the way it was written, it was as if I had to keep it to myself. Like it was speaking to me personally."

"Because these are most likely spells used in battle. We don't teach them, never had a need to. Whatever was on the parchment, they are your tools for defeating what evil lies ahead, I'm sure. No one knows Robin Occamy better than yourself," Said Lillian.

"But I don't think I wrote it, the list on the parchment - I think someone else put it there. I was gone before I had a chance to think of the consequences, all of these diaries and books, they weren't for my benefit, they're just who I am. I'm a family man, I like to write, I like to help. This time someone is trying to help *me*, but I don't know who."

Lillian and Yuri came to a stand still, Teppi had now caught up and was already scratching at his scalp.

"I think I have an idea as to who it could be..." Lillian began, glaring up at the Institute tower where Silverstein and Magenta were stood, barely visible behind the veil of snow.

* * *

His eyes were sore from the cold, but they had

not deceived him, he couldn't believe what he had witnessed.

"Robin destroyed a Celestial with a Hybrexio assault charm. This amateur Morient decapitated a *Celestial!*"

Magenta looked down towards the training grounds where the three professors and Robin were standing.

"How do you know that's Robin, it could be anyone? And I'm sure it's only part of the training."

"*He's wearing a vomit coloured coat!*" yelled Silverstein, with his fists clenched firm against the balcony ledge.

"We - wanted - a weapon."

"We need Robin, we don't need him getting ahead of himself. Now, come on. We're expected at the briefing!"

Silverstein stormed inside the bedroom, brushing off Magenta as he passed, leaving her in the chilly midst of the storm outside where she stood alone and confused, yet still completely besotted by her sleek, silver man. She gave a heavy sigh, looked over the edge then decided to follow Silverstein inside, seemingly in no such hurry.

CHAPTER 14
To Shoulders Heath

The heavy side door slammed behind them, shutting out the cold and the stark white glare of the outdoor land. They were covered from head to toe in ice as they came to a halt, patting and stomping away what they could from their coats and boots. *It was nothing a vigorous shake and a little warmth couldn't handle, it would soon dry off once inside the chamber, once under those scorching torches*, Robin thought as he ran his hand through his hair and waited for the others to lead the way out of the dim lit corridor.

"So it all boils down to this. It's really happening, isn't it," said Robin, rhetorically.

"It's problematic. I just hope everyone is willing to listen and drop the fascination with this bloody Phoenix!" replied Lillian, urging them forward, leading the way towards the light that sat at the end of the narrow corridor.

"I may still be a little rusty and misplaced, but I suspect I have similar questions to those that are burning away at each of you," Robin added.

"Like what kind of future lies ahead for the

Institute? We bring the Phoenix back and the school becomes unsafe for the children. We kill the damn thing and we're murderers, no better than the people who left us in this situation!" Said Teppi with an obvious tone of frustration.

"And leaving the Phoenix, or vacating it to the skies would only delay its capture. The Count is desperate, he has to be. He's been separated for far too long, I dread to think what he looks like now..." The echoes of Yuri's voice travelled around the entirety of the hall as they emerged from a secret passage, located behind the Vinemoore tapestry that hung from the foyer walls.

"But the Phoenix was kept here originally, was it not?" asked Robin as he pushed aside the heavy fabric and suddenly realised where they were.

"Oh, we're here! Outstanding," he added, casting an admiring glance about the vastness of the hall.

"The Phoenix was housed in the Institute dungeon, to yours and *only* your knowledge. No other professor knew, I don't think anyone even believed in the myth of a starlight Phoenix, only the Count and even he had no clue of its whereabouts. So since then I drew the conclusion that you seem to have a knack for hiding mythological treasures, don't you!" chuckled Yuri, wiping away the condensation from his spectacles.

"Hey, It was on your doorstep. I would hardly call that hidden; but then again, so was I and it took you this long to find me?"

"Sometimes one forgets to check the doorstep." Yuri smiled and then joined the crowd that had formed outside the chamber doors waiting impatiently for the head masters arrival.

Robin chose to hold back and told the others to go on as he noticed at the corner of his eye, the small silhouette of an Imp, polishing the head of a golden Ferret high amongst the many animal statues that lined the ceiling.

"Arlie!" called Robin, trying to grasp his attention.

"Arlie, it's Robin. Robin Occamy!"

The Imp paused and gave the dirty rag a whack against the Ferret, knocking away the last of the dust.

"Sir, how may Arlie be of help this time?" he grumbled.

"Well I wasn't really after anything in particular. I just wondered if I could speak to you for a moment, in private?"

He looked across to the crowd outside the chamber doors - none were paying attention to him, they were too busy with their own conversations to notice the Morient speaking to an Imp. It was a good job really as it was never seen to be acceptable in the eyes of some governing Enforces, who were present at the chamber, representing the Minister of Morient defence.

"It'll be quick, I promise."

"Arlie does not care for being seen, Arlie is not afraid of grey coats."

An extremely long ladder suddenly materialised down from the ceiling and Arlie slowly began to make his way down, one step at a time.

"Why do you work here? I mean around people like that..."

"Does Arlie not have a right? The Institute is

warm, outside is cold, Arlie chooses to stay," he explained as he reached the bottom and retracted the ladder away, "What is it you wish to speak to me about?"

Robin looked back, then shuffled Arlie to one side, a little further down the foyer.

"I found something inside an old spell book. Something only you were capable of putting there, but I know it wasn't you who wrote it," whispered Robin, removing the screwed up parchment from his trouser pocket, "Someone must have requested that you put this inside the book. It was slotted in at the back and no one else had access to my room in my absence."

Arlie sighed and looked down at his toes.

"Please, Arlie!" begged Robin.

"Someone *did* ask Arlie. They were trying to be helpful. Others disagreed but Arlie felt it was the right thing to do, so you can protect us."

"Who asked you to put it there, Arlie?" Robin lifted the little Imps chin to meet his gaze, "you can tell me, I'm only curious."

Suddenly the chamber doors clonked as they pivoted open and the crowd began to flow inside, but as the last grey coat entered, Arlie caught a glimpse of Magenta who was under the arm of Silverstein as they strutted their way around to the chamber entrance. Robin couldn't help but notice her eyes bearing a look like daggers, before turning to Arlie who seemed to be frozen with a look of fright plastered on his face.

"Magenta? Professor Aline Magenta gave you the parchment?" questioned Robin in confusion.

"You mustn't speak of it!"

"Is she this unspoken sister or something? Why would she want me to learn this kind of power?

Isn't that what Silverstein is for? I'm only here to help with tracking the Phoenix."

Arlie's eyes had widened as he pulled on Robins coat.

"He didn't want this, she felt it was right. You must not speak of it, Arlie will be in fear of his life. Arlie likes his quiet life."

"So you don't think I should take it up with her, in private?" asked Robin.

"Perhaps, when the dust has settled. Just get back here alive, don't underestimate the task at hand, Arlie knows what can be expected of the enemy!"

Moments he had shared with the terrifying Reapers began to flash before him as he blinked away the dryness of his eyelids.

"You've just reminded me why I'm dreading this - and I've only had a taster of what's to come. *Brilliant!*"

Robin took a gentle step towards the busy chamber, trying to spot someone he knew.

"I'd best be getting inside and on with this briefing. Thank you, Arlie. Once again you never fail to enlighten me and I appreciate it!"

Arlie smiled and reached for Robin with his extremely long spindly arm. He gave him a pat on the lower back for all that it was worth, then he departed across the foyer and went back to his duties, leaving Robin to the mercy of Professor Grimtale, who was already in position and waiting to start the briefing ceremony.

Grimtale was stood upon a raised platform, overlooking the crowds that were standing amongst the chamber. The thrones were left empty out of respect, stood as equals, a sea of grey and sparkle swamped around the ruby Phoenix statue, waiting, glaring up at Grimtale who watched carefully on as Robin strolled in, slotting himself amongst the closest group he recognised, which consisted of Yuri and Vargov, surrounded by the many grey coats, looking grim and disillusioned.

"Not very friendly are they?" said Robin, gently rubbing against Yuri's shoulder.

"They're not here to be friendly. It's not in the job description. I doubt many of them take much pleasure from their jobs though, can't be much fun being used as pawns," he replied, whispering in to Robin's ear.

"I guess it's easy to forget that such miserable beings have families to go home to."

One of the nearby grey coats suddenly turned and scowled at Robin.

"What? It's true!" Robin chirped, shrugging his shoulders, "What are they gonna do, anyway?"

Yuri leaned in, and spoke in a low voice.

"Protect your ass, then make sure we get the Phoenix back here safely!"

"And what happens then..."

"Your guess is as good as mine, but I suspect it won't be without it's drama. There's now rumours of further corruption within the Morient defence..." Yuri glanced to one side then back to Robin, "something or someone are infiltrating their way towards the heart of the Institute, the centre of what we stand for. Grimtale is overly suspicious, *especially* today."

Robin looked up at Grimtale who had now raised his hands, silencing the crowds and drawing their attention.

"Could I please have each of your undivided

attention. This ceremonial briefing is now in session so I would like you all to listen carefully, then raise an arm to address me with a question if you so desire," said Grimtale, bound by his heavy brown coat with two hands set firmly upon the bulbous handle of his walking cane, "Today we head to Shoulders Heath, and for those we have here present who do not know of the land beyond the black mountain, it's only faithful comparison would be Hell - until we pass the crossing, where Miss Bilshore will meet us." Grimtale paused, making the speech as carefully as possible for the vast audience stood below him, then continued...

"We owe a great gratitude to Miss Bilshore as not only has she secured the crossing, she has supplied us with a team of Slitherback, which will be ridden by the advance guard to take care of what we know already lurks within the caves and forests surrounding our route."

"Who will be part of the advance party?" asked a grey coat, stood in the foreground of the crowd.

"Myself for one. Our asset, Mr Robin Occamy. Professor Vargov, Leonard Silverstein and Professor Magenta. Then once clear, the ground parties will be able to press forward and accompany us. However, I've called you here today to highlight the dangers that may or most certainly *will* lie ahead." Grimtale looked down at Robin to make sure he was listening - it was incredibly important after all.

"There *will* be opposition. We don't know when or how they will strike but they are in motion and have eyes on our every move. The Count is believed to be amongst them, whether truth lies in that statement we do not know, but we must be prepared!"

Robin suddenly raised a nervous hand as he stood in the crowd and was immediately recognised by Grimtale, who called out his name.

"Robin."

"This Count, could you elaborate? Tell us a little more about him. I for one like to know exactly what I'm squaring up to."

His voice echoed about the chamber, bringing it to a deathly silence as the people around Robin turned to one another with an uncomfortable look upon their faces, for most already knew the significance of the infamous title.

"For any rookies we have with us today: The starlight Phoenix is known to possess a number of eyes, it's said to be the final thing you notice before being mutilated by its viciously sharp beak. Munder Mortal was a unfortunate pairing. The man that became a monster. Instead of being killed, he was bitten, but he bit back, being the brute that he is, forcing a bond with the creature. Many years later, you know the story. Mr Occamy obtained the trust of the Phoenix and used it against the pillaging hoards of darkness, vanquishing the Count, or so we believed. The point of the story is that with each Morient or human who pair themselves with the Phoenix, it seems to grow an eye. Our researchers say that there is a far deeper meaning to it, but based on assumption and a little common sense, we've been able to come up with this pattern."

Grimtale took a breath and drew his wand, pointing it towards the Phoenix statue that stood in the centre of the chamber. He muttered a command under his breath and a spark of light erupted from the end of his wand and illuminated the solid Ruby, casting a diagram that looked somewhat similar to a map on the wall.

"We have managed to track the flight path and account for every enemy movement since its disappearance. It always knows when danger is near and it has always known that Robin Occamy is in the vicinity of Vinemoore - yet it returned. We believe with what minuscule information we have, its eyes are a form of infinite vision, a connection that allows it to see through the eyes of each who have bonded to it. The perfect defence to those who seek its power to cause chaos. The Phoenix will know we are coming if this theory is correct. We will have to act fast, then hope it recognises Robin as a friend and not a foe."

Grimtale paused and glanced around the chamber, "I understand it's a lot to process. We capture, we return, then we assess what happens next."

"You can't possibly bring a war back to the Institute. It won't be safe for the children. The attacks will multiply and Vinemoore, both sides of the town will be left in tatters when the day is over!" said Teppi, unleashing his frustration.

"The Phoenix needs to be secure and we are the only ones with sufficient knowledge to ensure its well being," explained Grimtale, remaining calm as foreign and friendly eyes lingered in his direction.

"And you expect the children to feel safe? What will you do? Increase the security? Expect a child to come to school knowing they might not make it home that night, knowing that the Count might pay them a visit? This is out of hand, this creature needs to be taken away and cared for by your experts!" said Robin, finally making sense of the situation and speaking his mind, to much of a surprise to those stood around him.

"I have done all I can with what authority I have but as you can see by looking over your shoulders, we as a school are now under the strict control of the defence Minister. The sea of grey is not only here for our people's protection, but to ensure the creature remains."

Professor Yuri emerged from behind the sea of grey, progressively becoming more and more impatient as he nodded in agreement.

"All five Slitherback are waiting in the pit," Yuri informed Grimtale, raising his voice to fill the room.

"Fantastic. Please see to Robin, Professor Yuri. Everyone else, those who are positioned here and those in the field with me, keep safe, stay alert and let's make history!"

The crowd had erupted into applause and then started to leave the chamber with haste, flooding out in to the empty main foyer with nothing but determination and a wand strapped to their inner pockets. It was then Robin felt a hand grasp his shoulder as he slowly made his way forward, following the wall of grey.

"The Slitherback have a genetic deterrent that seems to cause the Count's disciples an excessive amount of discomfort. You'll be ok though, just hold on tight, it's like riding a horse - a horse with a snakes head!" said Yuri, nudging against him.

"But, I've never ridden a horse." replied Robin, aware of Yuri's presence by his side as he casually peered over the heads in front of him.

"Never mind, it'll be ok! Professor Grimtale

asked me to take a look at your wand, he's given the go ahead on my latest charm. Would that be ok?" asked Yuri, seemingly eager to give it a shot.

"Sure, here - but what is it?"

Robin handed over his wand to Yuri, who snatched it up and began running his fingers along the spindly roots that ran the length of the shaft.

"I like this one. The subtle green glow deep within the core, that's a sign of unfaltering allegiance. See here..."

Yuri pulled out his own wand from inside his waistcoat - it was a little shorter than Robin's with a speckled texture on the handle.

"You see that orange glow within the cracks? It's bright and full of life, but that's because I'm not one for combat. I just invent things and my wand agrees it's what I'm best at."

Robin looked confused again, frowning down at the dim green light pulsating within his wand.

"Then what must I do to keep the spark alive in mine?" he asked.

"Protect. Stay true to who you are and never give up on those who matter the most. We are your old life, your family now need you more. Just remember this... to rise above monsters, you abandon your humanity. We don't need heroes today, Robin. Just people we can trust."

Robin bit down on his lip and nodded.

"I'll do my best," he replied, in awe of Yuri's calming nature as he transferred the energy from his wand. The orange trail of lava-like residue seeped inside the core of Robins wand like a virus, the orange and green energy were like oil on water, pressing apart but swirling as one.

"What you're seeing are the cores of the wands communicating. Yours is receiving the brand new mapping for a charm. It's a rather special one, which Grimtale will explain a little more about when you arrive at Shoulders Heath. He asked that this remained strictly between us, because the enforcers and Silverstein would soon create a scene if they knew they were going in to battle without it."

"Why can't they have it as well?" asked Robin.

"*Diplomacy*," he whispered, anticipating the presence of a sleek silver figure passing beside him, "he trusts you. He never stopped trusting you," he added, watching as Silverstein and Magenta pressed their way past the chamber doors and into the crowded foyer.

"He's right to trust me, but even I wouldn't trust the man I used to be! He was a grade A, bastard," stated Robin, collecting his wand from Yuri before passing under the chamber arch.

Lillian was already making her way towards the main entrance with Silverstein and Magenta now in tow, working their way around the huddled enforcer groups.

As he passed, Robin glanced up at Arlie who was still sat high on a ledge, watching below, the swarms of strangers preparing to protect his home.

It was then Robin suddenly realised, he wouldn't see Yuri again for quite some time - a few hours to be precise. He stopped in his tracks, turned and pulled him to a tight embrace, thankful he was still following closely behind.

"My things are still in my room, I'll be coming back for those," Robin ensured Yuri as he took a step back and shook his hand.

"You'd better, because this ain't no hotel, that's a perk of being a Professor!" He grinned, with an unfaltering trust in Robin to assume he was simply pulling his leg.

The two men then went their separate ways - one to accompany the grey coated enforcer captain, and the other towards the grand doors that were left ajar.

Now the sound of the chilling breeze whistled, whipping back and forth through the tall railings of the pit. Robin glanced back over his shoulder, already impatient to return. He took a deep breath and pulled his mustard collar high around his face, proceeding to step outside the Institute, out in to the storm that had now begun to settle. But the pit was still covered by a thick blanket of white and stood in the centre of the grounds were the five astonishingly large Slitherback. They waited patiently with their cumbersome gorilla-like fists planted firmly in the snow.

There was a sudden pressure of anxiety that Robin felt tightening around his chest as he approached the creatures, while keeping a keen eye out for Grimtale as he passed the tall metal gates. He intently watched the Slitherback, taking in the sight of their long snake-like necks that rose high above the height of an average man. They had a piercing *hiss*, similar to that of a rather unhappy Cat. The Slitherback was unique and the closest representation of a Horse-snake, Robin thought as he watched their tongues slithering from their mouths.

"Marvellous creatures!" he called out, hoping someone would come forward to meet him as he wiped the snow flakes from his brow.

"Invaluable!" came a familiar deepened voice. Grimtale moved in to view from behind the front Slitherback, patting it gently as he moved away and approached Robin.

"They're harmless, for as long as you pose no threat to them. They shall keep us safe." Robin couldn't help but notice uncertainty in his voice, entirely warranted of course – he knew anyone would have to be off their head not to be somewhat afraid - unless you're Leonard Silverstein, who made a great job of seeming fearless as he stood at a distance, watching Magenta attend to the final Slitherback, impatiently flapping its wings.

"I think we're set. They're all harnessed up," said Magenta, fastening the last strap.

"Professor, I understand this is a specialist field and that it suits Magenta and Vargov, but I'm worried for their safety."

Grimtale sighed and frowned at Robin.

"Because they're women, Mr Occamy?"

"No! Not at all, not in a million years would I suggest them being inadequate. Just as a man, I'm concerned, if anything were to happen to them..."

"Mr Occamy, as grim as it sounds, there's a much higher chance of something happening to *you*..."

Robin trembled at the thought, but knew he was right.

"You're quite scary, you know that? But yeah, I'm the rookie, now."

He paused for thought then followed Grimtale's lead as they stepped up to the five Slitherback.

"Ground units can now disembark!" Grimtale called out back towards the foyer where the grey coat squads were waiting for the command,

"Mount your steed, Mr Occamy!" he added as he pulled himself up and on to the back of his ride.

"*I wish I knew how...*" muttered Robin, staring up at the creatures tiny beady eyes.

"There's a foot brace right there, and a reign right here," said Silverstein as he passed, trying his best to be helpful.

"Cheers," replied Robin, reaching for the reign and climbing up on to the steady hide of his Slitherback. He slotted his feet within the braces and held on tight, waiting for what had to come next:

The flight to Shoulders Heath...

CHAPTER 15
The Veilers

Robin peered over his shoulder towards the others who were waiting patiently, sat on the hide of their Slitherback rides. For the moment there was calm as the last of the snow swept by the faces of the mounted sorcerers, then Robin turned his gaze towards the Institute entrance, watching as the grey coats in the foyer began to cast their Senteer charms, opening up a series of portals that led directly down the black mountain route to Shoulders Heath. Robin could see the path they had planned to take as he looked into the openings that bloomed clearly like portraits in a gallery. There were three that remained suspended under the archway of the main entrance, torn into the fabric of reality.

  For a split moment he felt that sickening fear

returning, churning in his stomach as his eyes remained glued to the dark depressing shape of the mountain, but before it had a chance to consume him as it wound heavy around his chest, Grimtale let out a roar, whipping his wand from his coat pocket and casting an opening against the rocky earth as his Slitherback reared on its hind legs and let out an encouraging cry of advance - the signal alerting its fellow brothers and sisters that the task at hand was now under way.

"Hold on tight!" Grimtale warned, inserting the wand in his pocket and grasping the harness reins as the five Slitherback promptly began to move, galloping forward, straight for the tear that bridged the bottom of the pit with the late afternoon sky of Vinemoore, high above the lingering snow clouds.

The fists of the Slitherback pounded the snow, launching them on, through the void in the rocky wall of the pit and into a sudden but graceful fall as around them became the open skies of another realm - the Human world.

They had leapt from one world to another and now the five Slitherback were diving, then after a drop of one hundred metres, they broke into a gliding motion until finally picking up momentum to rise above the fluffy whites of the clouds, pushing onwards to the Black mountain and the hidden land that laid ahead of them.

Shoulders Heath was purposefully shielded by the same enchantments that surrounded the Institute; no animal, witch, wizard or absurd creature hell-bent on revenge could gain access to the community that lived there, without firstly crossing the dusty plains and requesting entry, which even then there was no certainty of ever being approved, for the people's safety was crucial in a time where the Counts return was believed to be imminent.

As they began their final approach Robin could make out the silhouette of the mountain, then as they emerged from behind the clouds, there was no missing it, even the finest of details, the vein-like cracks along the surface were gaping wide, even at this distance. The distinct dark shape that had been a part of the view from his bedroom window for as long as he could remember was now way too close for comfort.

It was somewhat haunting as they passed it, swooping overhead of the grey coated Enforcers as they spilled out from the portal openings, down on the rocky road below.

They looked to the horizon as the Slitherback party descended, shifting like shadows in shade, blackened by the amber glare of the sun as it began to set, the last gasp of light falling to the dull, dusty path that ran between the mountain and the surrounding cliff edge.

Magenta was first to touch down, followed by Silverstein who was already adjusting the shape of his silver tipped hair that bounced with the stride of the Slitherback as it landed and began circling the others, waiting for Robin who was the last of the arrivals. He clung on tight with both arms wrapped firmly around the creatures neck as its fists quaked against the earth, breaking its fall with a clear run ahead to the others, who were catching their breath and patting down their rides with words of encouragement.

"Valiant effort my scaly friend!" said Grimtale, running his hand along its spine. He had keenly taken up an interest in the animals that he had grown very fond of, ever since his romantic bond with Sachester had blossomed. He knew she would be relieved to see them back safely, and he felt proud of that as he cocked his leg over the harness and made his way down to the ground, holding tight to the reigns around its neck, peering around at the other four who were already dismounted and were gathering.

From a distance they could have been mistaken for a pack of bandits, as the light began to slowly diminish and the lake in the distance sparkled a shade of vibrant orange, reflecting the last of the sun light before it disappeared behind the rocky landscape surrounding them.

Then as day became early evening, where sunlight had charged the land, it was suddenly altered sharply, glowing an icy blue as if a light switch had been snapped on, instantly changing the colour of the world around them.

The skin of the Slitherback creatures now gave off a cold blue hue and their black beady eyes glistened, much the same as the five Morients as they admired the immediate surroundings. Their eyes reflected wonder at the sight of the place as the snowflakes fell around them.

"I had better make sure the captain and his men are unharmed and headed this way."

Silverstein marched away; his coat shimmering as it flapped behind him and his shoes crunching against the snow and rubble beneath him.

"Leonard! I'll -" but before she had a chance to complete what she was going to say, Silverstein was already making his response as he turned back around, stepping slowly backwards in the direction of the grey coat regiment that was set to meet them.

"I can look after myself, Magenta," he said in a commanding tone, "- besides, you're much safer here, by the water," he concluded, his final glance at her served as a brief reminder of his love and just a hint that this was his way of looking out for her, then he turned back to face the gloomy route ahead of him, remaining vigilant, aware of what was lurking unseen in the shadows.

Magenta watched with an aching heart as the man she adored disappeared beyond the luminous blue hue and into darkness. She couldn't help the worry that clutched at her heart, even though she knew there were twenty armed enforcers closing in on his location. It was safe to say she had lived a little and she also knew the dangers that inhabited the ground around them - nothing was ever certain, no one was ever truly safe, not even the seemingly invincible Silverstein, not here in this place...

"Please be careful," she whispered.

Silverstein drew his wand, taking advantage of the faint white glow radiating from its core - it was colourless and just about managed to light the path ahead as the silver man walked on with haste, keeping a diligent eye on the rockery towering around him.

There was a gentle whistle as the wind swept down the narrow route. The moon sat low in the skies overhead, unable to light the path as Silverstein continued onward, knowing he didn't have far to trek if the others were safe and unscathed, *they wouldn't be far off now*, he thought as he trampled over fallen rubble to reach the clearing. It was then with relief, his eyes fell upon the wandering Enforcer regiment as they appeared ahead of him, they were bound together and moving with their wands at arm's length.

"Captain," called Silverstein, as he carefully approached, giving the open space a once-over.

"Leonard," the Captain replied, picking up the pace, breaking away from the others, leaving them to trail behind.

"You haven't ran in to any... *trouble?*" asked Silverstein, with his wand glowing dull in his right hand.

"None as of yet; we've been overly cautious. Thank you for coming back for us."

"My pleasure," replied Silverstein. Then suddenly the Captain came to a halt, grounding his advance as he noticed Silverstein's right hand rising.

"Leonard… at ease..." ordered the Captain, unsure of Silverstein's intentions. But before anything had the chance to escalate as the two Enforcers opposed one another, a loud gasp came from the regiment.

"*Look! Look there!*" cried an Enforcer, pointing towards the shadows that were hovering at the foot of the crater.

Silverstein glanced at the Captain and shouted, "*Veilers!*"

Now the warning had been given he began backing up to witness, as multiple pairs of black glistening eyes approached them through the darkness, sparkling like freshly polished diamonds lodged in the body of something so hideous, that the sight of them left their victims scarred for life - if they lived - which was unspoken for a human, and rare for a Morient...

The Captain had already pushed aside the stand off with Silverstein as they stood their ground, attempting to anticipate the advancing creatures next move. Their backs were pressed firmly together as they followed the eyes with their wands, prepared for a moment's notice to deter the looming assault - but nothing had prepared them enough for what came running: The needle sharp claws and blade-like teeth, the deep black eyes and pale white skin...

The Veiler creatures leapt high into the moonlight and dropped down sharply on top of the Enforcers, impaling them with their long mutated claws. Others narrowly escaped their clutches, casting deterrent spells to knock the creatures away and across the frosty rubble. As Silverstein and the Captain turned to assist their comrades, the Veilers had already worked their way through a third of their men, tearing their limbs from their bodies, biting hard into the cores of their wands and slicing the flesh of their throats wide open, releasing a river of crimson to gush over their long grey trench coats.

The bodies began to fall one by one as the creatures continued to ravage their way through the Enforcer ranks. The Captain had frozen in fear, staring into the deformed faces of the pale humanoids - he couldn't move no matter how desperately he tried. The sight of such horror was too much, it was as if an overwhelming force had grasped at his chest and pressed him down into the ground, leaving him unable to move, stealing his breath. Then projectiles suddenly erupted from the end of Silverstein's wand as deep orange hues of energy, striking at the hearts of the Veilers as they pounced, forcing them back in to the ground where they laid, instantly lifeless. At last the Captain managed to break free from his mental restraints and followed Silverstein's lead as they began to work their way back to the regiment, casting projectiles left, right and centre at the infinite eyes surrounding them, casting them back to the darkness from which they came.

"Clear them!" yelled Silverstein.

He ran amongst the chaos and threw his life on the line, tackling a Veiler to the ground before it had a chance to slay another. He pressed the end of his wand to its chin and dealt the fatal blow. The creatures head erupted like a firework - just without the pretty colours. There was bone, flesh and bloody matter blown against the ground, staining the white of the snow as Silverstein shielded his face, looking away with no remorse. The arrival of the silver man had brought a steady footing amongst the remaining Enforcers. With their backs now covered, they began to work together, slaughtering the aggressors, putting an end to their vicious rampage.

* * *

Lakeside, as the conflict raged on, the tremendous light show caught the attention of Grimtale who was stood apart from Robin, Lillian and Magenta. They were knelt beside the glowing water, admiring the peaceful wash and the piercing sparkle as moonlight caught the surface. None were anticipating the cries for help and boulders being blown from the cliff edge as the battle began to echo from the funnelled rocky route. They turned simultaneously and glared towards the orange bolts of energy that were filling the night sky.

"What is that?" asked Robin as he rose to his feet, eyes fixed on the colours exploding in the distance.

"The first wrong turn," said Grimtale.

"Leonard needs our help!" Lillian remarked, making haste for her Slitherback and wasting no time in mounting it. The others followed her lead, making clear they were up to the task, no questions asked.

"Please be okay, Leonard..." muttered Magenta, as she pulled on the Slitherback's reigns and launched into a vigorous gallop, heading at speed towards the piercing light, where her lover was fighting what she feared could be a final stand.

* * *

They weren't an endless horde, but yet for now they kept on coming, emerging from the shadows and snarling as they ran in broken ranks towards the wounded regiment. There was only so much the remaining Enforcers could withstand. They were down to ten men. The Captain and Silverstein were huddled together, defending their lives with the wands in their hands; however, where one counter spell struck a fatal blow, another missed or maimed at the most and this was no longer free practice - the Veilers were closing in for the kill. Silverstein could sense it, realising the gruesome mutations were becoming noticeably more defined and glossy as they leapt, attempting to break the circle and slaughter them from within their tight, compact formation.

"*Brexio!*" declared Silverstein, blasting away a pair of Veilers as they fell at his feet.

"They're not gonna stop. How many are there?" cried the Captain, proving a burden on his men as his charms bolted by the aggressors head as it ran, licking its lips with a fierce craving for the Morient's blood. The Veiler slashed the nearby Enforcers wands in half, then pulled the Captain from under his feet, deterring his feeble attempts to fight back as it sunk its teeth deep in to the Captains forearm and sliced the necks of those grappled to its back, trying to pull them apart.

Silverstein could sense now that he was all too late. The sight of the Veiler feasting and the bodies against the snow, reflected in his eyes. He pressed his way towards the Captain and cast a bolt of destructive energy between the Veilers eyes - its head imploded and ran dry of blood as its body fell limp and lifeless upon the Enforcer corpses beneath it. In that moment it was as if time had come to a stop. The fighting had slowed around him as Silverstein cast his gaze to the last of the grey coated Enforcers, who had fallen to their knees at the mercy of the monsters standing over them.

The loss of Morient life seemed not to bother the silver man, it was the thought of what the Veilers would do to *him* that sent the most chilling of sensations down his spine.

One was flanked by three more, three then became five and before there was even a chance to take a breath, he knew it had to be the end. The remaining Enforcers were chopped at the neck and left to bleed out against the already crimson coloured snow that had turned to bloody slush, leaving Silverstein the lone target of their rage and hunger as he stood wearily amongst the fallen: the blood, the sweat, the tears... he was defenceless.

The land was dark but the Veilers appeared like insects on the snow, swarming over the perished blood soaked bodies as they surrounded the last opposing Morient. Silverstein glanced down at the diminished white glow seeping through the cracks of his wand, he then locked gaze with the Veiler creature approaching him, looking on with disgust as the final glimmer of hope he held, began to fade away. The Veiler sniffed at Silverstein's metallic coat, then pressed its beak-like nose against his face, inhaling the bitter sweet scent that wafted from his flesh. The creature's milky white eyes widened and it's already pale face turned deathlike as it backed away, snarling with its teeth glistening sharp like pins. Its finger shook as it rose, pointing at the mutated growths and scarring on the surface of its head.

"*Evil!*" it grunted, "*Evil!*" it repeated in an aggressive tone, but Silverstein remained calm and collected, with his head held high.

"You were shown mercy. You rebelled, and now you must live with your mistakes," said Silverstein, standing his ground, "Everyone are out for themselves, and themselves, only!"

The silver man's final words were met with a sudden burst of rage, the Veiler swung for his face with no hesitation, slicing a claw along his brow, narrowly avoiding his deep dark eyes that reflected instant panic. The cut was shallow, but far from painless as he grasped the left side of his face.

"*You're scum! Human scum, the lot of you!*" he yelled.

Then as he flinched, with one eye covered, the pack began to approach him, reaching for his coat and pulling him towards the blood soaked ground at his feet. The metallic silver fabric began to tear as the Veilers clamped their fingertips into his body, forcing him down on his knees. He could feel their claws piercing his flesh as they held on to him. Every twist and every jolt was agony as his hair was yanked back, exposing his neck as the vocal Veiler moved closer, its instinct set on tearing Silverstein apart, one piece at a time...

CHAPTER 16
The Return of Munder Mortal

The Veiler creatures were out of touch with their humanity. Some didn't even resemble that of a human anymore, except the one hovering in front of Silverstein as his head remained braced, his bare neck exposed. Something terrible had happened to these misshapen people, and now with no guidance, they had become bearers of the terror that had terrorised *them*.

Silverstein didn't break eye contact with the creature as it approached again. He tried to look deep beyond the frosty glaze that covered its eyes, but there was nothing but emptiness. It was as if the human mind had perished completely and churned up and out amongst the thick, foamy residue that dripped from its mouth as it snarled. Its skin was hideous with fluids leaking from its pores as its mouth widened and its body suddenly lunged.

It happened too fast. All he could see for that moment was white, then as he raised his hand and began to feel around his neck and face his sight returned and the Veilers were gone, retreating to the shadows from which they came.

"Leonard!" cried Magenta, who was followed by the team as they formed a protective circle around the wounded man.

He could barely hold himself up, but the pain was minimal now and he was just so relieved it was over, amazed in fact. In his mind he was certain he was done for, but fate obviously had other plans for him. He put away his dim lit wand and pushed himself up off the ground, taking a moment to find his balance as his head began to throb from the gouge along his brow.

They all had a look of horror on their faces as they cast their sights to Silverstein; especially Magenta as she trampled over the mass of bodies to get to him.

"Leonard!" She cried again as she threw herself around him, pressing her face against the damp crimson that had spilled on to his waistcoat and shirt. She had no care in the world for whoever's blood it was, all that mattered was that he was alive - but he was badly hurt, more than he chose to believe as he placed his arm over Magenta's shoulder, surrendering to his weakness.

"I'm okay. Honestly I'm okay," he muttered, barely able to see from his left eye, "It's all cosmetic, a few scratches, it's nothing. I'll be ok."

Magenta knew it wasn't serious, but it did look nasty and certainly painful. His beautiful metallic coat was torn at the seams and various puncture wounds were leaking on to the fabric, but he still had a little fight in him, she could sense it as she looked up at him wishing he'd call it a day so she could take him away from the dangers that still remained in Shoulders Heath - but that was never going to happen.

"I wish there was a spell for situations like

this," she remarked, wiping the blood from around Silverstein's eye.

"Well there was in the war. The great Morient war of eighteen seventeen. It was seen as a way of cheating death. So to make life more difficult, it was made obsolete by the Prime of the Celestial Institute. No wonder mad men hunt this god damn Phoenix," explained Grimtale, making his way over to assist as Lillian and Robin stood at a distance, processing the sight of slaughter laid before them.

"What were those creatures, Grimtale?" asked Robin, staring at the Veiler body parts, detached and scattered amongst the fallen Enforcers.

"We've always called them Veilers - but they're Human," he explained, stood with severed arms and teeth beneath his boots.

"The mutation hides their true identities but they were once all like us until the Count got his hands on them. You've encountered his repossessed clowns and now you've seen what happens when you oppose him, when you stand your ground. Brave souls, the lot of them."

While Magenta helped Silverstein over the bodies, the Slitherback gills continued to flutter, casting a wave of piercing deterrent across the open plain, having already forced the Veilers away to their hives, it was a reliable call, and it had saved a vital life.

As time passed, the land had fallen silent. It was peaceful as Grimtale pulled Robin aside and took a step away from the others.

"It wasn't ever going to be pleasant," said Grimtale, ushering Robin along, "- there's no way of preparing anyone for a job like this. Just remember what you've learnt. Your wand is the most important tool you have to hand."

Robin reached for his wand and drew it from his pocket.

"Unless it fails you," he replied, watching the Luminous green running within the core of the wand.

"That wand will never fail you, Robin. It's just getting to know you again, the new you." explained Grimtale.

"I guess that could take some time."

"Perhaps. But then again, do we ever trust anyone completely?"

Robin reached back in to his pocket and pulled out a small photograph. It had a crease down the centre where it was folded in two: he opened it up and his eyes fell glassy at the sight of his family.

"I trust, Kirsten. I'd trust her with my life."

His eyes were glued to the photograph, a sharp reminder of how much he missed home. He had only been gone for a day - not even that - but jumping between the two realms was like being on a completely different planet. There wasn't any certainty that he would even see his family again, not after what he had just witnessed, those bodies slaughtered amongst monsters. All he had to do now was survive the night, bring back the Phoenix and hope a normal life was still on the table, one without danger to those he loved.

There was a quick fasten of his mustard frock coat, then he climbed aboard his Slitherback, reuniting with the group who were ready to set off, heading east, back to the lake at the foot of the black mountain.

The returning journey was met with no further

threat. The path ahead was clear and Silverstein had begun to feel far better, given time to calm himself from the pain and panic. He just felt numb now the bleeding had stopped.

"I'll be ok..." he whispered, reassuring Magenta who still looked traumatised by the sight of him, covered in his own blood - a rare turn of events for the both of them.

Even Robin had a rush of concern as he slumped back in his harness, his eyes were fixated on Silverstein, he was staring at the blood-stained silver coat. The fabric was shredded and cotton strands were dancing in the cold winter wind as they rode along the dark canyon route.

There was an unspoken realisation, they had barely even arrived and it seemed as if there was already an ever looming defeat. Even if Silverstein denied it and told them otherwise, it was a blatant state of fact that they were damaged, and working any less than one hundred percent was going to hinder the next step, indefinitely. But with the odds against them, as a team, they pushed on, watching over their shoulders for hostiles, and keeping their eyes peeled for the beautiful lake that was sat a little further ahead, sparkling under the glow of the moon that had climbed high, peering down over the landscape.

"Was that the worst?" asked Robin, leaning over to Grimtale who rode beside him.

"Potentially," he replied, with a comforting twinkle in his eye as he glanced high to the disfigured rocky shapes that lined the very top of the mountains around them.

"If the Count shows, he won't come alone. And

his men are strong, they're precise - unlike the Veilers. They're just savages, now."

Grimtale met Robin's gaze for a moment before glancing at Silverstein, just to make sure his attention was far from the two of them in tow. Grimtale quickly made a swooshing gesture with his hand and pointed to Robins breast pocket.

"Take out your wand," he muttered.

Robin glanced to Silverstein, then back to Grimtale with a look of confusion.

"Why are you whispering?" asked Robin, backing away from the others in front.

"I never showed you what Professor Yuri did to your wand," he explained, as he sunk in to the black sheep skin of his coat, relaxing as they dropped back a few lengths.

Robin whipped out his wand and held it to his right hand side, down beside his thigh.

"He said he was mapping something to its core, something that had to be kept to myself?"

Grimtale smirked beneath his thick bushy beard.

"It's not been field tested, but I can assure you it works. If things get out of hand and you feel it's necessary to protect yourself, you have a means of defence that Silverstein and Magenta do not."

Robin's vision suddenly became washed by the deep red hue of Silverstein's jacket. He didn't understand why there had to be a divide that was costing people's lives.

"This could have all been avoided if he had what *we* have!" said Robin angrily.

"Perhaps I was wrong. But I must follow my gut feeling, Robin. The majority have agreed, until we return, we must be weary of those who are involved with the Morient Defence," explained Grimtale, pushing aside the overwhelming sense of guilt as his eyes kept falling on to the back of the limp and wounded Silverstein.

"*Shielz-ignite*. Remember those words, they will activate the defensive charm that may be essential to saving yours or someone else's life."

Grimtale looked away and glared towards the open ground where the vast waters of the lake began, washing gently on to the dark, damp gravel beneath the patchy snow. He was undoubtedly conflicted, but lives had already been lost to no fault of anyone, except that of the evil that they had come to suppress. If there ever could be peace, there wouldn't be a need for such extreme measures of protection; however the world had grown dark and cold, and only a small minority of the towns in the Morient realm remained enchanted by the joys of life and the love their communities had to give. Shoulders Heath had become something sinister in the human world, but further beyond that, on the other side, the Heath was known as quite the opposite. Some would say a hidden paradise, others thought of it as a target for those who yearned to steal all that paradise had to offer.

As they neared the foot of the lake, Grimtale's Slitherback pressed on towards the front of the group, moving in position to bridge the passage to their next location.

Lillian had already arrived and was sat patiently by the water while Magenta and Silverstein carefully manoeuvred beside her as they waited for Robin, who was plodding along extremely slowly.

"Sorry guys, not quite got the hang of this yet," he remarked as he neared.

"Lucky for you, the next part is on foot," grunted Silverstein as he leaned forward to pat the neck of his Slitherback. Their long snake-like necks were thick and heavy, with hard scaly skin which shimmered as it caught the moonlight. Thankfully they seemed to be unfazed by the sharp stench of fresh blood, soaked deep in the fibres of Silverstein's coat. Being somewhat peaceful creatures, their training allowed them to keep a calm and collected attitude, even when their heightened sense of smell detected the concentrated levels of iron radiating from the silver man and the land from which they came.

Their tongues flickered and their black, beady eyes followed Robin as he arrived beside them. In an attempt to fool their judgment he smiled, stemming an unbalanced flood of emotion. No one expected it, as it was rare enough for any of them to be afoot in Shoulders Heath, which meant none were familiar with the entrance that Grimtale had chosen to open, but he was the most frequent visitor to the land and knew it like the back of his hand - his judgment was trusted by most. He remained mounted as he reached for his cane and pointed it towards the water ahead of him.

There was a gentle rippling motion, then as the bulbous handle of the cane began to glow, a tiny pit hole emerged in the water and then it churned as if pulled like a drain as the lake water rushed down around the oval opening as it widened, until it was large enough to fit a Slitherback.

The water at their feet suddenly began to push

apart, forming a path that ran along the bed of the lake, directly to the edge of the opening. Ready to re-enter the Morient realm. Grimtale rode his Slitherback on towards the opening. Robin watched cautiously as Grimtale faded, then disappeared beyond the dark veil.

One by one they entered, until finally it was his turn. None of the others had batted an eyelid, but now he was sat over the dark mass, he felt somewhat anxious, staring aimlessly, waiting for that kick of courage he needed as precious time ticked by. The mounted Slitherback was growing restless and was eager to climb down, knowing its home was waiting on the other end, but it could also sense that Robin was worried, it could smell the nervous sweat as it looked back at him, curiously mapping the expression on his face; but before it had a chance to aid Robin, its gaze was distracted as it noticed movement along the mountain in the distance: There were dark silhouetted figures climbing down towards them, they wore familiar metal half masks hiding their faces and gauntlets covering their hands that sparkled as they crossed into the path of moonlight.

Without a second thought the Slitherback turned to the lake and leapt for the void that was still being held open by Grimtale's cane, disregarding Robins discomfort. He yelled as his head was forcefully thrown back, trailing his body as it was led away, and even though he'd done it twice already, this time felt different, it was just as bizarre but before he knew it, in the blink of an eye he had arrived and the gaping void had closed behind him. It kind of made him feel silly as he rubbed the ice from his brow and looked around in amazement at the new world that was waiting to be discovered. Whatever was lurking down the mountain side, back on the human side of Shoulders Heath, it was no longer a threat to them now.

The Slitherback had done them all a favour and wasted no time to warn Sachester, it's beloved keeper who was already at its side with her long dark hair held up in a messy bun as she caressed the creatures chin.

"You understand what it's saying?" asked Robin, looking down in fascination.

"Of course. I've raised them since birth, trained them. This is Edmund, he says you were being followed..."

"We were? I was too caught up with my own demons to even notice," said Robin as he climbed down from Edmund, the Slitherback.

"It sounds like Reapers," Sachester added as she turned to Grimtale, "- You suspected they wouldn't be far behind, if not already a step ahead."

Now dismounted, Grimtale made his way over to Sachester and Robin, leaning heavily on his cane.

"They missed their opportunity. They now have no other means of gaining access," explained Grimtale, "- we exhaust their advances, then the upper hand resides with us, my dear."

Sachester was glad to see them all, especially Grimtale who never failed to make her blush as she greeted him with a smile. There was a charm about him that kept her heart burning, a growing bloom of love buried deep within her chest. He wasn't what most would consider the common kind of heart throb, but he had style and a powerful presence that overshadowed those around him. He was perfect for Sachester, she realised that more deeply every time she saw him; it was rare, but she sometimes caught him smiling behind his black wiry beard as he turned his attention away.

"What on earth happened?" she asked with her eyes wide as Silverstein staggered forward, holding on to his rib cage.

"Veilers, that's what happened," he replied abruptly.

"But I don't understand... the call of the Slitherback was proven effective?"

Sachester was confused. The sight of Silverstein with bloody stains drying against the threads of his coat had shaken her. She may have never liked the man, but he was the last she ever expected to see in such a rough state.

"Well I was stupid enough to return on foot. But if it wasn't for your creatures, I wouldn't be here. I would have died with the twenty Enforcers who were pulled apart."

Magenta placed her hand on his back as a sign of support. They were all stood in a ring, facing one another as the Slitherback group wandered aimlessly around them, exploring the hillside they had arrived on.

The grass was frosty green and at the bottom of the hill was a town, similar to Vinemoore but far larger with rivers streaming as far as the eye could see. It was still night time in the Morient realm so the town was quiet from the outset, but the buildings were vibrant and unlike anything Robin had ever seen. The others had seen it all before but for Robin it was another pleasant surprise that left him speechless.

There was something quite abstract about the landscape and the metal plated tiles that sat tall and piercing along the rooftops. But as Robin's curious eyes strayed from the architecture, he noticed a chunky figure staggering towards them, climbing the path that led from the town to the hillside.

"We need to get you seen to, Leonard," said Sachester, dismissing the sight of a seventh figure.

"No," he replied, "it's just blood, a few scratches. I'm fine."

Sachester looked to Magenta who gave a nod of her head.

"He'll be ok. The wounds aren't fatal," said Magenta as the pink fur of her coat continued to ruffle in the gentle breeze that swept across the hillside.

Lillian suddenly turned as she felt the ground beneath her feet, shift.

Robin hadn't taken his eyes off of it as it arrived beside Sachester, much to the surprise of everyone as they noticed. It was a tall copper man - or machine. It rattled and creaked as its body came to a halt. Its head had two luminous green eyes and a heavy jaw with a protruding under-bite that looked to be riveted into position against the sides of its head. It looked aggressive as it towered over them, but Sachester seemed somewhat relieved to see it, and the Slitherback creatures were completely oblivious to its arrival - it couldn't of been a threat, most concluded as they stared high into the green of its eyes.

"There's no need to look alarmed. it's merely a mechanical man; plenty of cogs and rivets. I was toying with the possibility of housing a consciousness within him, giving the deceased a new means of living. I just never got around to it, call it a hobby of mine."

Everyone seemed fascinated, and no one denied it being a good idea as Sachester explained what she wanted to achieve some day, in the convoluted future that laid ahead.

"Does it have a name?" asked Robin, who was met with a look of alarm from Magenta.

"What?" he asked, taking a step closer to the bronze bodied man.

"We just call him Coggo. He runs off a charm that keeps him ticking, but one day I shall give him real life."

Its body rang as Sachester gave it a gentle pat on the back.

"See that my children make it back to their barns, safely. Thank you my friend," said Sachester, waving on the cumbersome tin man, who immediately began rallying up the five Slitherback creatures and leading them down the hillside, towards the town where their barns resided.

"Now, you'd best follow me," ordered Sachester as she darted past Robin and Lillian, following the same path as Coggo, the tin man.

"Is it far?" asked Robin, brushing his frock coat against the bare of her arms.

"We're certain it hasn't moved, which means it must be in the crater. There's a cliff that overlooks it, right at the other end of this road. We just have to cut through the town. They know who you all are, they've been waiting."

Sachester reassured them that the people were safe, then they left the hillside and slowly made their way down towards the town of Shoulders Heath. Silverstein followed Sachester's lead with Magenta in tow, while Grimtale and Lillian cautiously guarded the flank, nervous in case of any unwanted visitors that were on their heels, knowing it was near impossible for them to cross over with the appropriate shielding charms in place, but they were never without their doubts. The stone of acceptance that empowered the charm was all but a slither, it would have to run dry one day, surely? And that day had always worried Grimtale and the folk of all the Morient realms under its protection; however for now, thanks to the great mind of Professor Yuri, it withheld the enemy threat and allowed the group to move on.

Robin couldn't help but have a nose around the neighbourhood as they passed. Everything was drastically different to home; the houses had a pearlescent shine and their chimney stacks were tall and dispersing an emerald green cloud that rose in to the evening sky. There was a haunting silence riding the wind; the people hadn't left their homes in days - since the Phoenix had made its untimely arrival. Robin had spotted them as he passed, huddled around their fireplaces, peering out of the windows. It must have been quite exciting for them - either that or terrifying - not knowing who had come for the bird.

The streets were darker than the hilltops, the shadows hid their faces. Some of the braver residents had left their doors ajar to have a peek, and gave a sigh of relief as they caught a glimpse of Sachester. She had become a beacon of hope for the town; unlike others, she seemed to have an endless drive, and she always put the people before herself. Watching her lead the Institutes finest towards the open cliff edge was solid confirmation that there was no one else more suited to protect, and uphold the community.

Grimtale caught Robin nervously looking back at him as they finally arrived at their destination. The cliff was a large plot of land, like a platform suspended over the deep, dark crater. There were farming mills sat far in the distance, and wooden windmills turning as the light finally drained from the skies and the evening fell in to darkness, leaving only the luminous green of the fumes overhead highlighting the shapes of their faces as they looked high to the sky, their cheek bones glowing a subtle green.
"It's eerily silent out here," remarked Lillian, watching on as Magenta and Silverstein wandered ahead, while Grimtale hung back and Sachester joined him, leaving Robin to pursue his curiosity.
"Guys, if the Phoenix is here, do you believe my presence is going to be enough to draw it out?" asked Robin, glancing back over his shoulder to Grimtale, who confirmed with a gentle nod.
"You have no ill intent, a friendly face would hardly go amiss."
Silverstein held out his hand and softly stroked the scarred side of Magenta's face. She held his hand in place for as long as she could before letting go. He gave her his reassuring wink before following closely behind Robin.
The two conflicting personalities were side by side as they arrived at the edge, where the land

had dropped and fallen to the depths which even in daylight was hidden by shadow. There was only the echo of the wind whirling by their ears as they stood over the void and waited.

Robin continued to look towards the darkness. He listened closely then slowly drew his wand, hoping its presence would cause a stir, igniting a long forgotten spark within the creature they'd come to secure. But it wasn't until the wands core began to glow that Robin noticed a collection of orbs glistening near the bottom of the crater. Then they slowly began to grow, as if they were getting closer. Robin and Silverstein both stood their ground as the orbs became clearer, now equally partitioned and bulging. There were six in total now, and as they rose to eye level with the two Morient men, an overwhelming sensation shot through their bodies. Their legs suddenly felt like jelly as the glowing clouds overhead caught the metallic feathers of the great Phoenix bird. They shimmered a hue of blue, purple and green as it rose high in to the night sky and made a shriek, followed by the sharp snapping of its beak as it glared down at the six Morients who were returning the look of alarm.

"My word, it's beautiful!" remarked Robin as the blue and green hues reflected in his eyes.

Silverstein was somewhat overjoyed, or at least it seemed that way to Robin as he fixated on the bird with a grin as wide as his ego. The tail of his coat fluttered in the wind, his silver tipped hair waved a riot as he then felt a sharp twinge along his spine.

He was certain it was just the excitement, the thrill of seeing the Starlight Phoenix in all its untamed glory; but as he turned his head, no longer was Robin stood beside him, instead there was the bearded face of Grimtale with a look of satisfaction on his face.

As he began to tremble the realisation suddenly struck - it wasn't the excitement at all that had sent the piercing pains along his spine, it was a dagger, and that blade was lodged firmly in his back with its leather handle protruding from his coat.

Silverstein staggered, trying to find his balance as Grimtale's face began to blur. A wave of shock had left the others stunned and frozen to the ground as they witnessed the betrayal.

"What have you done?" cried Sachester.

"*Leonard*!" Magenta's voice echoed pain as deep as his fatal wound as she tried to pull herself along the ground. It felt as if all the energy had suddenly evaporated from their bodies. Robin's jaw had dropped as he began to fall back against the ground, trying to scramble away from the scene. Grimtale held out his arms to catch Silverstein as he fell to his knees. His body slumped but his eyes continued to follow the large bearded man as he made sure his face was within his field of vision.

Surprisingly, the Phoenix had remained in flight, hovering over the cliff face as Silverstein took his final breath. Grimtale's expression of anger then loosened to one of concern. The sight of Silverstein's corpse had triggered a panic as he realised, he may have made a grave error...

"*You're having us on! I know that I'm right, I have to be!*" he yelled, shaking the lifeless corpse in his arms.

"The wounds, they've healed. And that limp had suddenly disappeared as soon as you left

Magenta's side! Tell me I'm right!" He demanded, glaring into the eyes of the lifeless man, *"You are not Leonard Silverstein. You're not him! Tell me, I'm right!"*

There was a moment of silence as Grimtale turned to Sachester, his eyes filling with tears as the shock of what he had done suddenly struck. But then as he averted his gaze to Magenta, pulling herself towards Silverstein's body, he also noticed something else: Silverstein's eyes were now a bright yellow and air was filling his lungs again, raising his chest in a fluid up-down motion. He was alive, and his raspy voice roared as he suddenly sat up and grappled his hand around Grimtale's throat.

"You're right, Professor. I am not Leonard Silverstein!"

His grip tightened and Grimtale gave a gasp as his lungs begged for air.

"I may have lived as the silver man, but he is not I! I am Munder Mortal, and after many years of confinement, my flesh can breathe again!"

The revived man with the face of Leonard Silverstein rose to his feet and released a hand from Grimtale's throat, easing the pain ever so slightly so he could tug the dagger from his back. He held on tight to the leather bound handle then gave it a pull, yanking it neat from his back and holding it high overhead where the blood dripped from the blade.

"You - were - him, all this time!" gasped Grimtale, his words broken by suffocation as the blade began to rest against Silverstein's forehead.

"All this time!" he confirmed.

Then he pressed the tip of the blade through flesh and against the bone of his skull and began carving it down between his eyes, along his nose and under his chin. He then began tearing apart the flesh from his face until he was no longer recognisable as Leonard - instead, he now looked as he really was - the monster that everyone had grown to fear.

The Count had returned....

CHAPTER 17
Edge Of Defeat

The last fleshy remnants of Leonard Silverstein struck the ground as the Count finally bared all. His face was dripping with a dark hue of crimson, and his eyes glowed a luminous yellow as he scowled at the choking man, held tightly in his left hand.

The Count had gained a remarkable strength, he was enhanced as an effect of the Starlight Phoenix overhead, and remarkably one of six to ever bond with it. The power he sought was now all too close; his wounds had already healed, his body may have been heavily scarred, but now he was restored. All that was left was the perpetrator, gasping for air, for something, anything but death.

Grimtale's life was fading, he could feel it slipping away as his throat continued to swell until it had closed completely, but as all hope was thought lost, a bolt of light struck the Count's hand, forcing him to release Grimtale, sending him hurtling to the ground, back in a position to fight the great evil towering over him.

By the time it had taken Grimtale to scuttle

back against the gravel, Robin had stepped forward, leaving the women behind him as they held tight to a broken Magenta.

"*All eyes on me you ugly, poor excuse of a man!*" cried Robin, wielding his wand at arms length like the powerful weapon it was.

The Count's poisonous yellow eyes switched from Grimtale to Robin as he carefully approached. They were stark and sinister, but for Robin he expected no less. He had prepared himself for this very moment as his gaze remained locked with the monster standing in Silverstein's clothing. Then as the Count began to speak, the illusionary shape of his human-like teeth crumbled away until all that was left were the sharp elongated remains that closely resembled fangs.

"Boy, you may have aged but your arrogance remains as firm as ever!" hissed the Count. As he reached in to Silverstein's tatty, bloodstained coat. He drew out a wand, the wand with the dying light. And his other hand reached deeper, drawing from an opposite pocket, a wand of dark and sharp qualities, only this one had a deep red hue, pulsating at the core and considerably brighter than the other, which was a pure white and seemingly on its last legs as it flickered.

"Another reason for my concerns, a wand in the hands of its rightful owner would never fail them *like that one is failing you! What have you done with Leonard Silverstein?*" yelled Grimtale as he climbed to his feet beside Robin, forming a wall to obscure the path behind them.

As the Count responded to Grimtales question, he began wiping away the blood and fleshy residue from his face, using a charm which manifested in the form of turbulent dark energy, brushing against his face and restoring him to the form which he was most commonly recognised.

"He's probably at home right now, wondering what he must have done wrong to sway fate down a terrible path. But what surprises me, Magenta, for someone who declares her love for the man all so often, why is it you don't know where he lives? Why am I certain you're going to abandon these associates of yours in hope of finding the man?"

Magenta struggled as Sachester and Lillian held her, restraining her. They were all too aware that she wasn't thinking straight as her eyes continued to burn with pain and fury, but they held tight, straining the seams of her bright pink coat.

"*I will find him!*" she roared, like a lion with its paws dug deep in the gravel, fighting to reach its prey, with her golden mane hung heavy across her face as she pulled against her restraints. But Sachester and Lillian's grip was firm, and she knew it wouldn't make a difference what form she chose to take - she was detained and her human guise was far more forgiving of the pain she was sustaining.

The Count remained humoured by each of their feeble attempts to intimidate him as he stood restored, bathing in the rays of moonlight that were beaming down from behind a band of clouds that had moved overhead.

Beneath the silver shimmer that had flaked away, his hair was a dirty blonde and held its swept-back look behind his ears. His stark yellow eyes only exaggerated the density of the newly exposed flesh on his bones. He was a ghostly white and far from the most handsome of the bunch as he remained grounded to the cliff edge, stood in the torn outfit of another man.

"My followers will stop at *nothing* to gain access to Shoulders Heath!" said the Count, targeting the opposing professors with his darker wand, as its bright red core pulsated.

"The fragment of the stone that protects this land is more than secure. Your mindless servants have no hope, and neither do you!" vowed Grimtale, taking a defensive stance and watching as the Count's grin faded.

Then while both wands were drawn, the Count quickly whipped Silverstein's wand like a lasso, which suddenly launched a rope of blistering energy high in to the sky and around the oblivious Starlight Phoenix. It gave a cry as it began to flap its wings, pulling against the magical restraint that was tightening around its feathered body.

Slowly, the Count eased the Phoenix down, countering its escape as he felt it pull. He was fully aware that Silverstein's wand was on its last legs, it's dimming core was constantly at the front of his mind as he inspected the energy streaming from the end of the Wand. But it seemed consistent and powerful as his yellow eyes raised back to the agonising scene in the sky, the struggle as the constraints remained unyielding against every effort the bird was making to flee.

Robin and the others had seen enough. As Magenta remained at a distance, now only held loosely by Sachester and Lillian, Robin made the first move, launching an attack on the monster opposing them.

The Count suddenly diverted his attention to the balls of energy hurtling towards his face, raising his personal wand and deflecting them to the ground beneath his feet. Robin could have sworn for a split second, his poisonous yellow eyes had widened out of fear, but Grimtale had sensed the true nature of his expression, lit in the burning fire around his eyelids. It was pure torment that the Count had begun to exhale from his body, as a source of energy that had taken the form of a spearhead attached to a tail of chains that stemmed from the end of his wand.

Robin and Grimtale both dived apart, taking evasive action to avoid the counter spells that the Count had hurtled towards them. They could hear the sound of the chains falling heavy against the ground as the spearhead struck, narrowly avoiding Robin's leg as he fell hard against the blackened gravel.

"You missed!" taunted Robin, much to the frustration of the Count who gave a light snarl, then detached the chains before firing a burst of bright red orbs in Robin's direction, as a hope of wiping out the frock-coated annoyance who watched on in discomfort as the dazzling red glow filled his vision, deterring his attempt to reach for his wand.

But then Robin suddenly remembered. It was as if he'd been transported back to the chamber that day, with Yuri at his side, whispering as a precaution, the charm he'd taught him. He heard it repeated as clear as the wind being swept by his ear as he picked up his wand and pointed it sharply towards the energy that was now so close, he could feel it burning away at his brow.

"*Shielz-ignite!*" he roared, in time with a wave of golden light that dispersed from his wand and wrapped itself around his body like a shield, deflecting the powerful red orbs into the ground where they could do no harm.

Grimtale was staring at the light, as was Magenta, Sachester and Lillian. They all bore witness as Robin's clothing began to stiffen and weld itself like a suit of armour around him, sparkling gold as he stood beneath the moon. The skies were now filled with escaping air loaches, drifting high like a swarm of sparrows, migrating until a promised safe return.

His armour twinkled, dazzling the Count as he admired the blatant handy work of Professor Yuri: the Phoenix-like helmet with a faceplate in the shape of a sharp beak, and his coat taking the form of a fierce breast plate, with mirror finish to repel enemy charms. He was quite literally a knight in shining armour, but instead of a sword, he wielded a wand - a very powerful one with a core as pure as its owners heart.

With all but his eyes now shielded by metal, Robin made an advance, and so did Magenta, seizing the moment as Lillian and Sachester remained distracted, in awe of what stood before them. She had broken free of their grasp and already drawn alongside Robin as he carefully calculated his next move, entirely unaware of Magenta's presence as she stupidly gave in to her rage and launched a volley of fiery projectiles towards the Count.

His wand sliced the balls of fire, causing them to violently explode in to a mass of tiny black fragments, before riding the wind away from the cliff edge.

"Foolish move," the Count responded, still with the Phoenix detained by Silverstein's wand.

They weren't making it easy for him, he knew

he had to make a fatal blow and buy himself time as he quickly conjured another spearhead and launched it with blinding force in Magenta's direction. His yellow glazed eyes glistening with Magenta's fear as she watched the tip of the spear hurtling towards her, knowing it was already too late to try and counter.

She screwed her eyes shut and her body tensed, preparing for what would come next - the weapon continuing its path, slicing through the flesh and bone of her chest. But strangely, there was first a *thump* and then a *clang*. Magenta reopened her eyes as he stumbled in to her gaze, in time to suffer the full force of the Counts efforts to pick them off. Robin stood between them, with the spearhead lodged in the backplate of his armoured suit. He could feel his heart racing, pounding against the metal that encased him. The war drums were carrying his soul in to battle as he looked on, Magenta's expression was one of most sincere gratitude for Robin.

"We do it *together*..." said Robin.

He briefly placed his hand on Magenta's shoulder, then turned, signalling behind to Grimtale, who immediately began the final assault. It was one last effort to thwart the Count as he planted his cumbersome cane against the ground and directed a purple stream of electrical energy towards the enemy, married with the turquoise stream of energy pulsating from Robin's wand.

Each came together, one after the other until there was a rainbow of colour crossing the cliff like a sea of hungry serpents, converging on the Count, who had turned his gaze back to the Phoenix before attempting to repel the oncoming threats.

But his wand made easy work of the serpent-like heads, slicing the streams as they neared, rendering them useless and allowing time to identify Robin's wand, and meet his assault with a powerful rope of red energy which soared from his wand, clashing against the turquoise stream and holding as the two warriors tightened their grip, Robin now with a second hand held firmly around the handle of his wand.

"*Disengage, Robin!*" yelled Magenta, watching as the streams pressed against one another.

"I can't!" replied Robin, trying to pull his wand away to break the connection. However, with each attempt, the counts grip tightened and yanked him forward.

"The core! He's going to pirate your core!" warned Grimtale, sheltering his eyes from the stark white light which began to erupt between the multi coloured streams.

Robin continued to try and pull his wand away as a final act of desperation, knowing everything Yuri entrusted him with was now under threat. He could feel the virus-like energy vibrating beneath his finger tips, squirming inside the body of his wand, attempting to breach the core and drain it of all its secrets. Even Grimtale and Magenta's defences proved ineffective as they cast their disruptive waves, hoping to distract the Count long enough for Robin to break free of his clutches - instead, it enhanced his focus. His piercing yellow eyes narrowed and Robin's heart skipped a beat as the reality of the situation clobbered him firmly against the chest. The Count was powerful, and it was clear that he was capable of taking whatever he so desired. But while the two wands remained connected by the cores, in a moment of madness Robin realised, he may be able to take something too... *The Count would never expect that of him*, he thought, then he closed his eyes and listened closely beyond the snaps of electrical energy, beyond the cry of the Phoenix as it struggled against the magical binds around its body. Then as the door of reality began to close, beyond that was a peaceful balance where his own focus resided, and it was enough to guide him safely to the enemy core, without raising the Counts attention, which was already well spent.

The Core of his wand was like a beating heart, a deep blood red that was shifting with every passing second in an organic motion. As Robin's body seemed frozen in reality, his consciousness roamed free within the dark heart, searching for a means of turning the tides, pulling at every string of curiosity in hope of accidentally flicking an off switch - or so to speak.

Meanwhile the Count held firm, entirely oblivious as he impatiently extracted the defensive charm from Robin's wand, while watching eagerly over his shoulder towards the binding energy around the Phoenix that had began to lose its strength, fading between matter. It was a moment away from escaping, he could feel his grasp loosening as Silverstein's wand made one final effort to breath, reigniting the rope-like energy which suddenly intensified, casting a blinding light in to the eyes of the Morient protectors, buying the Count a crucial moment to integrate the pirated charm with his wand and break the connection, the force of it threw Robin backwards against the dirt.

His vision blurred, and his ears rang with the sound of grinding metal on gravel. As he laid there, everything around him had fallen silent. He was oblivious of how far the energy had propelled him as he quickly attempted to pick himself up, peering towards the Count as the piercing light in the sky once again began to dim. Only this time, it had run its course.

Robin's eyes narrowed from behind the golden helm as he watched the bonds break apart from around the Phoenix's body. It then began a frantic flap of its enormous wings in hope of escape as the Counts attention turned to Silverstein's wand. The white core had finally gone cold, and the light that had once burned at its centre was no longer ignited.

The pale hands holding tight to the carcass gave one final clench, then the body collapsed, shattering in its entirety to ash, which fell sharply beside the Count's feet.

The final remains of what Magenta believed to be the real Leonard Silverstein, the man she had fallen in love with, was gone. And the Count seemed somewhat relieved, no longer suffocating behind the tools and skin of what he considered an insignificant other.

He chuckled to himself as he glanced to the fearful protectors, each battling an inner demon of their own as they stood wearily with their wands directed towards him.

"Go! *Get out of here!*" cried Sachester as she caught sight of the Phoenix suddenly making for the clouds.

The Count's eyes widened, his body turned with his wand raised as he watched its mystical blue stardust fading away behind the dark night sky.

Then Magenta's bombardment continued, followed by Robin's and Grimtale's. A flurry of coloured orbs bolted from their wands and against the Counts back, knocking him forward, face first towards the cliff edge, kicking up a trail of dust in tow as his body came to a halt, his head hanging limp over the vast deep pit that resided below.

Magenta spared a moment for the dirt to settle, taking the first step forward, exchanging nervous glances to the others as she approached the Count.

"Wait there, Sachester," ordered Grimtale, as he followed behind Magenta with Robin at his side.

They took cautious steps forward as their vision remained hindered by the lack of light and clouds of dirt. But there was a defined outline of the Counts body, it was still and lifeless, yet no one believed it to be over just yet, it had been all too easy - unless the Count had underestimated his opposition. Yet they anticipated retaliation, as his body finally began to move.

"Shielz-ignite!"

Robin looked to Grimtale and Magenta who had been silent upon approach. Then suddenly there was a burst of red energy that engulfed the Counts body, transforming the leftover fabric of Silverstein's jacket in to a dark metallic armour which concealed his devilish form, giving him extra protection, similar to Robin's; however, the Count had also acquired a pair of bat-like wings, which rose high over his head as he effortlessly climbed to his feet. His face was also concealed like Robin's, although this newly formed helmet had taken a long, rigid form with tall, sharp ears, opposed to the beak like structure that Robin's possessed.

The armour glistened as moonlight fell upon it. His yellow eyes were now staring back across the cliff, through the tiny gaps in the metal. Then they were gone as he took to the skies, following the direction the Phoenix had already taken, disappearing behind the clouds.

Robin knew that every second was now even more precious than before as he imagined the Phoenix making a desperate flight for freedom, with the Count hot on its tail. He desperately needed a plan. And plans, as he stood amongst his fellow Morient protectors, were few and far between...

CHAPTER 18
The Volcanic Duel

"*What* just happened?" exclaimed Sachester as she and Lillian met with the others,
throwing her arms around Grimtale and holding tight to the battered coat that hung heavy from his shoulders.

"There's no time to re-evaluate. We need to act, and I have a plan - but it's a risk," explained Robin, as all eyes turned to him, stood at the cliff edge.

"I have a hunch - I think the Phoenix will be heading for the Institute, it's the next safest place and its life is under threat. If the Count can't capture it, he's going to kill it."

"*No,*" replied Grimtale, " - he might have blood on his hands, but he'd never take the life of the Phoenix. There's *always* another option with him."

"It will do everything in its power to remain free of the Count's clutches. I'm certain it's going home to the dungeons where I raised it."

Magenta scowled at Robin.

"You *remember* that?"

"*I* don't, but it seemed a good story - and that's

all this will ever be if we fail. A tale of how good was overturned. You four need to return to the Institute and warn the others."

Lillian stepped forward, visibly shaken as she clutched her wand.

"W-what do we say?" Her voice trembled as her thoughts remained tormented by visions of the Count and the devastating power he had left in his wake.

"We warn them of the Counts imminent arrival, and to arm themselves. Deep down they knew this was coming, it will come as no surprise," said Grimtale, resting his weight on his cane as he addressed those around him, " - the Count always wanted a war. We might not be able to give him that, but we can most certainly deny him the simple transaction he expects. Even if it means the permanent closure of the Vinemoore Institute."

"I think education is the last of people's concerns, now," Remarked Robin as he approached Sachester, "I'm gonna need Edmund, and possibly Magenta, I might need the back up. I'll pursue him, I'll buy you some time before side stepping to the Institute," he added, trading confirmation with Magenta as he spoke, knowing her rage would only be wasted elsewhere - at his side, she may find the justice she sought.

Sachester drew a breath then pressed her index fingers against her bottom lip. She blew firmly and suddenly - her piercing whistle echoed about the vastness of the surrounding area, riding the gentle breeze and reaching the barn, where an alert Slitherback suddenly rose its head, stark and tall as it climbed to its cumbersome feet.

"*Danger - danger*," sounded the metallic tones

of Coggo, the copper tin man as he moved between the gates, blocking the pack of Slitherbacks' as they attempted to race to Sachester's aid.

"There will only be fatalities." Coggo added, warning off the creatures which had already began to cower and back away, while watching in the distance as Edmund, already galloping away from the old wooden barn, headed straight for Sachester, at the cliff edge of Shoulders Heath.

* * *

Robin watched towards the horizon, waiting impatiently as Edmund's silhouette suddenly appeared, racing over the frosty mountain that sat between them, galloping through the twilight glow, and on to the frozen path that stooped and climbed before the cliff.

"*There he is*," Robin smiled, beginning to feel a companionship with that one particular Slitherback. He was overjoyed to see him, certain he'd improve their chances of catching the Count, who was already a great distance away, but moving at a slower pace than that of a Slitherback.

"Grimtale, you guys need to go. I'll see you at the Institute."

Robin reached for Grimtale's hand and pulled him in, giving him a firm pat on the back for luck.

"I'll hold you to that," he replied, remaining unusually stern behind his black wiry beard. No one was used to seeing this side to Grimtale. They were all so used to his positive, relaxed temperament. But where *his* fear did nothing for the team's morale, *Robin's* versatile attitude lifted spirits, and revitalised the energy around them to carry on fighting.

Reminded of everything they had to lose, they began their final move, knowing the Institute would be the final battle ground between good and evil, where failure would certainly result in many fatalities to young and old, rich and poor. There was no segregation, not in the eyes of Munder Mortal as he fulfilled the reputation that came with the feared title of *the Count.*

Robin gave Edmund a rub on his snout as he stood at his side, bound to his gaze as he saw no fear in his eye. The creature was selfless. It seemed to have an understanding of the dangers, yet it had still found its way after countless warnings from Coggo. Robin adjusted his helmet then mounted Edmund, reaching down to Magenta with his right hand as he turned back to the many faces that were staring up at him, as he overcame the fear that had sat dormant at the pit of his stomach for far too long. He had already stood eye to eye with the embodiment of evil.

Nothing would stop me now, he repeated to himself, silently. Lowering his shoulders and straightening his neck, the armour wasn't the comfiest but he sure did look the part from Magenta's view as she looked up at Robin.

"Just until we find him, then a little freestyle wouldn't go amiss."

Magenta nodded as she took his hand, climbing on the back of Edmund and holding tight around Robin's stomach.

Grimtale, Sachester and Lillian had already dispersed through a Senteer charm, *they must have been at the Institute already*, Robin thought as he gave Edmund a pat on the neck and braced for launch.

There was one final slither of Edmund's snake-like tongue, then his head bowed and his legs pressed firm against the ground before taking to the cliff edge, the creature carrying the weight of its body and its Morient passengers with ease as it leapt over the bottomless pit below them, before pulling against the laws of gravity, slowly ascending towards the glow of the nights sky and leaving the Morient town of Shoulders Heath to the peace it deserved.

* * *

His speed was sluggish in comparison to the Phoenix, but his raw might carried his armoured body high as he pivoted his blade-like wings and descended back through the thicker clouds, with his eye on the Starlight Phoenix as it manoeuvred between the scattered clouds below him. It took a sudden dive to the left, then moved to the right to avoid the tips of the falling spearheads thrown by the Count in a desperate attempt to damage its wings and slow its momentum.

The skies were still dark and sunrise was far from due as the Count's eyes remained fixated on the turquoise sparkle breaking away from the phoenix's feathers as it hurtled across the heavens, marking a path which only made it more difficult to shake the Count, who was hot on its tail.

After another series of ducking and weaving, Robin and Magenta were already catching, held on tight to Edmund who instead of moving around the clouds, shot straight down the centre, biting at the vapour like a playful puppy as they travelled blind, until re-emerging. They could now make out the faint turquoise sparkle and the flame tipped spearheads that the Count was conjuring from a bottomless quiver on his back - coated in the same dark metal that encased his body.

"There they are! Great work, Edmund!" said Robin, pointing towards the Count as more clouds breezed by.

"Should I jump off yet?" asked Magenta, squinting to make out the dark blur in the distance, she figured it had to be the Count.

"No, hold tight!" replied Robin, slowly making headway as the pursuit pressed on.

Where blurred lines became refined and moonlit armour shimmered, even beyond the heavy snow clouds that were stationary up ahead as Robin glared on like a hawk - one hungry for justice - he was back in reaching distance, but not long enough to deter the Count. The Phoenix performed a barrel roll manoeuvre, before swooping through a torn opening in the fabric of reality that led directly to the human realm. It was similar to a Senteer charm, however this magic was mind induced, by the sheer power that surged through the Phoenix's feathers – making the shift easy. The tear was being held open by a cluster of minuscule orbs that shined as bright as stars, just enough so the Phoenix could fit. The Count followed closely behind, entering the realm before the tear came to an abrupt close, snapping together and shutting off Robin on his approach.

"Did you see that?" cried Magenta, pointing to where the passage had closed.

"It was a Senteer charm, but was it the Count's?" asked Robin as he glanced over his shoulder at Magenta.

"Looked like the Phoenix's to me. It was too precise. But did you see where they went?"

Robin shook his head as he turned back.

"It was the human realm - Shoulders Heath. I saw the Black mountain, they were right overhead."

"Then that's where we need to be!"

Robin pulled out his wand from an armoured sheath around his waist and twisted the vine-like handle, pointing directly ahead of Edmund. Robin closed his eyes and began imagining the shape of the black mountain, while recollecting the land around it as he attempted to open the fissure. Magenta knew she could have done it quicker, but she respected Robin's efforts as they suddenly found themselves amongst the crossfire of Reaper projectiles, landing them in the eye of the storm.

The cliff tops opposite the mountain were overrun with the Count's disciples as they jumped in to a series of Senteer charms that crossed them to the dark surface of the Black mountain. The ones that had already arrived were immediately aware of Robin as he dropped from the Morient world, through to the skies of the Human realm. The Reapers had been waiting for this moment, as the Count had warned, stood higher up the mountain, with the Phoenix back in its magical restraints, pulling against the energy that had once again entangled itself around its feathers.

Robin could hear the cries of the Phoenix as he helped Edmund negotiate his way through the bombardment of incantations that hurtled in their direction.

"I can buy you some time, I'll hold off the Reapers while you deal with the Count," said Magenta as Edmund began to climb the Mountain, averting its path to avoid the projectile threats that were never-ending.

"Just be careful! Use the craters, play a defensive game. If I can free the Phoenix, I'll see you back at the Institute!"

"Be careful, Robin!"

Those were Magenta's parting words as she held firm on Robin's shoulder piece, before leaping off the rear end of Edmund and transforming back to her brightly coloured bird-like form. She rode the winter's spell as it fell towards the mountain surface, peering back as Robin and Edmund disappeared beyond the white haze.

Now the Reapers were climbing towards their master, guided by the turquoise storm that lit the night sky, overhead. The surface of the Black mountain was like charcoal, with cracked channels and craters, large enough to swallow half a dozen people. Some of the debris was partially glazed and reflected the stark blue bolts of lightning as they struck the mountain. Even with the continuous snowfall, the surface was patchy in places, which made life a hell of a lot easier for Magenta as she threw herself against a bare, levelled stretch, using her arms to break her fall as she began to turn back into her humanoid form, before rolling in amongst the gravel that sat at the bottom of the nearest crater.

As she laid on her back, for a moment she felt the mountain vibrating, a few rocks had dislodged themselves and fallen amongst her wild blonde hair as it fanned out, resting between her head and the crater wall. Her eyes widened as she coughed up a few pinkish feathers and spat them at her side.

"You've gotta be kidding me..." she grunted, as she scrambled to her feet and glared towards the height of the mountain with a hand shielding her face. There was another tremor; she could feel it beneath her feet, she could see the tiny stone marbles shifting around her; then a bright wash of light was cast over her face - The Reapers were once again on the move.

Magenta made her way to the crater wall and began to peer over, looking out for the advancing Reapers as their aimless projectiles continued to plummet against the ground, stamping their presence into the surface as more potholes and craters exploded in blinding flashes of light, hoping the hurling fragments of stone would maim or wound their cowering enemies as they made their way towards Magenta, whose striking pink collar stood out like a man riding a Slitherback.

There was nothing less conspicuous as Robin crossed the moonlit crest of the mountain. Then as the snowy haze cleared, the silhouette of the Count appeared on the mountain, no longer dressed in his armoured attire. He was once again back in the war torn, silver jacket that had belonged to Silverstein. His dirty blonde hair was waving in the breeze as he whipped his wand back and forth, electrocuting the Phoenix with powerful bolts of energy, which manifested from his wand as a series of bright red ropes, slicing across the pained creature's face and blinding many of its eyes as it slashed across them.

There was a shriek that filled the skies, then as Robin dived, the Phoenix pulled at the Count, lifting him off his feet and hurling him into the jaws of Edmond, who snapped at the scruff of his neck and launched him as far from the Phoenix as he possibly could. The Count landed hard against a boulder and dropped his wand on impact, which then glowed an evil shade of crimson that stood out like a beacon amongst the glazed charcoal shards beneath it.

The Phoenix - now partially blinded on one side of its face - took back to the skies, in time to pass through a Senteer charm that had been swiftly forged by Robin as he remained mounted on the back of Edmond. The charm closed firmly behind it as it arrived over the Institute, much to the dissatisfaction of the Count as he found his footing and glared with fury, across at the heroic pair, who exchanged a pretentious smirk as the armour that encased him returned to its original state, back to the mustard coloured coat, waistcoat and shirt.

"She's safe now," claimed Robin as he dismounted Edmond and patted down the distressed seams of his frock coat.

"It's a female, now, is it?" questioned the Count, reaching for his wand.

"One would assume. That face of yours has rejection written all over it!"

There was an awkward moment between the two as they slowly approached one another. Both their wands remained at their sides, each with an eager eye - two rivals watching their enemies every move.

"Look, Munder. We didn't come here for trouble. You can go on your way and we can all put this behind us. You live your life, and these humans and Morients alike can live theirs. There needn't be any more hostility... "

The Count frowned, then took a step closer. As the snow fell, a thicker haze filled the air, distorting Robin's vision as he tried to focus on the Count, squinting and brushing aside the ice from his brow.

"In good time you will come to understand that hostility is our only tool for bargaining. For all too long I have been labelled a traitor. If there was justice in this world we live in, I would be understood."

Robin felt uncomfortable, after all, he had never expected such a civil response from the man he had considered his enemy. Many questions swelled at the front of his mind as he met with the menacing yellow eyes of the Count, who had far more hidden truths burning within. He seemed like a monster; acted like one, too. But there was a sense of redemption in his voice as he expressed his fury towards those who sought control over the Phoenix, and the people who inhabited the Morient realms.

"If you think that I'm a monster, then you haven't seen anything yet, my old friend." he added, as the ground beneath his feet began to tremor.

"They want the Phoenix as much as I, don't you see? You've led it back where they need it, precisely where they want it. All I ever wanted was to restore life, life that was taken from *me!*"

"And those you've killed and hurt, don't matter?" remarked Robin "- does that not make you the selfish one? Being destructive because your life turned to shit?"

The Count forced a smile, "I wonder how alike we would find one another if Kirsten or Emily were at the receiving end of a killing curse. What kind of man would *you* then become, Robin?"

The ground shook again as boulders dislodged from the mountain and hurtled by, between the two men as they stood face to face at arms length.

"I'd make those responsible, pay. With their life!" said Robin, aggressively.

"Then we aren't so different..."

"I'd be less obsessive!"

As the Count's face began to soften, a crack appeared beneath them both, pushing apart the crest of the mountain until a subtle orange glow appeared like a sea of veins down beneath the ridge they stood upon. There was another rumble, and vibrations caused the gravel to chatter against their boots as they stood alert to the looming danger.

"If you insist on sheltering the Phoenix... then I must draw our moment of civil exchange to a close."

Robin looked him in the eye one last time, noting the gaunt impressions and burning redness as evil took ahold of him, warping his second hand life force that had been stimulated by the Phoenix's bitten curse. The Count was now an engine of destruction and Robin knew there was only one solution, one with many painful consequences.

The Count drew his wand as his sights sunk deep into Robin like a hawk, immediately conjuring a cluster of destructive energy that Robin managed to turn away, slicing the face of the projectiles with his wand and deflecting the blasts against the ground, which was now amass with debris. As more thundered down the side of the mountain, the ground shook, knocking them off balance as they scrambled back and forth, finding their footing.

"Brexio!" yelled Robin, returning fire towards the Count's feet, knowing the mountain would likely collapse beneath him, but as the charm exploded, more of the mountain came away, wounding the Count, knocking him off his feet, as he tumbled bloody and raw amongst the shattered debris. When his body finally came to a halt, he found himself laid across an abnormally large shell, one of a long deceased arachnid, its remains perfectly positioned to bear witness as the crest of the Black mountain suddenly blew wide open, into the heights of the sky, the explosive burst was followed by a stream of molten lava which came crashing down the sides of the mountain with boulders in tow, rolling and burning across the bright orange rivers as they followed the cracked channels.

The mountain surface had gotten a whole deal brighter as lava exploded from shattered pockets, illuminating the look of shock on Robin's face as he glared towards the skies, where the eruption was spewing from the neck of the mountain, like a collective of severed arteries. Edmund had returned to Robin's side, pressing his head against his arm - the creature was in fear of the frightful surroundings.

"You need to get away from here, boy. Head back to your brothers and sisters, the sky over there is clear..." Robin pointed away from the mountain, but Edmund shook his long, snake-like head, followed by a slithering, in-out motion of his tongue. He didn't want to leave Robin, but he was terrified by the lava erupting from the core of the mountain.

Robin took Edmunds head in his hand and rubbed him gently along his snout, then looked in to his eyes, "You're going to get hurt!" Robin warned, admiring the Slitherback's unfailing, faithful companionship.

Further down the mountain, as glowing hot boulders pounded the ground, so did the bodies of pursuing Reapers as Magenta turned to the killing curse as a final resort.

"*Vanphineer*!" she cried, feeling bitten by the will to survive, spurred on by the rage that burned inside her as she thought of this, the consequence of the Count – a man who had masqueraded as the one she loved. Her words had been as good as bullets as she stumbled and fell, landing sprawled across the mountain surface, avoiding the shots being fired by the Reapers.

"*Vanphineer!*" she cried again, closing her eyes as the stark red energy separated a Reapers head from its body, before falling to the bottom of a nearby crater.

"*Robin!*" she yelled, taking a glance over her shoulder as a stream of lava surged past her face, filling the crater, and incinerating the fallen Reaper body.

Robin turned a searching glance down towards Magenta, following the flow of the lava until his eyes fell upon the approaching Reapers, scrambling over the broken surface of the mountain.

"Get out of there! Get back to the Institute!" yelled Robin, directing her away with an eccentric wave of his arm, *"What are you waiting for?"* he added, before a blinding light shot past his face.

Robin stumbled back, then turned to the Count, who was advancing towards him, again, scowling as he flung another charm in his direction. Robin dropped to the ground to avoid the magical energy, which hurtled over his head and dissolved against a river of lava that was descending down the side of the mountain. The ground was still vibrating and the air littered by glowing ash as lava melted away the plant and wildlife that inhabited the surface.

Pockets of air were exploding as they rose from within the core of the mountain, launching molten particles across the black surface, further panicking Edmond, who suddenly leapt from Robins side and made for the skies, swooping over the Counts disciples on their uphill climb - his shadow drawing the eyes of the Reapers, and gifting Magenta with a window to disappear, while their heads remained turned, watching the long, scaly tail of Edmond as it disappeared behind the rivers of molten fire.

Magenta turned back to Robin, but his attention was entirely fixed on the Count's efforts. Robin was deflecting his every move, biding his time until Magenta had got away - but still she stood, hoping for acknowledgement, as blinding light burst from the ends of their wands as their streams of energy clashed, knocking them off their feet.

"Go now!" Robin yelled, *"Go now!"*

Magenta gasped, then cast the Senteer charm beside her; holding a clear image of the cliff and the Institute at the foreground of her mind. Then before the Reapers had a chance to act, she dived through the opening and closed it behind her, leaving Robin alone with the Count, much to her displeasure as she landed sharply, laid against a field of frozen grass, far away from danger and a short trek from the Institute which peacefully called to her with its colourful stones, glistening under moonlight.

* * *

The lava had cut off the path ahead as the Reapers attempted to climb the mountain. Their sights burned on towards the crest and the fighting silhouettes of the Count and Robin as orange light simmered around them in each desperate attempt to disarm, or highly likely, kill each other, as fumes thickened, filling their lungs. Robin thumped his chest and cleared his throat before returning fire, taking a wild shot with a standard Brexio charm, hoping to throw the Count's focus and buy himself some time to get away - but the Count was quick to the mark and denied his efforts, slicing the ball of turquoise energy in two.
"I'm going to kill you now, Robin!"
He glared towards the luminous yellows of his eyes as they appeared from behind the smoke and falling ash.
Robin was now on the ground, scrambling

backwards to escape the face of death as it emerged ahead, towering over him as the Count came to halt, planting his boots against the mix of brittle bone and charred earth beneath him.

Robin noticed the Count's wand was still at his side as he leaned back on his hands, trying to gain balance.

"You've really got a lot to live up to, Munder. Here I am, living and breathing -"

Robin coughed to clear his lungs, "- if you're to be this master of death, next time, have your wand at the ready…"

The Count drew his wand and directed it towards Robin's head.

"And I wouldn't allow time for any last words, like this. It may invite an easy getaway!" yelled Robin, as he threw a handful of shards in to the eyes of the Count, before rolling back through a Senteer charm in the ground that he had prepared as he spoke, working silently to pull up a magic doorway to salvation.

Robin's body dropped through to the Morient realm, landing firmly against the rocky cliff edge that overlooked the pit, and the tall Institute entrance.

He could hear the Count yelling as he tried to clear his eyes of the gravel, and the dust of bone fragments.

"Edmond!" Robin called, holding his wand high towards the opening in the air, eager to conceal himself and his companion Slitherback - but he was nowhere to be seen.

"Edmond!" He called again, aware of the risk he was provoking as the charm remained open.

"Come on, Edmond. I'm not leaving you!"

Robin muttered, as he watched the floating tear, anticipating the worst, which then suddenly arrived in the form of lava, building against the fringe of both realms. It *hissed,* then seeped through, dropping heavy against the fresh earth like a molten slug.

There was no longer any time in hand. Robin reluctantly began to twist his wand and draw the charm to its close, but as it shrunk, it froze, then began to rip open again, followed closely by the dark silhouette of the Count as he stepped up to the verge and glared down at Robin through the tear, with his wand pulsating red, holding a deadly upper hand.

"*Last words, you say? They may well be the death of you!*" the Count said darkly.

His eyes remained fixed on Robin as the molten waterfall poured at his feet, scorching the bottoms of his rubber soles, before dripping down towards the foot of the pit. Robin quickly backed away, finding a patch of earth to safely stand - his shoes steaming as they cooled.

"*Shielz-ignite!*" commanded Robin, hoping to coat himself within his protective armour; however, his wand was already engaged, fighting to close the bridge to the human world.

"*You're out of your depth, Robin. You never knew when to give in!*" bellowed the Count, sensing victory was near.

The Count prepared to climb down. But as he went to jump, a familiar beacon of hope appeared in the skies, exhaling its resounding war cry. Robin could only look on in awe as Edmond struck the Count, lifting him away and into harm's path, leaving Robin with the spectacle that was the burning ring of fire, and the vastness of the skies as he listened closely to the torturous sound of a dying Slitherback as they were swallowed by the raging fires...

Robin swallowed hard and took a quick breath as Edmond's deafening cry rung sharp in his ears, forcing a tear to run down his cheek as he slowly pivoted his wand, severing the Counts lead, and silencing the voice of his friend.

There was nothing he could do, but no matter how many times he told himself, "*there was no other way*", a heavy weight of grief weighed down his shoulders as he carefully stepped away from the lava, and stood silent.

CHAPTER 19
Cry Of The Phoenix

Morning was creeping on the horizon, yet the skies were still dark and the wind had a bitter chill, which numbed the tips of his ears and fingers as he reached for the tall metal gates and swiftly drew them to their close.

Assuming Magenta was already inside, Robin closed a large padlock around them, which had been hanging from an old hook in the wall. There was also a plaque underneath it, which looked a little worse for wear, having endured many winters. But most importantly, what Robin had noticed as he fastened the lock, the entrance was completely unmanned and its cumbersome doors were both ajar for those coming and going, those helping to construct the defences within the main foyer. Robin looked around at his surroundings as he awkwardly wandered across the threshold, watching the remaining Enforcers hard at work as they lumbered past, carrying wooden cabinets and chest of drawers on their shoulders.

It was not an accustomed sight to anyone who worked there. It brought a deep sadness, and a lump to their throats as they helped to fortify the hall, in hope of thwarting any further confrontations with the Count - who was now undoubtedly on the back foot, yet never to be underestimated.

Even though some had their wands at hand, fashionable tools were still being hammered against nails as Robin carefully stepped past, giving the Enforcer's handy work a once-over, before his eyes began to wander, searching for Magenta - or any friendly face, for that matter.
"Teppi!"
There was no one else by that name, yet it took him a moment to register who it was approaching. He was working beside one of the stone plinths as Robin made haste towards the back of the hall. And only then, as he neared, did Teppi finally click. From behind a sea of grey, the distressed looking frock coat and brown quaffed hair emerged.
"Robin! It's good to see you made it!" said Teppi, climbing to his feet to greet Robin as he rushed over.
"I didn't think I would, for a moment."
Teppi drew Robin into a tight embrace. They held each other with no care in the world what anyone else was thinking, and Robin rested his head for a moment, on the shoulder of his fellow professor.
"Have you seen Sachester?" mumbled Robin, his face still pressed against Teppi's robes.
"She's about the foyer. Why do you ask? Did something happen?" asked Teppi, eagerly.
"I need to speak with her, but I don't know how. I don't even think I can look her in the eye."
"Whatever happened out there, you did all you

could. No one doubts that."

"I should have sent the creature back..."

Teppi held the weight of Robin's guilt, grief and sadness that was still lurched on top of him, anchoring him towards the shiny marble floor. Even though Teppi had never been too fond of the creatures that inhabited the Institute, a shiver ran cold down his spine as he listened to each and every word Robin spoke.

"Those creatures are like children to her. What am I going to say, Teppi?" Robin brushed his hand against his swollen eyes as he took a step back, almost pleading to Teppi for advice.

"I think Sachester would agree that you being alive is a cost worth paying - no matter what the price, Robin."

Robin raised his hand and pointed his finger sharply towards Teppi.

"To trade a life? Those creatures have families! Their lives are in no way less significant than ours. I studied and worked with them for *thirteen* years, I should know. I had them eating pellets from my hand, and comforting students during times of distress -"

Robin's eyes widened, and his chest fluttered as detailed memories came flooding back to the front of his mind. Sharp, significant memories of his time as a Professor, and the smiles that the Slitherback brought to his students, "- no wonder my practises were questionable! But they were safe, no one was stupid enough to pose a threat. If I hadn't been so selfish and just followed the rules, maybe they wouldn't have suffered, yet now, even after all this time, they *still* want to help. Why is it that the ones who want to do good are so often punished?"

Robin frowned as he remained lost in the depth of thought.

"I didn't mean it like that, I just meant -" but before he could finish, he was suddenlly interrupted.

"More people would miss me, but that's not fair, he has a family waiting for him, too. They'll be waiting a very long time..." Robin's lip quivered as he looked to the ground. A single tear drop splashed the marble surface, which reflected his face back at him as he cleared his eyes with the clean side of his hand.

He drew a long, sharp breath, then lifted his head towards the ceiling.

"I'm sorry, Teppi. I don't mean to be a jerk. I just don't respond well to loss, I can't bear to look her in the eye..."

"You hear me now: You were never a selfish man, you are everything *but* that. You said it yourself, Robin. The good are punished, and you saving the institute: It's students, it's all forms of animal and spiritual life; it came with consequence. The real enemy has returned now. When the sun is risen, we can mourn and celebrate the lives we lost, but we have to move forward and appear strong for those who look to us for hope..."

Teppi's eyes began to wander as Robin looked to him for reassurance. Then a cold, nimble hand fell gentle on his neck, and ran across the back of his collar and along his shoulder.

"*It's ok,*" said an understanding voice. Sachester had seemingly heard everything, and was now stood at his side, fighting the urge to turn him around as he stood nervously, glancing at her reflection beneath him.

If the weight he felt was real, and his heart hung as heavy as iron, the ground beneath him would have already fractured, making way for his body to sink, but the psychological weight was something he had felt before. As his memories gradually returned to him, sparking life within his mind, they also unveiled the scars. Reminders of the times he had already survived and lived to tell the story.

Robin took ahold of what courage was left and slowly turned to Sachester, glancing at her dark wavy hair before meeting her gaze.

"Edmond knew the dangers. Slitherback aren't stupid, they're decisive. And even though he must have been distressed, he would have died proud, with a heart enriched with love. And that's one hell of a way to go, wouldn't you say?"

Robin's frown slowly softened.

"If, that was the case, he went proud, so I may be able to find some forgiveness for my guilt, but we shall never know, not really..."

"Don't think I hold you or anyone to blame, Robin. These times we live in, they were never going to be what the Morient realm had hoped for. Loss was always expected, and as Teppi said, we have to make sure we bloody celebrate the lives that were taken as a result of our triumph over the darkness that threatens to cast our love, and passion into shadow!"

In that moment, Robin found the courage to look Sachester in the eye.

"I feel a bit silly," Robin chirped, forcing back a smile, and wiping the back of his hand against the redness around his eyes.

"I wouldn't do that, they're a mess, Robin. Why don't you go have a wash, freshen up," said

Teppi, pulling at Robins arm.

"So I can wine and dine the Count? I think not. Who I need right now is Grimtale, have either of you -"

"Follow me," Sachester interrupted, haven just come from speaking with him - so she led Robin all the way back across the foyer, towards the bellowing voice of the Institute's headmaster as he called out for Professor Yuri.

He was stood amongst the working Enforcers; jacketless, with his shirt sleeves rolled to his elbows, his arm reaching as Yuri moved under his wing from behind a stone archway.

"My friend, I'd like one final check on the stone fragment, just to be sure. We need an optimised acceptance charm to ensure the Count doesn't waltz his way in here," said Grimtale, walking beside Yuri with his bare arm hung over his shoulder.

"I was going to suggest something along those lines. I'll make my way down to the Dungeons, now -"

"On second thoughts," Grimtale interrupted, "Take this strapping young fellow with you."

Robin cracked a smile as he approached, with Sachester at his side.

"It's good to see you, again," said Robin.

"I had no doubt," Grimtale added, as he placed his palm on Robin's shoulder.

"But truthfully, we never imagined getting this far, did we?"

Grimtale gave a subtle shake of his head and glanced at the ground.

"A little improvisation might be necessary. What happens once we defend this Institute, is something I wish for you to decide yourself,

Robin. But right now, I feel your presence is needed by the side of an old friend."

Robin nodded.

"Quite possibly, Professor. In the meantime, while I accompany Yuri, I can only wish you the best. And I hope the defences hold long enough for my return."

"If not, we will die fighting, won't we." Grimtale cast his sights to the chamber doors, "Go now. Take Robin with you, Yuri. Time is fleeting."

"Absolutely, Professor. Come on, my friend," said Yuri as he made his way towards the back of the hall, cutting his way through the sea of enforcer bodies, as they brought more furniture to the barricade structure that was beginning to take shape across the centre of the foyer.

Grimtale watched over the crowds as the heavy chamber doors opened and closed. He then turned to Sachester, who was lost in thought, clutching his arm and staring out at the gloomy looking pit outside the gates.

"His Slitherback didn't make it. He seemed pretty torn up about it," she muttered, still fixated on the view beyond the gates.

"You didn't think he'd care?" asked Grimtale, with surprise in his tone.

"Of course I knew he'd care, at least, I knew the old Robin would. He adored those creatures as if they were his own."

"See, the difference between the Robin we used to know and the one now, is not so clear. But his love now has a much greater meaning to the man who never wanted to settle, yet he has a wife to be, and a daughter he has taken on as his own. It's simply struck a nerve that we didn't realise was there..."

As he explained, his words turned Sachester's fearful expression to one of delight as she wrenched her attention from the cold metal gates to the dark brown iris of her lovers weary eyes.

Under any other circumstances, the gatekeeper and the Headmaster would have never aired their true feelings for one another, however, with the strong scent of uncertainty, a lack of care glistened brightly as Grimtale drew Sachester close, held her firmly at the waist and pulled her body against his own. He seized his moment and sealed it with a long, drawn out kiss. Sachester smiled as she drew back.

"Why don't we just go back to Shoulders Heath, release the herd and fly. Build a cottage where no one can find us..." she fantasised, as she held tight to Grimtale's hand.

"Are you being serious?" he asked, with a look of surprise, "Is that really what you want?"

"A future, no matter how we have to live it out. I know what this place means to you, but Grimtale, we really don't stand much of a chance..."

He glanced towards the golden chamber doors, then back to Sachester.

"Chance..." he muttered to himself.

"Yes, we could all disappear from here. We'd probably stand a far better chance that way!"

"Sachester, Reapers *would* eventually find us, and kill us off one by one when we're at our most vulnerable. Here, we can stand together and potentially put an end to many years of living in fear. Understand, I've lived in this fortress since the day of my promotion, that's a *very* long time!"

Grimtale reached into his trouser pocket, rummaging around before pulling out a coin and a heap of damp tissue paper. He shook the coin clear of tissue and placed it heads up in the palm of his hand.

"Tails - we run through those gates and never come back…"

"That's not what I'm asking! I just meant that we can avoid any more death!"

"For how long… tails, we abandon the Institute, my home. Heads… we stand, we fight, we endure the consequences, together."

As he stood there with his hand outstretched, the work carried on around them. The construction of the barricade was nearing completion and the front doors were being pushed together, shutting out the cold and the darkness.

Sachester nodded as she glanced at the Morient coin which was cast in silver, with the likeness of sovereign Ambrax (Ruler of all the Morient realms) embedded at its centre, and made of ruby.

Grimtale met Sachester's gaze, then proceeded to flip the coin, swiping it from the air as quickly as possible, before it reemerged with one of its two ruby heads facing up towards a pair of eager eyes, and one, not so much. Sachester was totally oblivious to Grimtale's bluff. He had never wanted to use his dirty trick on someone he wholeheartedly adored, but he couldn't always agree, so he had placed his double headed coin against his palm, much to his discomfort.

Sachester looked disappointed for a moment, then her expression changed to one of fear as the cumbersome front doors slammed together, pushed with a heavy hand by two grey coated enforcers.

"It will be okay," Grimtale reassured her, wrapping his heavy arms around her, suppressing fear and trying to ignite a long lost hope in her heart.

* * *

Yuri insisted that they pick up the pace as Robin's curiosity got the better of him.

"Have you seen Magenta? Did she make it back?" asked Robin, as he hurried past the Ruby Phoenix statue which stood alone at the centre of the dull, unlit chamber.

"I haven't seen her. Plenty of grey coats though - no surprise there. Would be nice to think they're here for our protection, but you and I know otherwise."

Robin nodded as he caught up to Yuri, finding his way around Grimtale's golden throne.

"Their entire regiment was slaughtered at the foot of the Black mountain. There were these very odd looking creatures, Grimtale called them Veilers. They didn't like the Enforcers one bit, or perhaps it was just the rotting stench beneath Silverstein's flesh ..."

Yuri turned to Robin as he approached an opening in the wall.

"Yeah I heard about that, he had me fooled, that's for sure. But not everyone, Grimtale had his suspicions, just nothing solid to act upon, good job he kept a close eye on him -" Yuri pulled a torch from the wall, then waved Robin on, "down here..." he said, as he took the first step down, into a tight descending stairwell, with only the light of the flame to guide the way.

Their shoes clapped against the stone slabs as they carefully made their way down, into the underground passages that linked the various cells and storage rooms which were once dungeons during the dark ages.

Robin could feel a slight breeze brushing against his sweaty forehead as he stepped off the stairwell.

"The Reapers won't be down here, will they?" he asked, dubious of further hidden passages.

"No one has ever found the underground entrance, it's still protected by the acceptance charm though. I wouldn't worry," said Yuri, lowering his torch towards the cobbled path.

"Great," Robin muttered, as he pulled his wand from his coat pocket. Its core was pulsating, it was still bright green, moving within the woodwork, flowing like blood.

It cast some extra light on the narrow tunnel walls as Robin and Yuri pressed on, keeping a keen eye out for potential threats, but most importantly, the Starlight Phoenix, which was said to be lurking beneath the Institute. An Enforcer had already spotted it when it arrived, he said it had taken the stairwell and headed straight for the dungeons, but no one was brave enough to follow it, given the fatal curse that its razor sharp beak could carry - the look of the Veilers was far from appealing, so they waited, hoping that someone was brave enough, or stupid enough to attempt bonding with the creature. Thankfully, Robin *was* brave and crazy enough to do so, not to mention he had already done it, if anyone had earned the rights of control over the

Phoenix, it had to be him. The one man that could show it his love and compassion, a life where it needn't flee from those it feared.

But the dungeons were far from friendly. There was a thick, unearthly presence making itself known to them as they advanced down what seemed like an endless tunnel. Robin felt uneasy - it was far too narrow, far too dark and there were strange noises echoing behind him.

"Try and ignore it, Robin," whispered Yuri, " - they mean us no harm"

"*They*? Who are *they*?" muttered Robin anxiously.

"This place is old. You probably can't remember, but some of the most devastating Morient wars took place in and around these grounds, above and below."

Robin hadn't noticed the brittle skulls and bones laid against the sides of the tunnel as they walked by, which was probably for the best, even though he had seen far worse, Yuri knew the parting of their way was approaching, and Robin had to go on alone. With barely any sleep for days, his imagination was understandably in overdrive as the ghostly footsteps faded and the gentle breeze began to whistle around the cross section of the tunnel. Its walls were rounded with many archways, leading away to further rooms and tunnels - one of which was the stone room, where the powerful stone fragment resided - exactly where Professor Yuri was headed. The others were detention cells, and empty armouries that were used in the wars.

"I didn't see the Phoenix, so there's no way of telling where it went..." said Yuri, as he glanced at all the openings, waving his torch in hope of casting some light on the situation; but it was far too dark, and the sound of dripping and the gusts of wind circulating the tunnels made it near impossible to further the search - Robin had no choice but to stand by his instinct.

"You go on... come and find me when you're done, if I don't find you first," said Robin, with a diffused green glow coating the side of his face.

Yuri nodded, then rolled up his shirt sleeves, "It shouldn't take me long - if I were you, I'd try that one, there," he pointed towards the largest opening in the wall, to which Robin proceeded to unveil, waving his wand around the shape of the archway. Stark green light reflected from the wet brickwork as his wand panned across it. Robin glanced over his shoulder, but Yuri had already taken his leave and was heading into the stone room.

The air felt heavier as Robin took his first steps towards the side room. The atmosphere was different as he crossed under the arch of stone, keeping an eager eye out for the Phoenix as he followed the green emissions, pulsating a path of light through what seemed to be the cell block. Made of tough iron, the cells were tall and wide - supposedly built to hold monsters, judging by the bulging metal work and missing bars as Robin carefully walked by, listening closely to the sound of dripping as it became distant, and the gusts of wind less aggressive the further he moved from the entrance.

The Dungeons were a dire sight to behold, left in an awful state of disrepair, it was obvious that no one had crossed the threshold in quite some time, as the cells that were still intact housed the remains of their prisoners - mounds of bones and hair, brushed against the walls to decay. Robin turned away as he passed, looking ahead to the distant glow as gravel crunched beneath his feet.

"Hello? It's me, Robin. You don't have to be scared anymore, I'm here to help..." his eyes glistened an emerald hue as they searched high and low for a trace of the Phoenix, but only the sound of the wind whistling, and the damp wet trickling could be heard. Robin gave a heavy sigh of frustration, it was followed by a whimper, which echoed around the underground. Robin knew for sure he hadn't made that sound, *unless it was Yuri? But it couldn't have been, surely? He was in the stone room...*

"You can come out," Robin reassured the unknown presence, hoping it was the Phoenix and not something worse.

"We're going to need a name for you. I know I wouldn't like it if I was referred to as *Human* everyday. Relatively speaking, that's not even true anymore, I'm a Morient Man, now. Crazy what a day can do..."

As Robin continued to mutter to himself, a turquoise glow began to brighten from beyond the shadows. It shrieked and squawked as a teardrop fell against the ground, dispersing in sparks like a firework. Its tears were brighter than its feathers, they glazed the gravel surface like molten lava, but cyan in colour, and as cold as ice to touch.

Robin couldn't believe his eyes as he managed to shuffle a little closer, desperate to help the Phoenix as it cried out in pain.

"It's ok, *he's* not here."

His hand reached carefully for the wounded

face of the Phoenix Bird as it skulked, growing wary of its surroundings and especially the sinister looking figure which had crept out from behind a locked cell and was now slowly approaching Robin, who was entirely unaware, casting his concerns to the Phoenix.

* * *

The walls shimmered as torchlight flailed past, being carried to the furthest side of the stone room by trembling hands, those hands had played a part in many conflicts - mostly the victories.

None of the granite looking walls were straight, it was like the inside of an egg shell, rounded high and low, encasing the large portion of the violet coloured crystals which were lodged within the surface of the walls. There was no way of telling them apart - the fakes from the genuine article - they looked identical, but Yuri on the other hand took pride in protecting the land - it was his job to uphold the charm that surrounded the Institute, and correctly locate the position of the Stone of Acceptance, which he always counted in from the left, seven steps, and central with his nose.

He raised the torch towards the wall, the stones glimmering under the flame. It was like the stone was speaking back at him as he looked into its core, his eyes alive with the tones of violet that swirled at its centre.

"You're quite happy, aren't you?"

He placed his fingertip on the stone, giving it a

final health check before taking a step away, and glancing at the imitation stones which sat comfortably around the authentic example, replicating its cores fluid motion as it slowly swirled, showing no signs of pain or rejection. They were part of a harmonious rhythm, which helped to calm his nerves as Yuri began to anticipate the fast, rampant movement and chaotic scenes within the Institute as he made his way towards the upper levels; but before he managed to reach the stairwell, the letter *R* began to materialise in front of him. A flame burned the air, leaving a red hot path which resembled letters as it burned across his field of vision.

Yuri was taken back by what it had spelled out, but what confused him most of all were the signed initials of the Institutes Headmaster.

The message had given a clear order: *Release the Stone, disarm all means of defence, leave the institute vulnerable to attack.* What was more worrying was the fact it wasn't a hoax, the signed initials that burned in the tunnel air were definitely his handwriting, there was no doubt about that - the message had come from Professor Grimtale…

CHAPTER 20
My Home Is My Battleground

Her eyes were wide as she peered up at him, her arm aching as his vice-like grip tightened around her fragile wrist. Grimtale had begun to make his way out from behind the barricade as the pit fell in to a further state of darkness. The yellows of his eyes were glaring back at him as he marched towards the open doors to deliver the news.

"The charm will be deactivated in a moment's time," said Grimtale, stood on the edge of the marble foyer floor, with his cane held firmly at his side, ready for any unexpected surprises. "Once entry is granted, the young one goes free, unharmed," he clarified, reaching out to Emily as she pulled away from the Counts clutches, only to be reeled back in by his sharp, pointed fingertips.

"A deal, is a deal, Professor."

Grimtale caught the yellows of his eyes, again, unsure if he was making a grave error, or if he would stay true to his word. Either way, it was now his duty to look after Emily in Robins absence - she was innocent, after all. Caught in the crossfire of Morient greed.

"Once she's safe, I cannot promise easy

passage. We will stand our ground, there may be bloodshed..."

The Count grinned at the thought, "I would encourage it, Professor," he smiled intently, "- however, it would seem you are extremely outnumbered. Perhaps we should try to even out the numbers?"

His yellow eyes returned to those of his own, as they stood with their half hidden faces behind personalised metal.

"You two -" the Count pointed with his spindly index finger, " - give yourself to the cause. Make your way through these grand institute gates..." he ordered, still bound by the remnants of Silverstein's clothing, fluttering with the wind and the stray snowflakes from the wilderness above the pit. The expression on the Reaper's faces suddenly sunk as they anticipated their fate, sights set towards the open foyer entrance where Grimtale looked on, flanked by a handful of Enforcers and fellow Professors.

"Please, sir..." the closest Reaper begged, stepping towards the Count, away from the iron gates. But before he could finish, a piercing red glow struck the Reaper's throat, slicing a channel for his blood to run cold. His body hit the ground, laid lifeless amongst pools of bodily fluids as they soaked in to the soil and snow. The Count's followers watched on, taking a detailed note of what to expect in their master's presence.

There were now at least twenty Reapers stood around the pit, each seemingly loyal and prepared to act when called upon. The second Reaper turned back to the gates and removed her hood. She took a deep breath of the bitter air as her shoulder length hair fluttered across the cold metallic surface of her mask. The Count watched with increased interest as she approached the gates, unaware of whether the protective charm that concealed the Institute was active, or not.

"This is a prime example of what I expect of you *all*. Now, go forth..." the Count waved on his entourage of Reapers, letting go of Emily's hand in the process. She looked lost amongst the blackened cloaks as they pushed her on, knocking in to her and forcing her away from the Count, washing her off on a Reaper tide.

Grimtale was still suspicious, hoping that Yuri had carried out his urgent request accordingly, otherwise, Emily was walking to her death... Even if the charm was no longer active, a battle was about to erupt. He watched nervously as the female Reaper reached for the iron gates and wrapped her hands around their oval bars, before giving them a firm shake. They were still padlocked, but Grimtale knew they could now gain safe entry, they had already stepped beyond the charms perimeter - but *they* didn't know that...

* * *

The stone slid in to his trouser pocket and the wall suddenly looked bare as Yuri took a step away to cast his sights over the shimmering stone room. The socket in the wall which had housed the stone was now nothing more than a placeholder, surrounded by the imitation stones, which continued to mimic the calming lava motion that still circulated within the originals core.

"I can't believe I'm doing this!" muttered Yuri, as he pulled the stone from his pocket one last time. He looked into its enchanting violet hue, knowing while it sunk in his grasp, the Institute was vulnerable to whatever the Count had planned. It made no sense to him, but he proceeded to store the stone inside his pocket, out of harm's way.

The placeholder remained empty, as he glanced back, before making his way to the tunnels, where the sound of light footsteps echoed, and a shadowy figure loomed in the distance, slowly approaching the open cross section...

* * *

Deeper within the dungeons, Robin was oblivious to the second mysterious figure that was edging its way towards him. The Phoenix had mistaken it as a friend, until it pounced at Robin, wrapping an arm around his neck and pulling him back. The Phoenix cowered back in to the shadows as Robin yelped, struggling to hold on to his wand as the assailant forced down on his arm, holding him against his will. He was still alive though, and there didn't seem to be any further aggression - he was just heavily detained.

"If you were here to kill, I'm sure I would be dead already. So you'd best have a good reason for violating my personal space, you coward!"

Robin tensed against the pull of the vigilante. He could feel his breath against his neck as his grip loosened, releasing Robin's wand and arm back to its resting position beside him. The attacker was no longer trying to hide his identity, Robin realised as he began to tilt his head and take a glance over his shoulder. He looked surprised as he pushed himself away, glaring in to the eyes of a seemingly old friend. He was staring back at him with no real sense of remorse, but it was definitely Kenneth Brown, as much as this had come as a shock, Robin could not deny it as he raised his wand to unveil his tired, wrinkled face, and golden framed spectacles.

"They're going to hurt my family, if not worse. I had to come, I had to return," explained Kenneth as he took a step closer, into the gloomy green light that was emitting from the end of Robin's wand.

"I never doubted you, I only wish you had taken my advice and saved the ones you hold dearest. You should have left this town! Now nothing is certain, but I knew it had to return here - to its home."

"And now it has me, because I don't run away when I'm asked, or advised, Kenneth. I like to use a little intuition, and on this occasion I came to the conclusion that a lot of selfish, vile people want to exploit this bird. So I'll make sure I'm stood right *here*," replied Robin, positioned between Kenneth and the Phoenix, which had tucked itself away, behind a veil of shadow and mist, staring out in fear of what the strange man had planned. He was itching to make a move: his hand was clenched around his walking cane, his eyes flickering in envy as the growing bond between Robin and the lonely Phoenix had never been so apparent.

"You - you have to let me by, Robin. You have

to let me take it, as a trade for my families safety..."

Robin frowned and raised his wand to Kenneth's chest, "Have you heard yourself? Everyone is out to capture this poor creature, without any consideration for how it feels!"

Kenneth paused for thought, casting his eyes to the remains of the prisoners that lay wasting in their cells.

"I believe this is the one time were a war is inevitable. Maybe it's not the only way to settle what's been started, but you have to hope that your family will be ok. We can fight them!"

"I just can't, I can't return home with nothing, I can't return empty handed..."

"Then use that brilliant mind of yours! You were head of security, So I'm informed. That's not a job you can take laying down!"

He didn't know if he was getting through to him, but anything was better than nothing. Any means of breaking down his mindset and protecting the Phoenix. He knew that Reapers were violent; they also lacked intelligence, which only encouraged Robin as he tried to muster up a plan. But Kenneth was firmly set in his way, with his family on his mind - it was more than enough fuel to cloud his vision.

"We can go back, together. We can settle this with our heads, and our words! If all else fails, we have our wands."

Robin smiled, nervously, but Kenneth still didn't look keen. He was eyeing up the corner, working out up a way to detain the Phoenix.

"They might already be dead," he muttered, with a vacant expression, "- I have nothing to lose, now..." Kenneth added, as he began to slowly raise his cane to Robin, who stood his ground, prepared to counter. But before there was time for any further action, the sound of shoes came clattering as Magenta and Yuri entered the Dungeon. With no time to spare, from her point of view, as Kenneth aimed his cane at Robin, Magenta snatched her wand from her coat pocket and yelled, "*Vanphineer!*"

The realms most powerful killing spell emerged from Kenneth's chest, glowing red hot, like lava, before his body fell towards the ground, into the arms of Robin, who cushioned his fall and laid him to rest on the damp concrete.

Robin glared at Magenta as he held on to Kenneth's body. The colour had already begun to drain from his skin. His lips were trembling, and his eyes rolling as he tried to speak his final words to Robin.

"*Time - it is running out…*" and that was all he could muster, before his eyes froze, struck still with his last breath. Robin lowered his wand, which was pressed against Kenneth's back as he cradled him, shooting a look of disgust at Magenta, who was still standing under the stone archway with Yuri, watching on, awkwardly.

"I could have convinced him. You didn't need to kill!" aggression sounded in his tone as he spoke.

"Maybe I did, maybe if I hadn't, he would have killed *you*. How about considering that?" argued Magenta, unable to believe what she was hearing as she retained her distance. Robin fell silent as he turned his concerns to the Phoenix, calling it out from behind the rubble..

"If I were in your shoes, I'd consider how you might explain that you took the life of Kenneth

Brown, and how his children will now have to grow up without a father. Unless, they *are* actually dead, then I suppose this has no consequence - to you, anyway!" said Robin, as he pulled open his coat pocket and began to coax the Phoenix out of the shadows, with nothing but his charming smile and the familiar scent he hoped the creature would associate with trust.

Magenta was looking down at the body as she felt Yuri place his hand on her shoulder.

"I would have done the same," he whispered, knowing how awful Magenta had to be feeling, "- If we survive, I will deal with the body, and his family."

"You care too much for others, Yuri. They wouldn't do the same for you…" said Robin, glancing back over his shoulder towards Yuri.

"The difference between you and I, Robin, is that I do not expect anything in return."

"Who even said that's how I roll? It's just a little thought that counts," Robin muttered as the Phoenix finally began to shake away its feathers and shrink to the size of his coat pocket, before hopping inside. "Care a lot, live a little. That's who I am," he added, as he climbed to his feet and forced his way past, brushing arms with Magenta and Yuri's scruffy shirt sleeve.

"The old Robin may have been a bit of a dick, perhaps I'm starting to see why."

Magenta frowned and picked up her pace as she followed behind.

"Because I tried to help you? Because I saw a man threatening your life?" she yelled, calling back Robins attention.

"A man you despised," he concluded before

disappearing behind the darkness of the Dungeon tunnels.

"Let him go. It's not worth wasting your breath on," advised Yuri.

Magenta spoke again as anger blazed in her eyes.

"No, because if it was anyone else, he would have taken the shot!" she glanced at Robin, "Kenneth was ready, he would have done it, that made him your enemy, and you were going to do nothing but try entice him with your godly words of wisdom, after a day living in a world that's completely alien to you. Here's a reality check, Robin: *Words don't win these wars, and I'm pretty sure they don't back in your adopted land, either!*"

Magenta was red in the face as she took a breath, watching as Robin remained quiet, thinking back to when he was held up by the christmas eve thug. A solid punch to the jaw had ended that altercation...

It was strange, it didn't make any sense to either of the two as they tried to work out why Robin was happier to let Kenneth dictate the future of his life when *he* also had a family of his own. What was clear though, was the fact that he fully intended on ending what he had potentially started all those years ago. Putting an end to all the Morient wars and banishing the Count, even if it meant killing him, an act he was blatantly opposed to perform.

"I'm sorry."

"For what?"

"For being the guy who landed us in this mess. I appreciate what you did, I struggle with consequence - always have."

Magenta knew what he meant, she'd be lying to herself if she couldn't grasp why he was upset, "We all struggle with what comes after, it's just a part of life."

Robin looked to his feet as he climbed the stone stairwell, trying to remind himself of the life he had led in recent years. The happiness he had discovered within himself as he remembered who was waiting for him back home - for all he knew.

"Robin, I was ordered to disarm the protective charm, I'm just warning you now, it could be hell up there," warned Yuri, following closely behind Magenta.

"Why would we need to lower the shield?" asked Robin, glancing back at Yuri as they climbed the stone steps.

"That's what worries me…" Yuri put on a brave face as they neared the top, ascending in to the orange light that had begun to fill the throne room.

* * *

The rusty padlock had already been shattered, and the gates yawned wide open as Reapers advanced across the foyer entrance. Grimtale had lost sight of Emily as he pulled back to find himself some cover behind the barricade.

"*Hand over the child, first!*" he yelled, peering by a mass of chairs and desks, which had been bonded together with a glass-like cement.

"They're not listening!" claimed Sachester, crouched amongst a group of Enforcers.

"She was tangled near the front. If we force

back the front row, we can pull her to safety." Grimtale looked high to the foyer ceiling and winked discreetly. Arlie was hiding with a polishing rag pulled over his head, he knew what Grimtale was suggesting as he took his hands away from his eyes and pulled along the extremely tall ladders, nodding to confirm, sending his spring loaded headband in to a frenzy, as the yellow smiley faces swayed back and forth.

"When you say *force* back, by what means, professor?" asked Teppi Lint, with an anxious Lillian at his side.

"By *any* means, my friend. This school is closed, we're now defending our home."

Teppi nodded, then turned to Lillian, "I'm not going anywhere, before you ask."

"I really don't desire our chances. You can't stay."

"Well, I do," said Lillian, darting to her feet.

"I thought you weren't leaving?" said Teppi, looking confused.

"I'm not, I'm going to warn Robin and Yuri."

"You can't mention his daughter, you must trust me, I can save her," claimed Grimtale, certain it was for the best that Robin was unaware of the dangers posed on his daughter, Emily, when his focus was most important for what would come next.

Lillian agreed, then began to run towards the chamber doors, slipping by and making haste for the Dungeon stairwell. She couldn't resist a quick glance up at the beautiful snow filled sky as she passed under the domed ceiling, and by the Ruby statue that had begun to glisten again in the wake of the sun. If this was the start of another war, nature wasn't so disenchanted by the odds.

"Robin!" she called as she caught him climbing to the chamber floor.

"Lillian, what happened?"

"Why did Grimtale order me to remove the stone?" Yuri interrupted, with a question of urgency.

"I'm not sure what to say… The Count arrived with a bigger problem than we had anticipated. We had to grant him entry - you'll understand!"

Lillian wasn't ready to answer their questions, so to buy Grimtale time, she cleverly avoided the reason and harassed them for information concerning the Phoenix, which was comfortably resting inside Robin's coat pocket.

"This is not ideal, to say the least. We must help, we should get moving!" exclaimed Yuri, seemingly panicked.

"Don't worry, I do have a plan, but I need to get to the Count, I need to speak to him," explained Robin, addressing the group as they stood huddled around the golden thrones.

"You must be joking, right?" Magenta glared at Robin.

She understood he was just getting up to speed, but there was no way of delaying the war by a bit of chin wagging. The Count was here for blood, and no mere words would stand in his way, *"- even yours,"* she muttered to herself.

"I just have a proposition, okay? Something the Count might be willing to agree to. Anything is worth considering, otherwise there will be needless death."

"What makes you think he'll listen? He's past that, now," said Magenta, as Robin rubbed his hand against the stubble on his chin, trying to recall the unexpected conversation that he had shared with the Count on the Black mountain, during its eruption.

"I think he'll listen, because besides the pain he's inflicted on people, he's after something. Not just the Phoenix, but something deeper."

Lillian and Yuri looked to Robin with interest as Magenta turned away, hesitant to forgive, with her heart still in pieces by his doing.

"I know you're hurting, Magenta. But there's always another side to the story. A reason, a moment that twisted his soul, and maybe, that's our means of turning this around."

Magenta shook her head, "I'll kill him, that's all I have to offer."

She stormed past, brushing by Robin the same way he had done in the Dungeon.

"You have to understand, she was head over heels for that man," said Lillian, looking up at Robin, "- disguised as a dead man, impressioning the idea of hope."

"Silverstein might still be alive… can't either of you see the good he may have done while fighting problems of his own? I need to find out his true intentions, The Count isn't evil. I'll prove it!" Robin swept back his hair with his hand and made his way past the thrones, drawing his wand and anticipating the scenes outside the chamber doors as falling debris began to rain down, smashing against the foyer floor.

CHAPTER 21
Devil Undone

The Enforcers had engaged with the advancing Reapers. From behind the barricade, a flurry of spells were flung like mortar shells, sweeping the front line off their feet as the marble floor exploded beneath them, burying them in debris and clearing a path for a frightened Emily who stood paralysed with fear, her small hands pressed against her ears.

Grimtale placed his hand on the side of Sachesters face and met her gaze. Remembering the first time he fell in love with her, he rose to his feet from a crouching position and pushed his way by the barricade at the very last moment before emerging into the path of the second wave of Reapers. The grey coats followed his lead, now down to ten men, they felt they had nothing to lose as they began to engage.

"Cover me!" ordered Grimtale, before making a dash to Emily, while watching in the distance as the Count casually walked over the threshold with his hands bare, witnessing the conflict like sport.

"Emily! It's going to be ok, your father is here!"

She suddenly perked up and removed her hands

from her face as they stood surrounded by amplified dangers.

"Where is he?" she asked with desperation.

"He's on his way, but I need you to be brave, now. You need to follow me…"

"I can't, I'm too scared!" she cried, glaring up at Grimtale as he deflected an attempt on his life, shattering a projectile with the blade-like edge of his wand.

The Enforcers were fully engaged in combat around them - and they were outnumbered by Reapers.

"Can I carry you?" asked Grimtale, which was immediately met with a gentle nod from Emily, who was eager to get away from the fighting.

"Great! Now hold on!" he added as he swept Emily off her feet and protectively cradled her as they made their way over to Arlie's ladder.

"Do you think you can climb it? It's safe up there, my little friend is hiding, he will take good care of you."

Emily looked unsure, but she grappled on to the ladder with no hesitation and began to climb, telling herself to be brave. Grimtale gave a sigh of relief then smiled as he watched her climb to a safe distance, before turning back to the chaos.

"This is my home, *our* home," he muttered as he caught sight of the Count again, taking delight in every stride as he stepped over the injured and deceased.

"Emily!"

Robin had never moved so fast in all his life as he spotted Emily climbing the extremely tall ladder.

"What's my daughter doing here?"

Sachester had already leapt at Robin, to hold him back as he forced his way towards his daughter.

"She's safe, Robin!"

But nothing could shake the fact his family were now part of the mind bending turn of events. His family were threatened, much like Kenneth's, and it only brought on further worry, which Grimtale had feared would happen as he asked the inevitable question, "Where's Kirsten?"

"He only had Emily with him," Sachester replied as Robin's face turned sour, and his cheeks flushed a bright red, glaring at the Count from behind the barricade.

"*He* - threatened *my* daughter?" he said, suppressing his anger.

"Removing the stone was Grimtale's only option," Sachester explained as Robin stood in the wake of his own fury.

"Still think he needs help?" said Magenta sarcastically, finally with a sense of being level headed.

"He will," Robin replied, as he looked away for a moment to wave to Emily, who had just reached the top of the ladder and was beaming from ear to ear, peering down at her father.

"I'll look after her," mouthed Arlie to Robin as he stepped out from behind one of the golden animal statues, much to Emily's surprise. She wasn't accustomed to seeing an Imp, but she wasn't scared, she just couldn't take her eyes off of him.

"I'm Arlie," he smiled, then reached for his headband and gave one of the springs a flick, which Emily found hilarious, then proceeded to reach for the swaying yellow faces - instantly amused.

Robin was still infuriated, he hadn't taken his eyes off of the Count as he stood at the centre of the Institute foyer.

"Let me take him out, I can do it!" pleaded Magenta, looking into Robin's eyes, "- *Please!*"

He shook his head, "He's enjoying this. Just look at him."

While Enforcers struck the barricade and Reapers bled out on the broken marble, the Count remained unarmed and bemused, staring into the soul-less corpses of his own. Life no longer mattered to him, not even those who had pledged themselves to finding the Phoenix. The female Reaper's body was nothing greater than an annoyance, now, as he passed by her sunken eyes as she laid lifeless against the ground. The Reapers heavily outweighed the Morient Professors and their Enforcer reinforcements, but they were far from outclassed.

"Are we done?" asked the Count, addressing the entire hall.

Silence fell, along with one more Reaper body that clattered to the ground face first.

"We will defend this Institution. The line is drawn," said Grimtale as he stumbled back towards Sachester, who was there to catch his fall.

"I'm not here for your precious facilities, Headmaster."

"We will also protect the Phoenix with our dying breath!" Grimtale added, as he caught a sight of Robin, stepping out from behind a pillar and into the open space to come face to face with the Count.

"I'll be honest, I'm disappointed. I didn't want to have to kill everyone, but if that is the only solution… I can live with that."

"You're lucky, because not many could," Robin added, "- you know, I must have been deluded to think there was any good in you. But the moment you threatened my family, I couldn't care less who you are, or what heart breaking story haunts your dreams - *if* you even sleep at night with a conscience as heavy as yours."

The Count's poisonous yellow eyes began to follow Robin as he paced, checking for any injured amongst the men and women on the ground.

"You've lost something, or someone, correct?" Robin asked, as he waited for a response he knew would never come, "- it's no surprise that love can drive mankind to such levels, it's a powerful thing. It's eternal in every one of us. I wanted to help you, Munder. But you had to threaten the life of my daughter, you had to carry on killing."

But Robin's point made no difference to the Reapers that were left standing at the Count's side, they had other interests, like the whereabouts of the Phoenix, which one of them asked, hinting that Robin may already have it.

"I might have," Robin replied, sensing everybody's eyes on him – everyone who was left. There only stood one Enforcer, the other nine had perished protecting Robin's daughter and holding back the Count's advances. There was only one way to keep alive the people he had grown to care about, and that was to gamble. *Protect the Institute at the cost of the Phoenix, or lose everything.*

"Convince me, Munder. What will you do with

the Phoenix?"

The Count's expression softened as it almost seemed like his true intentions were resurrected. Robin could sense the innocence reflecting back at him, but those eyes were not to be trusted, he knew that, but as the Count tried to cast away the anguish that had pulled what felt like a lifetime of shadow over him, there was a ray of light that lifted the darkness. His cursed yellow eyes shimmered, then an emerald green began to glow as the yellow faded. Empowered by hope, he remembered the shape of her face, that perfect face, he painted clearly in his mind; her eyes, her lips and then nothing. She was gone, and it never got easier, like the day it happened, his heart shattered all over again - what was left of it.

The Count looked startled as his awareness returned - everyone was staring at him, as if they had witnessed an unravelling of his soul. But for them, only a few seconds had passed. The same hatred filled eyes were glued to him and his followers as they stood blank faced, expecting a reply to Robin's question, however, what Robin wanted to hear and what the Count wanted to say did not materialise, instead, the Count raised his wand from under his tatty, silvery linen and pointed it towards Robin's chest.

"I'll forcefully reclaim my power, and with the Phoenix under my control, I will kill every last one of you, before taking the head of Sovereign Ambrax and his insufferable guard!"

Magenta took a step forward, opposing the six Reapers that stood amongst the fallen rubble and wooden fragments of the late barricade.

"No! You're lying…" said Robin, as if he knew more, "- I've read my notes, I read everything that I left myself. You *know* the final gift of a Phoenix is life, which is why you wouldn't kill it!"

Robin turned to Grimtale, then to Sachester who had stepped out from behind cover, feeling less threatened as Robin continued to explain.

"Its bite is fatal, its bond is powerful. It grows an eye to watch over you, for times when you are not at its side. I don't know how, but the gift of life is supposed to manifest before it's reborn from its ashes."

The Count looked uncomfortable again as he felt his image crumbling. The face he had painted was coming unstuck as Robin tactfully scattered ideas across the foyer.

"The damage is already done. Nothing can change how any of us feel," said Grimtale - much to Robin's surprise, who showed his concern with a simple glare. Grimtale wasn't entirely up to speed with what Robin was conducting, but it had seemed to have worked.

The Count was embarrassed and furious, and all he could see was red as he yelled at Robin, conjuring the deadly spell that struck down the mortal with instant effect.

Robins heart trembled as he turned his head. It felt like time had slowed to almost a halt as he saw at the corner of his eye, what he had always expected. The Counts wand continued to glow red, but it had disobeyed his command.

"*Vanphineer!*" he cried again, tilting his head to inspect his wand as it continued to fail him.

This was the moment that Robin had been waiting for. The Count had initiated what was meant to be the final blow, the move on his life.

Now, nothing could hold him back as he flourished his wand and sent a bolt of powerful green energy down the centre of the Count's wand, shattering its fiery core and rendering it even more useless than before.

The wand exploded in his hand as the spell followed through, leaving shards of the handle lodged in his palm as it dispersed in the air. The black remnants of the wand began to litter the ground and Robin smirked, having anticipated these events unfolding, ever since the first encounter on the cliff of Shoulders Heath. He never anticipated it feeling *that* good though.

"That wand was never going to kill again. I thought you might had known, but I guess it goes to show, your reputation is inaccurate. You're just a fear monger, who occasionally likes getting blood on your hands to maintain your image, when really, you just want her back!"

"How did you -"

"The same way you hacked mine. When our wands connected, I took a little wander inside your core, pulled a few random plugs. But it wasn't till just then I realised that I've been drip fed memories and thoughts. Like our minds and wands were one. I couldn't have tethered the connection. I don't know how, but maybe, it's just a perk of being a little bit human."

"Go, Daddy!" shouted Emily, which brought smiles to everyone's faces. All, except the Count, who seemed to be backing away. His hand was trembling: his dirty blonde hair was covering his face, and his eyes were burning with defeat.

But before he could get far, Magenta appeared by Robins side, watching him cower and stumble. There was no greater satisfaction, she thought as she indulged at the sight, choosing how she would follow up on Robin's unsightly move.

She gave him a moment, still enjoying events unfold, then whipped her wand from right to left, like a lasso. A powerful pink energy erupted from her wands core and hurtled across the foyer, connecting with the side of the Count's jaw as it swept by his face.

There was a shriek of pain as the Count turned back to Magenta. Flesh was gaping open along his cheek, and his jaw was barely attached as a river of crimson poured down on to the marble from the hole in his face, filling the cracked channels beneath his feet.

The remaining Reapers took a hold of him and shielded him as they pulled him clear of further spells being flung across the foyer.

"Don't let him escape!" she yelled, launching another which severed the Counts right index finger from his hand. He yelled, and gargled, now completely incapable of speech. He was heaved away, dragged through a one way Senteer charm that was torn open by one of his associates. Once they were through, the charm closed rapidly behind them, leaving four Reapers to the mercy of the Institute - prisoners of war, with their arms held high towards the ceiling.

Their wands were placed on the ground and collected by Grimtale, who proceeded to tuck them in to his inner breast pocket.

"Professor Yuri, Lint and Vargov. These four are to be taken to the Dungeons to await sentencing by the Ruby Citadel."

The Reapers hair fell from behind their masks as they were carefully removed by the Professors.

Their heads had dropped considerably, and the prospect of them paying for their crimes was all too real as they were escorted away. While most were dead, one Enforcer remained able and made his way over to Grimtale.

"Don't forget to reinstate the stone, Yuri."

There was a short acknowledgement, then Grimtale lowered himself against a mound of stone, taking a well earned rest from the chaos that had now begun to settle. He could have laid back and drifted off without any care in the world who was stood over him.

"The Minister will have to be informed that the Institute is now back under the protection of the stone, and that the menace has been overcome." explained the Enforcer, stood in his battered grey coat, glaring down on Grimtale.

"But it's not, not yet, soldier," replied Grimtale, "- you're going to have to inform the Minister that it is still unsafe to step foot inside here."

The Enforcer frowned, then looked to the others who were stood around him, including Robin, pressing the tip of his wand against the young man's chest.

"We don't have much time, so if you will…"

The Enforcer looked alarmed as he carefully took out his wand from his pocket and began to draw out the message in the air, similar to the message that Yuri had received in the stone room. He proceeded to construct the sentence, waving his wand, spelling out the message to the effect that the Institute was still a war zone, and that it was unsafe at this time. While the Enforcer finished and signed off his communication with the Minister, Emily had begun to climb down the ladder with Arlie.

The bodies didn't seem to distract her as she hit the ground, which was quite worrying for Robin as he made his way over to his daughter with wide, open arms.

"You're a very brave girl, you know that?"

Emily nodded, but she looked worried, and so did Arlie for that matter, standing side by side.

"Mr Occamy, Emily shared with me some important information," said Arlie, clenching his hands together and stepping forward.

"What is it? Is something wrong?" Robin panicked.

"It's Vinemoore. The Count is attacking both human and Morient homes. It's how he found Emily, and your partner, Kirsten."

"Is Mummy ok, Emily? Do they need help?"

Robin took out his wand and held Emily's chin as he raised her innocent gaze.

"I think Mummy is hurting," she whispered, as worry grew in Robin's face.

His hands had started to shake from all the anger and frustration - it didn't help that everyone was overly tired by this time, haven been on their feet all through the night and early hours of the morning.

"You were right, Magenta…" glancing over his shoulder to where she was stood, "- I should have…" he paused, then stood up to look her in the eye, "- would you come with me?"

Magenta remained silent with a blank expression, but she came across to stand beside Robin as he turned back to Arlie and his daughter.

"Arlie, please just keep an eye on my daughter."

"You needn't ask, sir. Arlie is already Emily's friend," he smiled, flicking the springs on his headband, which he knew would get a giggle from the young girl. Robin also chuckled, then blew Emily a farewell kiss as he moved to the opposite side of the battle scarred foyer, to join Grimtale, who was finalising with the lone Enforcer, exactly what he expected of him.

"If you're done, please do send it."

The Enforcer reluctantly waved his wand and the message dissolved. There was no real way of telling if it had arrived with the Minister of Defence, only time would tell if he would prove to be a trusted informant, but until then, it wasn't safe.

Grimtale knew the risk the Enforcer posed, so as he looked away to the approaching Robin and Magenta, he threw a right hook, knocking the Enforcer to the ground, unconscious.

"He went down easier than expected. Young lads these days - posers, the lot of them."

Robin was shocked to see Grimtale throwing punches, but he understood why it had to be done. Grimtale knelt beside the unconscious body and began to filter his memory, wiping the past few hours so he wouldn't have anything further to report back when called upon to do so. The bruising on his brow would only add to the story when Grimtale was asked to recall the turn of events. *It was simple really, he was in the wrong place at the wrong time.* He couldn't argue, afterall, he had no memory of it.

"Professor Grimtale, I need to go home. Emily told us some worrying news. The town is under threat, Kirsten might be hurt."

Grimtale froze from shock, then forced his head around to look into Robin's eyes, "Go now, waste no time, my friend!"

Robin nodded, he then pulled his collar high around his neck and began to cross the foyer, climbing the rubble back to Emily.

"Robin. Make sure you return, because the Minister will want that Phoenix. We have to make sure it never happens, okay? I can help with the next steps, just get your family back."

Robin tensed as he raised his hand to Grimtale, who then turned back to the unconscious Enforcer. Memory wipes weren't so simple, they took time - time they may or may not have. But there was still no sign of the Minister, or any reinforcements, which had to be a positive, to ensure Robin and the Phoenix's safety.

Emily would always smile when she saw Robin, even though they were not blood related, she knew no different, he was her father, her Daddy. She made him proud, growing up with an unwell Mother and a Father who worked long days. She deserved better, in Robin's eyes.

"I love you, Em. I'm now going to get Mummy."

"Ok, please don't be long," she replied, holding on to Arlie's spindly hand.

"I'll try not to be," he smiled, climbing back to his feet with Magenta waiting patiently beside him.

"You definitely up for this? You don't have to come, I'm just a little worried, It's okay to be scared."

"Oh, shut up!" Magenta remarked, swiftly opening a Senteer charm and pulling Robin by his larger than average, ear. "Be good!" he added, waving as he disappeared through the charm and reappeared on the streets of Vinemoore.

He was home now, he realised instantly as he held his collar across his mouth. The air was far colder here, and the snow that had fallen overnight was no longer fluffy, instead it had turned to solid ice, set along the window ledges like slugs.

Both of them knew that something wasn't right; the town was silent - they expected chaos, but it was eerily quiet as they peered down the alley ways, looking out for those in need of help.

CHAPTER 22
Family

There were no Reapers in sight as they stood on the slippery sidewalk. Robin didn't like it one bit. It made his stomach churn as he discreetly peered up towards the hillside to his family cottage. It seemed to look the way he left it, at least that's how it seemed, but Magenta wasn't so sure.

"Is this a trap? Do you feel like we're wandering in to something here?"

Magenta kept her eyes peeled, panning the street as they crept along, fighting to retain their balance.

"I hope the Count has learnt…" but before Robin could finish what he was saying, a front door creaked open, nearby. They scrambled into the closest alley and pressed their bodies against the wall. Hidden by shadow, they listened closely as leather boots crunched against the ice at the side of the doorframe. A cloaked figure scoured the street high and low, then proceeded back inside - the house belonged to Kenneth Brown. It was the family home they were looking for.

"The Reapers *are* here…" Robin glanced around the corner, "Kenneth was telling the truth, that was his front door. They'll have his family, and I need to get home to mine."

Magenta looked down at the ground, reaching for Robins hand.

"We can come back for the Browns."

Robin agreed, but he wasn't quick to respond. He didn't like the fact he was being selfish, but there was nothing more he wanted than to be reunited with Kirsten and Mrs Jillings, who were far more important to him.

"I can meet you on the hill," said Robin, expecting Magenta to take her animal form, but she didn't want to leave him - especially surrounded by Reapers that were hiding away behind the village walls.

"I'm staying on the ground with you," she informed him.

Robin didn't argue, instead, he smiled, knowing there was no time to waste trying to convince her he would be okay. They both glanced back around the wall.

"Why is it so quiet?" he muttered under his breath, carefully stepping out in to the open.

Magenta followed, watching the doors and windows for movement.

The sound of the wind was whistling between the alleys, distorting the sound of their boots as they crunched on the ice.

"We'll go under," Robin pointed to the window where the Reaper group stood watching. They had their backs turned, but they were still too strong for just the two of them, Robin assumed, as he peered through the glass before leaping past the door that had been left ajar.

"There's at least four of them in there. I wonder why they're hanging around?"

"Maybe we're still playing the Count's game? Maybe he expects us to be here, I mean, they're the perfect bait. I'd do the same in his shoes," Robin agreed

As he stood hunched against the wall, he began to wonder just how bad the Count's injuries were. It wasn't the prettiest sight, but even in his defeat, he was still dictating the turn of events in the town...

"I think they've targeted Morient families. Look here," he pointed, observing a man across the street as he pulled apart his curtains, "- they don't have a clue. And what's so strange about people in long dark robes?"

Magenta watched the man in the window as he smiled and waved, recognising Robin - the local pharmacist.

"This pink coat seems to be attracting more attention…"

"And you thought it wouldn't?" Robin sniggered, "- come on, watch the windows, most seem to be drawn."

"That's because it's dawn."

Robin looked back, curiously.

"What? You think I didn't notice?" he remarked, glancing at his watch, which pointed to the seventh hour.

The sun had risen, but clouds kept rolling in as their journey to the cottage unfolded. The first stop was the market: then the stone staircase that led to the upper streets, and finally the stretch that Robin took each day on his travels to work. They could see the cottage far clearer now.

The windows glowed orange from candle light flickering on the walls. But on the hillside, something - or *someone,* curiously stood, watching over the land, observing the collection of humanoid bodies - all of which were still and silent as ghosts.

"Who is that? Do you recognise them?" asked Magenta, as they arrived at the bottom of the hill.

"Probably a Reaper," Robin replied, climbing the icy paving stones with urgency.

As he got closer, the Phoenix was growing more and more agitated, flapping around inside his pocket as he neared the figure.

"Hey, it's ok, you're safe in there…" whispered Robin, lifting the flap of his pocket to inspect the Phoenix. It was staring back at him with its beady black eyes, each curious as it sensed the presence of great darkness. Robin glared at the figure, which was stood in the same black robes that the Reapers wore. As they got a little closer, both Robin and Magenta were relieved when the bodies on the ground were blatantly *not* who they had feared - they were also Reapers.

Their wands were freshly simmering with the residue magic that had torn them from their owner's hands. Robin had noticed that the mysterious figure's wand was at their side. All but their eyes were still, focussed on the bodies beneath them, watching for any rising chests, any sign of life, or any means to warrant further aggression.

Robin turned to Magenta, "Are you also adding two and two, and getting four?"

"I'm getting three," she muttered, looking at the bodies sprawled across the snowy hilltop.

"I thought as much," said Robin, cautiously stepping closer to the robed figure, yet, still completely unarmed.

"Good morning…"

"*Good morning?*" Magenta sighed, which was met with a shrug of the shoulders as Robin took another careful step closer.

"We owe you our gratitude. I assume you handled these - these…"

"*Monsters.*" the figure added, lowering her hood to reveal her long blonde hair and soft, fair skinned face.

"Wait a second, I know you…"

Magenta looked surprised, eager to discover how he had recognised her.

"I saw you before, you were having a difficult time with your comrades, here."

The woman looked at Robin as if she had been reunited with a very old friend. Her eyes glistened like stones of sapphire, and her hair was bound in curls, much like Magenta's, but far more wild.

"You wore their mask, the mask of the Reapers. But I don't understand what brings you here. This is my home," Robin explained, as if he thought she didn't know.

"My name is Sapphire, I…" her eyes fell in to Magenta's gaze as she looked away, then reverting back to Robin, she stuttered, "- I owe you a debt. I couldn't let them carry out their orders, I did what I could, but it wasn't enough."

Robin's attention suddenly fell astray, to his family who were still inside the cottage.

"I'm sorry -" but before she could finish what she was going to say, Robin had already pushed past.

"Keep an eye on her, Magenta. She might be able to help with the other Reapers. Then she can answer to a higher power. The ruby guy, or whoever it is who deals with criminals."

Sapphire looked fearful, watching Robin run across his front yard, towards the heavy wooden door of his home.

"I doubt you'll remember me, but I know who you are. Don't you even *think* about telling him," Magenta warned, drawing her wand from her coat.

"He's better off without me."

"Too right, he is!" claimed Magenta, trying to make sense of it all, "Come, help me. There's a family being held against their will. If you help me, you'll be free to go. You'd be wasted imprisoned inside the Ruby Citadel."

Sapphire breathed a sigh of relief.

"How - how many are there?" she asked.

Magenta held up four fingers, "no more than four - maybe five?"

"Then let's take them," chirped Sapphire, stepping beside Magenta like equals. But there was something else urgently burning away - a question that was most important.

"The Human, his fiancée - is she ok?" Magenta asked, as cold blue eyes fell upon the cottage door, looking on with uncertainty.

"She might be, now," said Sapphire with welcomed optimism in her tone.

"Come along, before the Enforcers begin their clean up."

Magenta let the cottage out of her sights and lead the way back down the hillside, headed back to the high street, with Robin in her best interests as she hoped he would be ok.

* * *

The floorboards *creaked* and *groaned* as Robin stepped foot inside his home. The passage was dark, and the furniture was barely held together. Wallpaper was torn and there was a slipper loosely perched on the foot of Mrs Jillings. Robin's weary eyes had widened as he leapt down the passage, pushing aside broken panels from under the stairs.

Mrs Jillings was laid across the kitchen floor. Her head had taken a fatal knock as she fell. And her wrists had been bound, Robin concluded as he carefully examined her.

"Mrs J, can you hear me?" he panicked as he tried to find a pulse. But there was nothing he could do for her, no matter how much he wanted to, she was beyond help. Her skin was cold to touch, and her fragile bones were broken. The result of Monsters that had found themselves part of the furniture as their robed bodies laid limp against the floorboards. It was evident that Mrs Jillings did what she could to protect the family, but she was overpowered. Her sunken eyes told a devastating story of the fear that had consumed them, as Robin gently moved her hair behind her ear, and then lowered her eyelids to a close. The terror that shaped her final expression was haunting. The way her skin had stiffened and the absence of colour and warmth just left a vessel that had housed the most sincere of souls. Robin removed the pale tablecloth and covered over her body. There was no magic that could return the dead, but there was something that the realms sought in the Phoenix:

Its ability to open a channel to the afterlife, where rare souls were believed to wander.

The world's passion for loved ones had driven many of them insane, unaware of right and wrong. Until Robin could understand it a little better, he swore to protect the bird, no matter who or what he would lose in the process...

"I'm sorry," he whispered as he looked down at the covered shape of Mrs Jillings.

The Phoenix had climbed from his coat pocket and was now perched on his shoulder, also staring down towards the body with an understanding of what she meant to the Occamy family. It chirped, and nipped at Robin's ear as a means of showing affection. It kind of hurt, but Robin knew she meant no harm as he rubbed his ear and looked in to all four of her remaining eyes.

"I wish you could stay that size," said Robin, holding out his finger, then gently stroking the Phoenix's neck, trying to suppress his swelling anger, while avoiding eye contact with the crippled Reaper bodies that were staring at the ceiling in the corner of the kitchen.

He was glad they suffered, and even more grateful that Mrs Jillings seemed to have passed rather suddenly. Not that it made it any easier to come to terms with... Robin eventually stepped over the body and re-entered the hallway, running his hand along the wall as he neared the bottom of the stairs.

"Kirsten? Sweetheart?" he called, fearing the worst.

"*Kirst -*" He couldn't complete her name as he tried to call out again. His hands were trembling and his legs had gone weak as he turned to the living room, where his eyes fell abruptly on Kirsten, who was lodged at the side of the sofa, facing the fireplace.

"What did they do? What did they do to you?" Robin's face was a flood of tears. He leapt over the christmas tree and fell at Kirstens side, wasting no time to check for a pulse.

"Kirst, can you hear me?"

There was no immediate response. She was still and cold while Robin held on to her. He had noticed a wound similar to Mrs Jilling's, where a curse had torn a path through her chest. It was no secret, the Reapers had been sent with one intent - to kill his family, and use his daughter as bait before killing her, too. Even though it hadn't gone to plan, Robin could feel his heart tearing in half as he buried his head against Kirsten's hair, holding on to her like there was still hope of something - anything but death.

He repeated her name tearfully, his voice muffled as he buried his face in her hair. He then began to tell the story of his travels, before apologising, realising it was all essentially his fault.

"If only I had listened to Kenneth, we could have escaped – all of us. But the Count would have taken the Phoenix..."

As he said those words, the Phoenix had been watching from the arm of the sofa, somewhat curious as it turned its head and hopped down on to the carpet.

There was a single Reaper laid under the bay window - its head was barely attached to its neck. Robin assumed he was one of Sapphire's victims by the way he seemed to have been attacked from behind. She must have been moments too late, but it still made no sense why she wanted to help him, no matter how unsuccessful she was. It was a sight he had become accustomed to seeing - but not in his own home, if he could even call it that anymore...

The day had become a living nightmare so quickly. The price that had been paid for the Phoenix's safety seemed too high a price to pay as he wiped his face and watched as the Phoenix stepped up to Kirsten, searching for her scent.

"It never occurred to me until now," the Phoenix pivoted its head and listened, "- you're my little Damsel. But it would seem I'm the one in distress."

Still pained by the gauge across its face, the Phoenix continued to stare up at Robin.

"I knew what I was getting into. I knew, the moment I left the house yesterday morning. I guess I underestimated everything."

The cottage was silent. There was only the sound of rustling feathers, and the occasional floorboard creak as the temperature began to rise - melting the ice from the window sills.

The sunshine shimmered in Robin's eyes as he finally found the energy to smile, "you look like a Damsel, you do."

The newly named Phoenix hopped on to Kirsten and made her way up to her wounds, treading carefully as Robin leaned in, watching with intrigue.

"I don't even think the *old* me knew if it was true. He always seemed uncertain in the books he wrote. Whether you could actually... *save* her."

Damsel was inspecting the flesh wound, then suddenly, Kirsten drew a breath.

"*Did you feel that? Did you hear?*" he yelled, as

hope ignited, "She's still alive, isn't she?" His eyes widened, then Damsel flapped her wings and peered down into the cursed burrow of flesh in her chest. Robin was calling to Kirsten, shuffling her body from the sofa and into a flat position along the carpet. Damsel closed her eyes, and a couple of tear drops appeared from the corner of her eyes and fell down in to the depth of Kirsten's wound.

Some believed it to be a myth, the power of a Phoenix tear. But not only did the wound suddenly begin to clear, but Kirsten's entire body began to absorb the healing elixir, ridding her of all her life long diseases and disabilities. She was slowly becoming brand new again, but still regenerating as her lungs refilled with air and her eyes fluttered open.

"Robin?" she strained. Her throat was sore from the screaming, and dry from the cold.

Robin ran his hand over her forehead and pulled her closer, gently.

"I'm here, I'm back. There's nothing to fear, now," he assured her, turning her head away from the debris, and the assailants body.

"Where did you go, Robin?" her eyes were weary, she looked like death, but colour was beginning to bloom in her cheeks as she gazed into Robin's deep brown eyes.

"We woke up and you were gone. Mrs Jillings said it was work, but you never came back last night..." Kirsten was playing with the stubble on Robin's chin. She always thought it suited him, but it wasn't very fitting for his line of work - in his opinion, but his attention had been well spent - it was the very least of his priorities.

"I wish it was simple enough to explain," he

replied, aware of Damsel in the corner of his eye, begging for attention.

"You're going to find out, though. Little by little. You'll be quite amazed by the things I've seen and the people I've met."

Kirsten cracked a smile and wrapped her arms around Robin's waist, "I love you," she chuckled, feeling abnormally well.

"Have you noticed my friend over here?" he asked, holding his hand out to Damsel, who rubbed her beak against his finger tip, before hopping on to his palm.

"This is Damsel, she's a very, *very* rare bird."

"She's beautiful!" said Kirsten, cautiously turning her attention to the five black, beady eyes, "- but, why has she got… *so many eyes?*"

Robin smiled, "Because she's rare. Something close to a myth to some, but if you trust your instinct, and ask yourself how you're so well, the answer won't be too outrageous."

Kirsten shuffled up against the sofa and ruffled her hand through her long brown hair.

"Try adding two and two, and getting three. Two normal numbers, but one unlikely result. One normal work shift, plus one casual Christmas, there's been nothing but fireworks!"

Robin wrapped his arm further around Kirsten as he carried on speaking.

"There's just so much I want to tell you, but our daughter needs us now."

"Where is she? Where's Emily?" she panicked, realising she was taken by the intruders.

She could barely remember what had happened…

"She's safe. Some friends are taking care of her."

"You have friends?" Kirsten looked surprised, "I'm sorry, you just always put *work* and *us* before a social life."

"I just met them. I guess I can't really call them friends, but when you meet them, you'll understand. When you're ready, we'll make our way back, because we can't stay here anymore."

Kirsten had already come to terms with that, as she didn't feel safe. Not after seeing the tall cloaked figures in her home, standing over her child.

"Mrs Jillings isn't ok, is she?"

Robin shook his head, "I've taken care of her. It wasn't a pleasant sight. But I don't think she suffered for long."

That image of her gaunt, ghostly face flashed before his eyes as he cast his memory back, reminded of the moment he stepped forth inside the kitchen. It wasn't a memory he wished to cling to, that was for sure. As painful as it was, he could no longer remember the times they had shared. So much had happened - too much. Now he could only focus on getting back and away from the posed threat that was now watching over the town of Vinemoore.

Robin opened up his coat pocket and prompted Damsel inside. Its turquoise coloured feathers rustled as she looked at Kirsten, then proceeded to climb inside the pocket, which had become like a temporary home for her.

"Robin, I feel great. I honestly can't remember when I last felt this way. Even when I was on the lowest dose of medication, it never had an effect like this."

Kirsten pulled apart her navy coloured dressing

gown and began inspecting the wound in her chest, above her left breast.

"You've never had anything like this. This medication is out of this world." he smiled, pulling his spindly wooden wand from his pocket.

Kirsten was still studying her wound and the miraculous lack of bruises discolouring her skin.

"I don't hurt, I don't ache...I..."

The emerald green glow of Robin's wand finally caught her attention, stopping her mid sentence as the green shimmered across her eyes.

"This is linked to those crazy ideas you had. All that speculation about the town."

"This makes them sound rather tame," said Robin, humorously. "If you feel up to it, we'd best get a move on."

"But what about our clothes, our money, our... memories?"

"We've never been materialistic. And the good memories have been very far and few between. We can create new ones."

Robin reached for her hand and drew it to his lips.

"You're right," she replied, glancing at the ring on her finger, "This - you and our daughter is all we need. But if we're moving, we'll definitely need cash."

"Quite possibly. Or perhaps not," he debated, as he cast his mind back to breakfast and all the food that manifested on the dining tables, "Where we're going, money is the least of our concerns."

Robin raised his wand, then began to paint the Institute in his mind. Once he was satisfied with its appearance, he turned the handle of the wand and cleared his throat, before chanting, "*Senteer*."

CHAPTER 23
Destination Unknown

Magenta was already back at the Institute, but she had returned alone and had kept her word. Sapphire was far better off out of chains and opposing the Reaper uprise that they now had on their hands. Wherever she had gone, the help would always be well received, and the further from the Institute the better, in Magenta's eyes. It had already taken a beating, and it showed as she crossed the entrance in a storm of pink feathers. Her body casually transforming back to its humanoid form with every stride, until finally her coat unravelled around her body, and her curls fell heavy over her collar.

The ground was clearer now than when she had left with Robin. The bodies had been moved against the walls and covered over. The debris was being cast aside into heaps for easy repair, and the barricade was slowly being dismantled.

Curious eyes had now begun to peep from behind the golden monuments set along the ceiling. Emily and Arlie were already best of friends, even though they were so different, at heart they wanted the same thing for each other.

Emily didn't care for looks, and Arlie was used to being one of very few Imps accepted to work in a building with so much history and function.

Emily brought Arlie happiness, and Arlie made Emily feel safe, even suspended thirty feet off the ground.

"Magenta, my dear. What news do you bring?" asked Grimtale on his approach.

"He wasn't joking around, Professor. Kenneth Brown warned that the Reapers were moving on innocents - Morient Innocents."

Grimtale frowned, and listened as Magenta continued to explain.

"We were lucky enough to cross paths with a deserter, a female Reaper who helped fend off the threat, but they had already done a ridiculous amount of damage. We cleared the town as best we could, but no doubt they will regroup, reform and recruit more. We've only delayed the inevitable..."

A million questions were begged for answers as Grimtale grasped and processed what he could.

"But the one thing we have now, that we didn't before, is time. Time that can be spent advancing the schools defences, and relighting the flame that so many have warmed to in recent years. The heart of the school will beat again, I promise you."

Grimtale glanced to the doors, " Is Robin not with you?"

The question stemmed interest from Sachester and Yuri, who were stood close behind him, clearing the last of the rubble.

"He'll be back for his daughter," said Magenta, who wasn't certain what had happened inside the cottage.

"What about Kirsten and Ethel?" asked Grimtale, with concern growing in his eyes. Magenta slowly shrugged, "I'm not sure - I'm not sure that they made it," she said, regrettably, "From what the Reaper described, it would explain why you haven't heard anything from their housekeeper. I know you were fond of her, Grimtale."

"She was a very old friend - taught me everything I know," he smiled, remembering his time as a student:

*There had been no wars back then. The only wars were those in the human world. The Morient realm had been largely peaceful. One hundred years had now passed since the very first recorded Morient war, and now it felt as if another was on the verge, brewing wherever the Count and his disciples had fled to...*Grimtale was now tired, they all were as they continued to clear the foyer, looking forward to getting some well deserved rest.

By the time Robin and Kirsten arrived at the Institute, it was nearing immaculate inside. The gates were still unhinged outside, and there were a few chunks of stone knocking around from the walls, but it was finally looking like home again, especially to Magenta, who watched with interest as Robin and Kirsten entered. Between them they carried Ethel Jilling's body. There was no way he could have left her. He had to bring her home, where she belonged. It was the least he could do, and that way he knew the chances of a heart felt send off were far greater for Ethel and Kenneth.

Robin was convinced that all the other bodies would end up in a furnace, forgotten. So he made it his first point of conversation upon entry, looking in to Grimtale's weary eyes, as he released a sigh of relief. Robin and Kirsten's safe return had to be better than none at all. But great sadness overwhelmed him as the lifeless shape of Ethel was carried closer.

"Kenneth Brown - his body needs retrieving from the Dungeon," said Robin, sadly,

"- they'll get a proper burial, won't they?"

Grimtale nodded, "Of course they will! What do you take us for, animals?"

"I just don't expect all of these other bodies will be given the respect of a place in either realm's soil."

"They knew what they were signing up for. Cremation would have come in their terms and conditions."

Robin wasn't feeling the humour, while Kirsten's eyes were a blaze with wonder, dressed in her underwear and covered by her dressing gown that hung down to her ankles.

"I'd like it if Kenneth could be taken to Vinemoore – some place local, for his family," said Robin, lowering Ethel's wrapped body on to the marble floor.

"Don't worry, Robin. I was going to have that done anyway. Everything is under control." Grimtale smiled, then turned to Kirsten, "I didn't mean to be rude, it's a pleasure to meet you," he added, to which Kirsten looked confused.

"And, you are?" she asked.

"This is the school's headmaster, Professor Grimtale. He made sure our daughter was safe."

Emily had already spotted her Mother and Father. She was on her way down as Kirsten began to search the foyer, completely ignoring Grimtale now, as her thoughts rested only with her missing daughter.

"*Mum!*" yelled Emily, as she jumped off the final step and raced past Yuri and Lillian. Kirsten fell on to one knee and threw out her arms as Emily leapt, and latched herself on to her waist, burying her head against her furry gown.

"My brave girl." Said Kirsten, as she wrapped her arms around her daughter.

"Have you made a new friend?" she whispered, noticing Arlie standing anxiously behind, kicking up dirt from the last few piles of dust and rubble.

Like Emily, Kirsten wasn't concerned. There was an Imp stood before her eyes, and it was okay. She was still incredibly overwhelmed by how well she felt, and her ability to walk again, without aid, that she was willing to accept anything - even peculiar looking creatures, wearing humorous headwear. Emily raised her face from the comfort of her Mother's dressing gown and waved to Arlie, calling him over.

"He's my friend, he's called Arlie." Emily smiled, beaming as she reached out to him.

"Arlie is pleased to meet you. Arlie did all he could to protect young Emily."

Kirsten rubbed her eyes then continued to stare at Arlie.

"*Robin!* Why didn't you tell me about all this?"

He walked over, and looked down at the bundle of joy that was grinning and excited to have her parents back.

"To tell the truth, everything happened so fast. Turns out it was a lot safer here than back home."

Yuri was listening in as he swept the floor, "The stone won't be removed again. No unwelcome visitors will get by!" said Yuri, much to the amusement of Magenta, who made no conscious effort to shield her laugh.

"We were living with the Count for months while that charm was active. I was sleeping in the same bed as him!"

Arlie distracted Emily as the conversation took a sudden turn.

"I knew you were on to him, Grimtale."

Magenta suddenly felt rather distressed. It was the thought of everything that had been done to her by the Count, and realising it could have been averted sooner...

"I had suspicions, but nothing concrete enough to act. You must remember where I stand. I am the Headmaster, a figure of security and safety to my students. I am yet still a pawn to the Minister and the Sovereign."

There was nothing else Grimtale could do or say, he felt guilty enough as it was. He even felt guilty that he was tired.

"I'm just mad - at myself," Magenta confessed, turning away and burying her head in her hands.

"There is plenty of rebuilding to do. Plenty of physical repairs, and most importantly, mental healing required for *all* of us. There can be a future, but now, we must plant the seed of virtue, and step across the void we find ourselves slipping into."

Everyone could agree on one thing - time would carry on ticking, the sun would set and rise again. The only thing standing in their way was banished, at least, for now.

"Grimtale, we don't have much time. The Minister will be expecting an update from his informant," said Sachester, reminding Grimtale of the urgency.

"We need to get you on your way, Robin."

Grimtale thanked Sachester as he passed, making his way over to Kirsten and Robin, "the Minister wants that Phoenix, and so does the world. You won't be making many friends, but there are those who will help with your journey, to find a peaceful settlement for your family."

Robin always suspected deep down he wasn't going to be returning to the cottage he had spent the last few years of his life. It was no surprise that from this moment on, they were homeless. They still owned the cottage. It was in Kirsten's family name, but it was no longer safe, and the Institute was no place for war. Children would be allowed to return for classes come spring. Besides that, the Minister would expect the Phoenix to be there. It had to be taken somewhere secret, under the supervision of Robin and his family, where it could live in peace, away from ill intentions, with people it now trusted.

Robin nodded, understanding what was expected of him.

"Security is about to tighten inside these walls, so I say to you all: My friends, my love. Be clever, and don't lose contact." Grimtale looked everyone in the eye one last time, then proceeded in saying his farewells, starting with Emily whose eyes were still aglow with innocent excitement.

"Now, you look after your Mother and Father, *won't you?*"

She smiled, and peered up at Robin, "Can Arlie come too?" she asked.

"I'm not sure, I think he's going to be busy here, sweetheart."

Emily seemed disappointed, she didn't have any siblings, and Arlie, even though he had lived for over a century, he still had the fun and energy of a child, similar to Emily's. He was the perfect companion, even her Mother could see it.

"Is it true?" Emily asked Grimtale.

"Well, I'm afraid Arlie does have work, however, I have a new assignment for him, *if* he wishes to accept?"

Arlie seemed interested in hearing more as Grimtale explained, "It's to complete your Father's training."

Robin looked confused, "My training?" he asked.

"You see, before the old Robin went under the wand and had his memory of magic withdrawn. Myself and Arlie took it upon ourselves to protect certain events, certain moments and knowledge that could one day be returned outside the law. Arlie holds that power, so I believe it's only fitting that he joins you on the next chapter of your journey."

Emily gave Arlie a hug, then clamped her arms around her Father's leg.

"Arlie must thank you, Professor."

Arlie held out his hand, which was quickly collected by Grimtale, held firmly between the warm palms of his gloves.

"It's my pleasure, my friend. You know what to do?"

"Arlie understands," he nodded, giving his wand a tap as he withdrew his hand,

"We really need to disband, before we get caught in the act." said Robin, adjusting his coat, while casting a fond farewell to those staring back at him: Lillian, Yuri, Teppi, Sachester, Magenta, and last but not least, Grimtale, who he pulled in for a tight embrace.

"We may no longer live in town, but home is

where the heart is..." Robin whispered, as the Phoenix popped her head from his pocket.

Grimtale was oblivious to what Robin meant by his words - he blamed the tiredness, but he knew that time would tell, that's for sure.

"Goodbye, Professor."

"Goodbye, for now, Mr Occamy."

They both departed on one final handshake, then before there was time to dwell, Robin had cast open a charm to the mountains overlooking the Institute, where his family could say one last farewell.

Robin turned back around, for what felt like the final time he would cast his eyes on the Vinemoore institute. The sky was clear and the air was brisk, the sun was now high and had begun to shine across the mountains, illuminating the dazzling gem stones and steel work.

It was certainly a sight for sore eyes, he couldn't help but leave it a parting gift, his farewell to what was once his school, his home, his battleground, and now, something as far from a safe house as it could ever be. He looked on at a loss, then drew his hand to his brow, saluting the past, present and future, with his head held high to balance the heavy sinking feeling that tugged at his heart, trying to bury itself in the gravel beneath him; however, before disappearing through the ripples of a newly opened Senteer charm, he smiled, then with the Phoenix safely and happily tucked away in his larger coat pocket, with Arlie and Kirsten holding tight to Emily, they travelled beyond, away from danger, some place brand new, somewhere they could make their own, without living in fear of what might be coming for them.

The fluctuation slowly shrunk to nothing once they were gone, shattering the chances of being followed as the sovereign guard suddenly began to materialise on the cliff edge, emerging from multiple charms that had opened up where Robin was stood, but no longer resided. They were too late - far too late, they realised as a rumble of thunder sounded from the heavens, rolling in on a cloud of snow that loomed on the horizon.

* * *

For Many months, the Occamy cottage remained empty. The entire town knew of the tragic loss that took place in their home, given the facts had been manipulated to fit with the town's human population. Most would of hoped it was purely out of respect that no one went near the cottage after that, but truth be told, it was more likely that no one was brave enough to make a life where one was lost. Its boarded up windows brought only sadness as residents passed by. There was no longer any warmth or love, even the gardens foliage had shrivelled up and given in.

But not *all* was bad in Vinemoore.

A few weeks later, the Institute for Morient kind was ready to reopen, and welcomed its brand new students to a reformed and safe learning environment. Given it would never be the same, with the increased security roaming the corridors, and sovereign guard at every entrance -

even the dungeons - the children still managed to settle and learn about their hidden talents, and what set them apart from the human residents they shared their lives with. Grimtale made sure that every child was given a fair chance, especially the likes of young Charlie Reed, who had always been extremely sensitive to the Morient movement and the magic within the towns community, but he was rarely accepted by the purists. Charlie wasn't born into the world by Morient parents, but Robin had made sure to put in a good word, and he was quickly accepted and taken under the wing of Professor Grimtale - he even made sure that all the first year students were given human worthy homework each day, just to protect and keep things a secret from unknowing eyes.

The sightings of robed figures had never raised any concerns amongst the town's people, and no questions were ever asked of it. Kenneth and Mrs Jillings were given a proper burial, one on the Morient hillside, overlooking the institute. The other, at the local churchyard in Vinemoore, opposite the courtyard by an old, overhanging tree.

Even Edmond was given a grave beside his brothers and sisters barn in Shoulders Heath. He would never be forgotten for his bravery on the Black mountain - which wasn't due an eruption any time soon, but the disappearance of the Phoenix on the other hand - that had caused a stir within the walls of the Ruby Citadel. Sovereign guard were back and forth daily at the Institute, scrutinising the professors, hoping *someone* would crack under pressure and reveal how events had unfolded that day. Their visits had become a strain on the classes; until sovereign Ambrax was finally ready to question a person of great interest to the enquiry. *At the start of the Morient inquisition, a warrant was finally released for Professor Magenta's arrest...*

Epilogue

Time had brought much change, but the Institute remained a home and a place of comfort, after four long months of self rediscovery.

Magenta had finally settled back in to her job, teaching the students about all the wonderful creatures that inhabit the realms. Even those that sometimes found themselves lost in the Human realm - which the majority of the youngsters had come from. The children born and raised in the Morient realm were often sent further afield, to the bigger Institutions. Vinemoore was still well populated, and its students were more than happy to be attending. Professor Magenta helmed one of the more popular classes, it was a favourite, which brought major disappointment at the sound of the bell - alerting them that class was now over.

"Now, don't forget that your next class will be taken by Miss Bilshore."

The children moaned and groaned as they pushed their chairs under their desks and slowly made their way towards the classroom door.

"Miss Bilshore has a real treat for you, I Promise!" Ensured Magenta, as she opened the heavy door, where there stood a trio of Sovereign guard, dressed in their crimson coloured uniform and sinister gold and silver plated helmets.

"Have a lovely weekend, everyone," said Magenta, trying to distract herself from the escort waiting outside. The children carefully and quietly made their way down the corridor, behaving subdued, somewhat out of character - as they were only too aware of the presence of the guardsmen.

Magenta was now alone in her classroom, tidying the chairs and desks as the three sovereign guard entered by the door. There was a short moment of silence, and a mutual understanding as they took their positions, watching Magenta redress the room accordingly.

"Will you be coming peacefully, Professor?" said the captain, who made his way to the front of the class, leaving his entourage beside the door, ready to apprehend Magenta.

"I'm not running, if that's what you mean," she replied, walking over to the chalkboard.

"Then as it's procedure to do so, I must inform you that as of now, you are under arrest by the Sovereign guard. Anything you say will be given as evidence, and questioned when mentioned in court - if this goes to court. You understand why we are here?"

Magenta yanked her fluorescent pink coat from the hat stand and glared at the Captain, whose face was hidden behind the metal of his helmet, "Procedure," she grunted.

"Your involvement with the criminal known as Munder Mortal, but more commonly, the Count, has sparked questions. We understand you weren't to know and we hold nothing against you, we simply require your side of how events unfolded and whatever information that might assist the search for the more recent criminal, Robin Occamy. We understand you were somewhat close?"

"No comment," she replied, still staring with unbroken eye contact.

"You are well within your rights to refrain from answering," the captain turned to the other guards and called them over, "Would you place Miss Aline Magenta under arrest," he commanded, to which one of the guards drew his wand and began to cast an enchantment around Magenta's restrained wrists. The energy was bright red, and it flowed like a river of magma, with the intention of doing great harm if broken, so Magenta kept still and followed their lead without any hesitation. It was a new experience for her, it was quite exciting, really. She knew she hadn't committed a crime, but she played along.

"Sovereign Ambrax awaits your arrival at the Ruby Citadel."

Magenta had known for a while that this day was coming, it had been forewarned, but with nothing to hide, and for all she knew, nothing to fear.

A Sovereign guard stepped to one side and began to tear open a bridge to the distant land where the Ruby Citadel resided. However, this Senteer charm was quite different, this charm bridged the classroom with the inner chambers, beyond the acceptance charm that fortified the Citadel within a metaphysical bubble. The guard's privileges allowed them to travel direct, being a class above the casual enforcers. The energy around the tear was pulsating with a crystallised crimson loop, which was a common trait to identify a genuine cast spell over one of an imposter, whose wand had no such power.

Magenta glanced to the Captain, who was stood at her side. She then proceeded to enter the rift, followed closely by the two Sovereign guard. The captain remained in the classroom, closing the charm securely behind them with a soft wave of his wand.

Grimtale had already put a plan in place for Magenta's authorised absence from teaching, which meant there was nothing further to follow up. The Sovereign Captain was now free to end his day and return to his life. His family were home, anxiously awaiting his return, for each day brought mountains of worry, even though they knew he was only assigned the follow ups, after the Enforcers had given their lives for resolution. The Sovereign guard simply had to piece together the fragments left over. But with the Enforcers recent failure to capture the Phoenix and detain Robin, a greater soldier would need to be deployed. The Captain knew that changes were coming, so making the most of his day, he left the Institute with hopes of seeing his children and wife before sunset. There was still time, as the shores of Cromer settled and the violet Swans swept in. Change was coming, memories needed to be made. He knew that as he took a breath of the summer air, peering into the distance where his home sat peacefully perched on the bed of a cliff, overlooking the beach.

"Home..." he muttered, already forgotten about Magenta and the hour that had led to her arrest. It was just work, but to Magenta, it was her life.

* * *

She had only heard stories of the Ruby Citadel, so to be stood inside its walls, seeing it for the first time brought a gut curdling worry. Still unsure what was going to happen, the nerves soon returned, killing any positive thoughts and replacing them with overwhelming concern.

The room around her was very dim, lit only by a handful of torches hanging from the walls. There was a oval table at the centre, and the walls glistened a sequence of colour, like oil on a path. She moved closer to the table, watching the light refracting from the tiles and casting rainbow patterns towards the floor and ceiling. It wasn't anything special, but the back wall had sparked intrigue as she remained stood at the centre of the room with her wrists still restrained behind her back, glowing brightly.

The entire wall was moving, like rippling tides out at sea, but vertical, defying all the human laws of gravity. It reached the ceiling which was tall and arched. There was no reflection, but it did shine and warp as if it was *alive*. Magenta had never seen anything quite like it before, but never had she been held by the Citadel. *Perhaps it was her cell, and behind it was the realm that criminals were thrown to endure the rest of their lives*, she wondered, as a dark silhouette of a man began to emerge from the wall.

The two Sovereign guard were stood to attention in the doorway as the figure stepped through the liquefied mirage, then casually approached the table, moving in to focus as Magenta's eyes adjusted to the shifting light.

The man was partially robed, with an excessive collection of gold jewellery hung from his neck. He wore a tall pointed helmet, which was also gold coated. It hid his face, but left his mouth and chiselled jaw exposed. The helmet, like the guard's, protected his mind from any attempt of invasive manipulation. It was the pinnacle and most reliable piece of craftsmanship the Ruby Citadel had seen in recent years. The mysterious figure wore it with pride, and now he stared into Magenta's hazel coloured eyes.

"I was mistaken in trusting the Ministers enforcers. I should have enlisted my own personal guard to the Institute all those months ago. You, however, you had a good idea of what was coming, *didn't* you?"

His voice was deep, and rough around the edges, much like his appearance.

Magenta remained silent, knowing she was well within her rights, with no intention of being intimidated.

"What you know, will need to be extracted, you understand? It will be as painless or painful as you choose it to be, professor. I must stress to you the importance of cooperation."

The figure pulled his wand, which was longer than the usual that Magenta had seen. He then waved it towards the table, and a wave of stardust spilled across the surface. It sat like a magical layer of fog, glowing red as it morphed in to the shape of Robin's face, and the Phoenix, flapping its wings.

"Robin Occamy, your friend, has been at liberty for far too long. As we begin to draw our inquisition to a close, I know you will be most useful in finding him."

Magenta looked unamused.

"Who exactly are you?" she asked, as her heart began to race a little faster.

The figure took a step closer, towering over Magenta, who stood at five feet tall.

"I am the supreme power of *all* Morient realms," he began, creeping closer, hovering over Magenta, "- I drop the hammer on how long your friend will serve for his crimes. I am Ambrax, the ruler of the Citadel, and soon enough, the outlaws *will* be apprehended. You will be the one that the people thank. You can restore peace across our land. You could be known as Inquisitor Magenta." Explained Ambrax, glorifying the role that he had crafted on the spot for her.

She was now trembling, her arms were still restrained behind her back, and Ambrax was breathing down her neck. There was nothing she could do but nod, while facing away, watching the menacing red eyes that had appeared from behind the moving mirage.

"It's ready to hunt," Ambrax whispered, forcing Magenta's face towards the wall.

She watched as the terrifying pale face pressed against the confines of its cell, breathing heavily: *Whatever it was, it was dangerous and becoming ever more impatient to be unleashed, to hunt Robin Occamy, the remains of Munder Mortal and the criminals that threatened the Morient realms...*

Printed in Great Britain
by Amazon